The
PROVING

Books by Beverly Lewis

The Proving • The Ebb Tide
The Wish • The Atonement
The Photograph
The Love Letters • The River

HOME TO HICKORY HOLLOW

The Fiddler • The Bridesmaid
The Guardian • The Secret Keeper
The Last Bride

THE ROSE TRILOGY

The Thorn • The Judgment
The Mercy

ABRAM'S DAUGHTERS

The Covenant • The Betrayal
The Sacrifice • The Prodigal
The Revelation

THE HERITAGE
OF LANCASTER COUNTY

The Shunning
The Confession • The Reckoning

ANNIE'S PEOPLE

The Preacher's Daughter
The Englisher • The Brethren

THE COURTSHIP
OF NELLIE FISHER

The Parting • The Forbidden
The Longing

SEASONS OF GRACE

The Secret • The Missing
The Telling

The Postcard • The Crossroad

The Redemption of Sarah Cain
Sanctuary (with David Lewis)
Child of Mine (with David Lewis)
The Sunroom • October Song

Amish Prayers
The Beverly Lewis Amish
Heritage Cookbook

www.beverlylewis.com

The
PROVING

BEVERLY
LEWIS

BETHANYHOUSE
a division of Baker Publishing Group
Minneapolis, Minnesota

© 2017 by Beverly M. Lewis, Inc.

Published by Bethany House Publishers
11400 Hampshire Avenue South
Bloomington, Minnesota 55438
www.bethanyhouse.com

Bethany House Publishers is a division of
Baker Publishing Group, Grand Rapids, Michigan

Printed in the United States of America

Library of Congress Cataloging-in-Publication Data
Names: Lewis, Beverly, author.
Title: The proving / Beverly Lewis.
Description: Minneapolis, Minnesota : Bethany House, a division of Baker
    Publishing Group, [2017]
Identifiers: LCCN 2017012332| ISBN 9780764219900 (hardcover : acid-free paper) |
    ISBN 9780764219665 (softcover) | ISBN 9780764219917 (large-print : softcover)
Subjects: LCSH: Amish—Fiction. | GSAFD: Christian fiction.
Classification: LCC PS3562.E9383 P76 2017 | DDC 813/.54—dc23
LC record available at https://lccn.loc.gov/2017012332

Special Edition ISBN 978-0-7642-3134-6

Scripture quotations are from the King James Version of the Bible.

Cover design by Dan Thornberg, Design Source Creative Services
Art direction by Paul Higdon

17 18 19 20 21 22 23   7 6 5 4 3 2 1

Mercy and truth are met together;
righteousness and peace have kissed each other.

Psalm 85:10

To Julie Marie,
darling first daughter,
long awaited . . .
one of the great joys of my life!

Prologue

My first-ever night away from home, I struggled with sleeplessness, having abruptly left with two other Amish girls. Linda and Vicky Zook had been ousted by their bishop in Ronks, not far from Gordonville, Pennsylvania, where I'd lived all of my eighteen years. I had agreed to split rent on a two-bedroom apartment with them after they encouraged me to join them in their flight to the world, saying they had a friend of a friend living out in western Kansas who knew of a place for the three of us.

And here we were at long last, though I never would've considered doing such a thing if I hadn't been in a hurry to get away. I needed time to think. *Just for a while,* I told myself. Truth be told, I was furious with my twin sister . . . and heartbroken. It was impossible not to keep replaying the horrid last moments between us. And I knew for sure *Dat* would be just sick over it, if he were still alive.

Sitting in the small, nearly empty bedroom, I recalled my father's fondness for Arie and me, and felt terribly alone.

Though it might surprise some, my sister and I had never been treated like twins. *Mamma* had seen to that. In fact, no one in our immediate family ever referred to us as *the twins*, like most families of multiples. No one ever said, *"Go tell the twins to dress around for Preaching service,"* or *"The twins are over ice-skating on Uncle Mel's pond."* *Nee*, we were called by our given names and, thankfully, weren't required to wear matching color dresses, not even when we were tiny. From the start, Arie and I were our own persons, each free to have our own interests. Nevertheless, an indescribable bond had connected us. We were more than sisters; we were best friends. *Till now.*

I got up and paced the floor, staring at the moon through the window. How had it come to this?

Jah, I had plenty of good reasons to put some distance between my sister and myself. And then there were Mamma's heated words to me, as well.

There was no getting around it, no way to sugarcoat the truth. Arie Mae had betrayed me.

OCTOBER 21: FIVE YEARS LATER

Pulling into the parking lot at the Scott City, Kansas, florist where I'd been working for nearly five years now, I couldn't help but notice the familiar white ornamental windmill near the entrance. The sight brought back visions of dairy farms and milk houses, waterwheels, and *real* windmills nestled among rolling hills tinted with Lancaster County's dazzling autumn display.

Leaves are turning in Mamma's yard right now . . . like flames of fire. I thought of my childhood home, roughly fifteen hundred miles away. For as long as I'd been gone, it was still easy to picture the stand of sugar maples near Old Leacock Road, and Mamma out raking the leaves into big piles with my sister.

"You're right on time," Karyn Fry, my employer's wisp of a

wife, greeted me as I stepped inside the small shop. I inhaled the heavenly fragrance of flowers, thankful for this job. Working with flowers was ideal for a young woman raised with hands in the soil, and arranging bouquets of all types and sizes gave me creative freedom.

I reached for my work apron and removed it from the wall hook, noticing today's date on the wall calendar. Oh, how I dreaded the coming weekend—tomorrow, October twenty-second, would be my twenty-third birthday. Instantly, my heart was tangled with memories of growing up in my family's sprawling farmhouse turned Amish bed-and-breakfast. "Five birthdays away from Butterfly Meadows," I whispered, slipping the apron over my head. It felt like a lifetime ago.

"Everything okay, Mandy?" Karyn glanced up from a fresh shipment of coral-colored roses. Her short dark hair revealed the dangling silver earrings she liked to wear.

Sitting down at the shop's computer, I checked on the latest FTD order and smiled over at Karyn. "Just feeling older," I said, rising to find the appropriate vase.

"Aren't we all." Karyn wrapped three long-stemmed roses in green florist paper. "By the way, Tom asked to meet with you before you leave today."

Her husband was the one who'd hired me, but meticulous Karyn ran the place. "Okay, I'll check in with him," I said, noting the strange, flat tone of Karyn's voice as I trimmed the thick stems on a few stargazer lilies.

········ ⚬ ········

Hours later, I rose from the work stool and stretched. Through the window, I could see a teenage girl riding bareback in the meadow across from the rural shop, her hair flowing behind her like a golden waterfall in the breeze. It stirred up recollections of riding Ol' Tulip, one of our faithful road horses . . . and later, my father's attempts to teach me to hitch her to the family carriage. I was just ten years old that first time, and real curious, so while I held the driving lines for him, I had asked what my name would have been if the Lord had seen fit to make me a boy.

My father chuckled and gave me an indulgent look. He knew me well enough to humor me with an answer. "Well, let's see. Ammon, it might've been," he said, twitching his eyebrows.

I grimaced at the notion. "Really, Dat . . . Ammon?"

His eyes twinkled. "Ain't ya glad ya were born a girl?"

Real glad, I thought.

"And Arie Mae?" I pressed.

"Oh, prob'ly Aaron."

"Were ya hopin' for more boys, then?" I held my breath.

He gave his big shoulders a shrug. "Your Mamma and I s'posed after four sons in a row, we might just get two more."

I waited for him to add something, but Dat simply leaned down to kiss the top of my head. "I'm glad we figured that wrong, Mandy Sue," he said with a grin. "After all those boys, it was mighty *gut* to have daughters."

Relieved, I beamed all the way back to the house. And later, while Arie and I dusted and mopped the front room, I relayed Dat's comments and could tell she was pleased, too.

After Dat passed away due to a silo-filling accident, our world became a whole lot less carefree. I felt I'd lost the one adult I could turn to with any question, no matter how fanciful, and always find a patient, good-natured response, despite my tendency to *"create drama,"* as Mamma sometimes put it. Perhaps too much drama for her liking.

It was ever so hard to say good-bye to Dat. I poured out my heart in a note of loving farewell, and late that night, while his long body rested in the hand-built pine coffin, I snuck downstairs to the gas-lamp-lit front room and slid it under his heavy right arm when no one was around, trying not to cry. It was the hardest thing I'd ever done.

.... ✿ ....

The shatter of glass on the cement floor startled me, and I brushed off the cherished recollection and glanced over at Karyn, who had never once dropped anything during the years I'd worked there. Her eyes were wide with embarrassment, and she shook her head as if to clear the clumsy cobwebs.

What's bothering her? I wondered.

Without asking, I went to help sweep up the jagged remains of the vase.

.... ✿ ....

At five o'clock sharp, Tom Fry opened the door to his office, having been gone most of the day. He was a clean-shaven man of modest build and graying auburn hair as thick as a horse's mane, and his rare frown concerned me. I followed him into the small space where he kept the books on his computer.

"Somethin' the matter, Mr. Fry?" I asked, taking a seat and folding my hands tightly, like Mamma when nervous.

"I'm afraid there is," he replied, taking a breath and letting it out slowly. "You see, it's getting harder to compete with the larger florists in Garden City, and since money is tight, I have to cut back."

My heart beat hard. I needed this job, but I managed to thank him after he said he'd allow me another week's work before letting me go.

"I'll give you a good reference," he added, clearly frustrated at the shop's predicament.

"Thanks . . . that'll help."

Afterward, I trudged out to my car in a daze, wondering how I could make the payments now, let alone cover my rent to Don and Eilene Bradley, reasonable though it was. While I'd tucked away enough to get me through until I found another job, I dreaded the idea of saying good-bye to the Frys. I'd found such pleasure in making bouquets, and sometimes even handling deliveries, bringing joy to various people in the area, seeing the happy expressions on their faces. Someday, once I saved up enough money, I hoped to start my own florist shop, determined to keep moving forward with my life.

Pressing the key into the ignition, I headed in the direction of the pretty house where I had a sunny, spacious room and private bath on the third floor. The Bradleys had been kind to take me under their collective wing when I met them at the community church up the road after the month-to-month rental arrangement with Linda and Vicky had fizzled.

Two good-looking English fellows had started showing up for supper with them, and the last I heard, both couples had married, the young women abandoning their Amish life, no looking back. I, however, was *"too wounded for a beau,"* as Linda had so bluntly put it a few weeks after we became roommates. Loneliness seemed to color my life back then, which was a discouragement to potential suitors, English or otherwise.

Although I've long since moved on, making a way for myself in the outside world, there are times when I miss the way my life used to be. Surprisingly, Arie wrote two letters in the months after my departure, letters I never opened, each one marked *Return to sender* by my own hand. Doubtless my sister had gotten my address from careless Vicky Zook, who'd written home a few times.

I figured Arie would have gotten the message after the first letter came back, and I suppose my actions might have seemed punitive to others. Still, I felt justified, considering what she'd done.

Oh, in time I regretted it, but it was too late. Besides, I simply could not bear to read what my sister might have written, to see the words that would confirm my deepest fears.

Chapter 1

The tale of the arrival of the butterflies had been passed down through the Dienner family tree for many years. It was said that butterflies of various species and colors had flocked like bees around a hive to the surrounding meadows that long-ago June when Ephraim Dienner's grandfather first flung wide the windows of his newly built farmhouse off Old Leacock Road. No one had ever determined what attracted so many of the fluttering beauties, but *Dawdi* Dienner had insisted they were a blessing from the hand of God. Certain Amish folk in Gordonville back then had wagged their heads at that, just as some did to this day, baffled as to which trees or wild flowers were the butterfly magnets.

Other folk around the area simply enjoyed the graceful creatures and let it go at that. Amanda Dienner had been one of them. And sometimes she wished she could better describe the return of the butterflies each spring, as well as The Butterfly Meadows Amish Bed-and-Breakfast, to Don and Eilene Bradley. There were no pictures or online ads—not even a website. For the past decade since her husband's death, Saloma Dienner's clientele had come mainly because of word of mouth, regular guests returning every summer or fall to sit in the rockers on the side porch and sip Saloma's delicious meadow tea as they watched the brilliant butterflies and whiled away the stress of their lives.

After this many years, Mandy had no idea how daily life at the inn was going. She had heard a few times from her mother, who had reached out by letter early on, but that correspondence had been infrequent. And while Mamma had written an apology for her words prior to Mandy's leaving, Mandy was certain she was just trying to get her to return to Gordonville.

"Mandy, would you mind jotting down another Amish recipe for me to try out on a gathering with my church friends?" Eilene asked while sitting at breakfast that Monday. "Something sweet, perchance?"

"Are you interested in baking a pie or cookies . . . or making homemade candies?"

Eilene stirred her hot Earl Grey tea and turned to look at her husband, who was dressed in a pressed blue shirt and tan trousers as though he were heading off to church again. "What do you think, dear?"

Don lowered the morning paper, his brow momentarily creased. "A slice of pie and maybe a scoop of ice cream for your hubby, too?"

Eilene gave him a good-natured glare. "More like a spoonful, I'm thinking, considering what the doctor said."

"That's hardly enough to taste," Don said, giving Mandy a wink.

"Be happy to get any, dear."

Mandy smiled at their happy bantering. "How about my mother's recipe for shoofly pie? I know it by heart," she told Eilene, who agreed and excused herself to get a blank recipe card and a pen from the side drawer of the nearby hutch.

"Here we are," Eilene said, returning to sit at the table and handing Mandy the card.

Printing neatly, Mandy began to write down the ingredients and instructions, then handed the recipe to Eilene, who looked it over and thanked her.

After helping to clear the dishes and place them in the dishwasher, Mandy asked to see the day's newspaper, anxious to search the help-wanted ads. Scanning the columns, she spotted an opening for a grocery store cashier, as well as a clerk at a family-owned bakery. She asked to borrow that section, saying the florist shop was cutting back on help. "I'm being let go after this week," she said.

Eilene frowned and shook her head. "So sorry to hear it." She pushed her chin-length blond hair behind one ear. "How can we help?"

Mandy appreciated the offer. "Please cross your fingers that something opens up soon."

"We'll certainly pray to that end." Eilene set down her teacup on the saucer with a clink. "Won't we, Don?"

Removing his reading glasses, he nodded repeatedly. "Why not right now?"

They bowed their heads, and Don led in prayer, asking for a "divine appointment" for Mandy. "Amen and amen," he said emphatically as he finished the prayer. "Now we'll wait in anticipation for the answer. And meanwhile, I'll ask around, too."

Mandy respected his confidence, though she'd never approached her own prayers in such a bold manner. Since leaving Lancaster County, praying hadn't been the easiest thing, though she still made a point of it. "I best be headin' out the door," she told them, taking up her tan all-weather coat. "I don't want to be late for the start of my final week."

"Good. Be conscientious right up to the last minute," Don encouraged her with an approving smile.

Same fatherly way Dat used to talk, she thought as she waved good-bye to the charming middle-aged couple.

On the drive toward town, Mandy hummed one of the praise and worship choruses from the local church. It hadn't taken her long to pick up the English words and new melodies, so unlike those in the *Ausbund,* the traditional Amish hymnal. She appreciated the songs, though when she sang in church, it didn't feel the same.

Thinking now of her upcoming job search, Mandy remembered applying for work at the florist shop, giving her only job reference—her work at the inn with Mamma and Arie Mae—and wondering if Karyn Fry would contact Mamma, and if so, what she might say. *"My impulsive daughter left us in the lurch."*

Nee, Mamma wouldn't have been unkind, she thought.

Yet if Karyn had contacted Mamma, she'd never said.

Mandy clasped the steering wheel and wondered how Mamma and Arie were getting along with the demands of running the B and B all these years later. Surely by now they had established new patterns of doing things, managing quite well without Mandy's help.

She hadn't forgotten what it was like to introduce wide-eyed *Englischers* to the Old Ways. New guests had arrived every few days, some coming from as far away as England and Germany just to spend time in Amish farmland. There had always been such good fellowship around the table with Mamma's regulars, too, while Arie and Mandy served them scrumptious high-cholesterol breakfasts by the cozy hearth in the large breakfast room. Eggs made to order, bacon and sausage, and fluffy pancakes topped with handpicked berries and real whipped cream . . .

Her mouth watered at the thought of Mamma's cooking, which never failed to draw rave reviews from the guests. Indeed, her mother's cooking was one of the primary reasons people returned year after year.

BEVERLY LEWIS

On chilly autumn or wintry days, Mandy had made extra-rich
hot cocoa for the guests while Arie played the harmonica Dat
had given her for Christmas one year. And when winter came
in earnest, Mandy and Arie had accompanied any guests who
wanted to ice-skate on Uncle Mel's pond up the road, the soft
snowflakes tingling against their cheeks. Sometimes, a few of
their boy cousins had built a bonfire in the late afternoon, which
brought contented *oohs* from the delighted guests.

But Mandy had especially liked the summer and autumn seasons, when she had showed families with small children around
the farm, letting them pet the barn kittens and giving carriage
rides.

Why am I thinking about this now? she wondered.

Glancing in the rearview mirror, Mandy noticed a yellow
school bus make a turn onto the road. "So many differences
here on the other side of the fence," she murmured, recalling the
initial jolt of becoming established so far from home—Kansas
might as well have been a foreign country. *But I've managed all
right so far. . . .*

Mandy spotted the florist shop and felt a twinge of sadness,
not for herself so much but for Karyn and Tom, who'd been so
good to her. During her coffee break, she would call the bakery
and hope for the best. And if that job or another didn't bring in
enough, she'd try to get part-time work on weekends.

Her father's words returned to her unbidden: *"The Lord's Day
isn't meant for work."*

Yet what would Dat say now if he knew of her plight?

I'll be fine, Mandy thought. *Someone will give me a chance.*

Chapter

2

*B*ack to the drawing board, Mandy told herself during her lunch break, setting down her phone after learning that the bakery position had been filled earlier that morning. *Missed it by minutes.*

The other listings in the paper led to similar dead ends, and her in-person inquiries at the other shops in town after work didn't turn up any opportunities, either. *Maybe one of my church friends will know of something. . . .*

.... ❀ ....

The next day, Mandy worked diligently, still determined to finish her time at the florist well.

When there was a lull in calls and walk-in customers on Wednesday, she asked Karyn if she knew of anyone hiring in the area. "I'd do most anything," Mandy admitted. They both knew her options were limited without a college degree, though she'd gotten her GED after leaving home.

Karyn stopped working on the arrangement she was preparing for a bridal shower and looked concerned. "I hope you know how much Tom and I dislike having to let you go, Mandy." She paused and then removed a stray leaf from a ranunculus. "You've been an excellent worker. And though Tom dreams of retiring, that's not in the picture."

At least now Mandy didn't have to fret that she wasn't doing a good job. "My father always said he'd work till he drew his last breath," she said softly. "Sadly, he died much too young . . . doing just that."

"I know you miss him terribly." Karyn's eyes were watery. "I felt that way when my father died, too."

Mandy nodded, not wanting to talk more about this, sorry she'd brought it up.

Determined to keep her chin up, she returned to cutting stems and arranging flowers, wondering as she often did about the people who would receive these bouquets her hands were touching. Was the birthday girl shy or excited about turning sweet sixteen? Did she already have a boyfriend? How sick was the man receiving these get-well flowers? Did his family live nearby?

All this giving of joy is about to end, she thought.

Sighing loudly, her neck and shoulders knotted up as the questions poured over her mind. *I shouldn't put myself in a stew.*

Her mother had taught her, as a little girl, to look to the Lord when troubles arose. *"Worry makes things worse,"* Mamma had repeated through the years.

"Okay, Mamma," she whispered, forcing a smile. "I can do this."

········ ❀ ········

On the way home from prayer meeting, Mandy turned the car radio to an easy-listening station, thinking maybe the music would ease her tension. The few people she'd mentioned her quandary to at church seemed to sympathize and had said they would put out feelers, but the search looked like it might take more time than Mandy had anticipated, and she didn't want to have to rely on the reserves in her bank account.

But by the following Sunday, not a single lead had materialized, other than an offer of baby-sitting.

"Something will turn up," Don said later while eating a fruit cup. "It's hard not to give in to discouragement."

Mandy shrugged. "I'm okay."

Eilene nodded her head, giving a ready smile. "You're in our daily prayers."

Don reached for a cookie. "It takes times of challenge for us to grow."

"My father believed that, too," Mandy told him as she looked at the collage of family pictures on the wall. "I never knew him to give up on anything."

"I would've liked your father," Don said.

Everyone did. And in that moment, she missed him and Mamma more than she could say.

.... ⚜ ....

Mandy rarely received any mail, so when Eilene called up the stairs to say there was a certified letter for her on Monday afternoon, Mandy was bewildered. "Who from?" she murmured, running down to see on this, her first day of unemployment.

Signing her name for the amiable mail carrier, she thanked him, as well as Eilene for alerting her, then hurried back upstairs, where she made note of the return address. Her pulse sped up. "Jerome?" Had Mamma given her eldest brother her address here?

Ever so curious, Mandy tore open the envelope. Whyever was he writing now?

Dear Amanda,

If you're reading this, this address is evidently correct. None of us is certain where you are, considering you don't stay in regular touch with Mamma.

Well, I dislike being the bearer of bad tidings, so I offer an apology in advance. You see, Mamma passed away unexpectedly yesterday morning. The coroner says it was likely a stroke. Only our heavenly Father knows for certain.

By the time this letter reaches you, the funeral and burial services will have taken place, but given the circumstances, the family wanted you to know directly.

When you receive this, please call my number at the bottom of the letter—my barn phone. There is something I need to discuss with you.

Again, I am sorry to burden you. This loss is a hard one for our family.

Your brother,
Jerome

Mandy's knees suddenly felt weak, and she settled down in her chair to catch her breath. Never had she expected such terrible news—Mamma had always been sturdy and hardworking, rarely sick a day in her life.

Getting up, Mandy paced about the room, then stopped to look in the mirror, staring at the young woman who now had lost both of her parents.

Looking at the date on the postmark, three days ago, she realized the funeral had most likely taken place this very day. It wasn't hard to imagine her four older brothers and wives, and their children—Arie, too—gathered at the fenced-in Amish cemetery a few miles from the inn to silently mourn with Mamma's many relatives and friends. Hundreds, perhaps, were in atten-dance, all having donned the black Sunday attire to pay their respects to Saloma Dienner, who had owned and operated the most highly respected and recommended Amish B and B in the county. *Always booked up months in advance,* Mandy thought of the spic-and-span place she'd once called home.

It was possible some of the regular guests had received word and traveled to be present, as well.

A numb feeling overtook her as she continued to ponder this dreadful turn. Who was keeping Butterfly Meadows afloat? Were sisters Sadie and Betsy Kauffman still around to help Arie Mae manage without the matron of the inn, the grandest cook and baker around? Not to mention the work of changing bed linens and towels and the careful cleaning each time guests vacated and new ones took their place. The heaps of laundry alone were daunting, she recalled. And then there was the care of the horses and chickens that remained after they sold off the goats and ponies to downsize following Dat's passing.

Feeling absolutely dazed, Mandy wandered downstairs with the letter in hand. She headed for the front porch, where she sat on the wooden swing and pushed her foot against the floor, rocking back and forth.

Oh, Mamma . . . how can this be? She wiped away a tear, then steeled herself against the knowledge that her mother was gone. Drawing a breath, she realized suddenly that there was no way to fix the past, or to face up to harbored regrets, though she wouldn't have known how to address them if Mamma were still alive.

Mandy sighed. *It's too late.*

Chapter

3

Winnie Maier pulled into the driveway a short while later, surprising Mandy where she still sat on the porch mulling over her brother's startling news. She must have looked downright peaked, because her closest friend wore a concerned frown as she walked to the front steps in black dress pants and a long-sleeved white blouse.

"Are you all right?" she asked, coming to sit with Mandy on the swing.

"My mother passed away." She lifted the letter, then dropped it back into her lap.

Winnie looked astonished. "Oh, Mandy! I'm so very sorry." Her frown deepened. "What can I do? Just say the word . . . anything at all."

"I'm still trying to believe it. She always seemed so healthy. . . ."

"Do you want to talk about it?" Winnie asked, turning to face her. She must have come straight from her office in Garden City, a half hour away.

Mandy expressed her sadness, though didn't offer much detail. Truth be told, Winnie knew little about Mandy's family.

"I've been trying to contact you," Winnie said. "You've been hard to reach this past week."

"Oh, sorry—I've been job hunting in my spare time." Mandy filled her in, trying not to make things sound as problematic as they were.

"As you know, it's not easy to find a good job in a town this small."

Groaning, Mandy said, "If I can't find a job here, I'll have to move."

The swing swayed with their combined weight.

Winnie's eyebrows rose. "Where to?"

"I haven't given it much thought . . . maybe to a city." Mandy laughed softly. "Can you imagine me in an office building? Former Amish girl goes urban?"

Winnie joined in her laughter, and they sat there, swinging gently for several minutes. Mandy thought of her brother's request to call him, and it made her nervous, wondering what was up. If only she could have been present for the funeral, difficult as it would have been to face her family again.

"Are you hungry?" Winnie asked, studying her. "We could go out for supper. My treat."

Not in the mood, Mandy suggested a rain check. "Okay?"

"That's cool." Winnie got up from the swing. "I'll see you later, then . . . and take care of yourself, okay?"

"Thanks for listening."

Bobbing her head, Winnie paused at the steps. "Text me if you need me," she said and then headed to her car.

"Thanks for dropping by," Mandy called and waved. Winnie had come to cheer her up at exactly the right time.

········ ❦ ········

The next morning, after a leisurely breakfast with the Bradleys intended to bolster her spirits, Mandy placed the call to her brother as requested. The barn phone rang so long, she was certain it would go to voice mail, but suddenly Jerome was on the line. "Hullo, Dienners."

Tempted to hang up, she hesitated before saying, "It's Mandy."

"*Denki* for getting in touch with me," he said. "I take it you got my letter."

She closed the door to her room and moved to the window, where she stood looking out at the landscape below. "*Jah*, what terrible news."

"Dreadful to hear by mail." He sounded apologetic. "None of us expected Mamma would die this young."

Like Dat, she thought.

"'Twas quite a crowd at the funeral yesterday. We held it at my place. More than six hundred. People from all over Lancaster County, and Arie Mae said she recognized quite a few guests from the B and B, too."

Hearing him refer to their sister so casually made Mandy more tense, but Jerome went on to say that their mother had gone to see a Lancaster City lawyer to update her will just a few months before she died. "She made me her executor."

Mandy couldn't fathom it. "But why bother with a will?"

"I was baffled at first, too. But I met briefly this morning with the attorney representing her wishes, and he told me that Mamma was quite astute. Evidently, she knew exactly what she wanted to happen to her treasured inn when she passed." Jerome fell silent for a moment.

Mandy waited for the pointed words she knew must be coming. But what he said instead was a shock.

"Mandy, you are to inherit the farmhouse, including the business of the inn."

She could scarcely find her voice to respond. "*Ach*, this must be a mistake," she told him, shaking her head as she talked into the phone, feeling befuddled. "The house . . . and everything related to the inn . . . shouldn't that go to Arie Mae?"

Jerome cleared his throat. He stumbled a bit as he explained how a will worked, sharing with her that it was the decision of the deceased to assign property. "The inn will be yours, although under certain stringent conditions."

Her brain was fraught with questions she wasn't sure how to articulate. Finally, still thinking of what this might mean to the rest of her family, she asked, "What if I just couldn't . . . accept this? What then?"

"I'm not at liberty to say," Jerome said flatly. "I'm sorry, Amanda."

This struck her as strange.

Several moments passed as she tried to make sense of this. *What am I supposed to do with it?* she thought. *I haven't been home in years!*

When she spoke at last, Mandy tried to joke. "Maybe you should just refer me to a real estate agent in Lancaster County."

Jerome didn't comment at first; in fact, he seemed all the more serious when he did speak. "Well, ya can't just sell it outright, Mandy." His voice had turned stiff. "In order to claim full ownership, you must manage the inn for twelve consecutive months. And it must remain profitable."

So there was a catch. Of course there was—one that would force her to return home. Her heart slammed against her chest.

Everything came back to her—the past with Arie, Mamma's parting words. All of it. Mandy had a mind to refuse the inheritance. Why should she move back there against her will?

Mandy remembered how her mother had sided with Arie Mae, all the while completely in the dark about what had been going on in the shadows. She cringed anew. "Who's running things now at the B and B?"

"Well, Arie Mae, of course . . . and the Kauffman sisters."

Her stomach clenched, and Mandy wondered what Arie would think of this turn of events—that is, if she didn't already know. *She'll feel perplexed, even slighted . . . if not offended.*

Still, Mandy couldn't help thinking of her present unemployment. It was downright embarrassing to be without work, enough so that it would be foolish for her to turn down the inheritance. Taking a breath, she worked up her courage.

"All right," she said. "I'll plan to arrive in Gordonville as soon as I can pack up and drive back."

"So you'll take over the care of the inn?"

"I will," Mandy said, noting the surprise in his tone. She brushed aside the fact that Arie was involved. She would have to deal with that once she got there, but she was pleased to know the Kauffman sisters were still assisting with the day-to-day responsibilities.

At least there's that.

They talked awhile longer, then Jerome told her, "We can discuss more when you arrive."

And because of everything that had transpired in the past, Mandy could only hope the months till the deed was signed over to her might pass swiftly. *A full year!* Once the conditions were met, she would put the inn up for sale.

All in good time, she thought, dreading to see her twin again. *How can we possibly work together?*

Chapter

4

Twenty-five-year-old Catrina Sutton got up later than usual that Tuesday morning for her weekly trek to her Rochester, Minnesota, grocery store. She chose black yoga pants and a long-sleeved pale blue top and, as she often did, lightly touched the elegant engagement ring she still wore on her left hand.

She thought of Shawn, gone more than a year now, and sighed. Her late fiancé had made even mundane tasks like grocery shopping fun.

At the store, she parked her car and headed through the automatic door, hungry for something besides a salad or sandwich for lunch. Fourteen months since Shawn's accident, and her appetite was finally returning. She had once mentioned her lack of hunger to the gracious elderly widow she cared for five nights a week in her work as a home health aide. *"How long before you felt like eating, after your husband passed away?"* she'd asked Gail Anderson.

"Months," Gail had told her, gray eyes blinking back tears. *"And I lost weight I didn't have to lose."* She had patted her nonexistent hips through her bathrobe.

The grief-stricken woman said she had worn sunglasses for months after her husband's funeral, and most days, Trina wished she might do the same. But there were other ways to mask grief, and it was her job to press on as best she could.

Trina reached for a sirloin steak in the meat section, thinking ahead to the meal she was formulating. She had a wonderful recipe for steak with garlic butter, and this noon was the perfect time for it. A side of green beans with lemon and almonds would be an ideal accompaniment. Her mouth watered.

Trina's only sibling, her younger sister, Janna, often said how amazing Trina was in the kitchen. But then, Janna was known to be lavish with compliments. Too bad they lived two and a half hours from each other—Janna in St. Cloud, where she worked as a consultant for a marketing firm.

To her credit, Janna had called and visited more often since Trina had lost the love of her life to a fatal car crash caused by a drunken driver. Janna seemed to understand the heartache Trina bore in the wake of the painful loss, one Trina had been reminded of twenty-four seven back when she still worked at a local nursing home.

I loved Shawn so deeply, Trina realized. *And it's made a mess of my life.*

If there was anything Trina didn't like, it was messes. She liked to be neat and efficient—a fact few of her acquaintances seemed to appreciate.

More than once, Trina had heard the words *control freak* thrown around when the other certified nursing assistants assumed she was out of earshot. But the fact was that her straightforward manner was the most effective way to get things done. As far as she was concerned, if people would just let her handle things, the world would be a better place. Hadn't Gail Anderson told her exactly this with a sweet smile? Actually, wasn't that what dear Shawn had always said, too? She glanced at her engagement ring and wondered how many other young women continued to wear theirs after the loss of a fiancé.

Is this normal? she wondered, hurrying to the checkout with a week's worth of items. Quickly, she paid for them and pushed the cart out to her car.

The sun hid behind the clouds, but autumn's scent lingered in the air. A few stubborn oak leaves still clung to the trees. The leaves had been raucous this year with the reds, oranges, and golds that Shawn Franklin had photographed through the years. His studio had been absolutely aglow with fall foliage, and Trina cringed even now at the memory of having gone there immediately after the funeral. She'd broken down and sobbed.

One year already seems like ten, she thought miserably.

Glancing in her rearview mirror, Trina was surprised at her disheveled state, her shoulder-length wavy brown hair tangled in places. Running her hand through her hair, she was anxious to return to her small condo and what had become her new normal. She remembered Shawn's attentive hovering as she worked in the kitchen the evenings they'd enjoyed dinner together. And his endearing grin and smiling brown eyes as he acted as sous-chef, allowing her to direct him.

"I can't argue with the results," he would tease.

It had been so easy to fall in love with him; he'd never minded her frank opinions and let her be who she was. Prior to Shawn, few men had made the effort to pursue her.

"I'm cool with that," she said aloud. *Better one Shawn than a dozen other guys.*

Trina was coming up on the street where, for three exhausting years, she had turned off for her former workplace. The nursing home had given her the boot six months ago. "Good riddance," she murmured, glad to have connected instead with the home health service and her affirming charge. Gail was a reminder that something wonderful had come out of recent difficulties.

In fact, Trina looked forward to her weeknight shifts at the Anderson home. Gone were the daily dustups with other staff, many of whom Trina thought took their responsibilities too lightly.

Initially, Gail's family had questioned the woman's insistence she employ someone at night, but Gail definitely had a mind of her own and money in the bank. More important, she was considerate and appreciative, and Trina prided herself on anticipating the woman's every need. It felt good to be so needed. A natural night owl, Trina also enjoyed the chance to catch up on her reading prior to drifting off to sleep on the daybed in the sitting room a few steps from Gail's room.

Typically, for the first few hours of their evening together, Gail sat and talked until she grew too tired, and Trina helped her to bed. Gail's mind was active and strong, and her body in fairly good shape for a ninety-one-year-old. Yet Gail confided in Trina that she feared being alone at night after the passing of her husband of sixty-six years.

"That's why I'm here," Trina would reassure her, patting her arm. "You can rest easy."

"Oh, and I do now," she readily agreed. "You have no idea."

Occasionally, one of Gail's granddaughters came to spend the weekend, relieving the weekend nurse, though Gail was always waiting near the front door for Trina's arrival following such a visit. Her apparent fondness was a surprise to Trina, who didn't often click with people . . . not anymore, anyway. "I was afraid you'd forget me," Gail would say, her eyes twinkling with mischief. "Then what would I do?"

At least Gail understands me. . . .

With her fiancé gone and buried, there was really no one else for Trina to look after. *I might adopt a child someday*, she occasionally considered, before just as quickly shaking off the fanciful notion. She still hoped to have a family of her own someday, knowing she'd be a terrific mom.

But men weren't exactly beating a path to her door.

Chapter

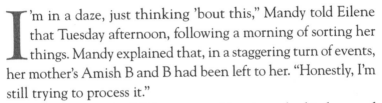

5

I'm in a daze, just thinking 'bout this," Mandy told Eilene that Tuesday afternoon, following a morning of sorting her things. Mandy explained that, in a staggering turn of events, her mother's Amish B and B had been left to her. "Honestly, I'm still trying to process it."

"Well, no wonder." Eilene steered her into the kitchen and pulled out a chair for her to sit down.

"There are conditions, though."

"Here you are sick with grief . . . and now this." Eilene sliced some applesauce bread and poured some coffee for Mandy, like a good Amish mother might. The gesture of kindness made Mandy smile, and she thanked her for the years of hospitality. "You and your husband have been so generous to me."

Eilene gave a small shrug. "It's our pleasure, Mandy. Besides, you're part of God's family . . . and we've enjoyed having you here."

"I hope my leaving won't be a problem . . . well, be inconvenient to you and your husband," she said, explaining that she needed to move back east as soon as she could to oversee her mother's inn. "I'll pay my next month's rent, of course."

Eilene declined and thanked her. "Don't be concerned about us. God will bring along someone to rent your room, just as He sent you to us for a time." Her mouth turned down slightly. "But we'll miss having you here."

"I'll miss you, too."

Eilene sat at the table with her, and they nibbled on the moist sweet bread and sipped coffee, talking softly, reminiscing.

"I'll keep in touch," Mandy assured her.

This seemed to ease Eilene's sad expression. "We'll look forward to that."

Glad to have been blessed with such a nurturing landlord and friend, Mandy excused herself to finish going through her few things.

········ ❁ ········

By the next day, Mandy had packed up her car for the two-day trip and left hours before dawn. Kind as she was, Winnie had asked if she might call her once Mandy was settled again in Gordonville, even though Mandy couldn't promise a return to Kansas at the end of a year's time.

"I don't know where I'll land ultimately," she admitted aloud now, certain it would not be Lancaster County. *Maybe someplace where I can set up a florist shop of my own.* She stared at the long road ahead as the car sped east through the flat prairie toward home. *For better . . . or for worse.*

········ ❁ ········

Mandy checked into a motel for a warm shower at seven o'clock, and later walked across the parking lot to the restaurant for a hot meal. Wanting to rise early again the next morning, she headed right to bed, hoping for a midafternoon arrival in Lancaster County tomorrow. *Lord willing.*

She was thankful for traveling mercies and let her thoughts fly back to her growing-up years on the farm. She recalled the severe June hailstorm that had wiped out her father's crops of corn and wheat, yet he had bowed his head at the supper table and thanked almighty God for His sovereign will. *Dat had such a strong, unshakable faith,* she thought.

After Dat died, no one sat in his oak rocking chair near the coal-burning stove in what had later become private family quarters when the B and B opened. Mandy could still picture that grand rocker with its slatted back, specially made padded brown seat, and wide, firm armrests.

It'll seem strange going home without either of them there. Mandy shuddered at the thought and turned over in the double bed, trying to stretch out the stiffness in her muscles after the long drive.

·········· ✿ ··········

Mandy felt all in by late morning the next day, weary of driving. To maintain good time, she'd limited her stops to no more than every three hours.

She felt trapped in a kind of limbo as she neared the Amish farmland of her childhood, not sure what to expect. She could almost hear her father's deep voice as he called for her and Arie to come inside for supper, his dear face tinted with sunburn. And the way he'd always held the driving lines when out in the family carriage, giving them a gentle snap, so Ol' Tulip would take off trotting. An image of Mamma in the big kitchen also flitted across her mind, Mamma hard at work to prepare yet another scrumptious meal.

If only Mandy could keep her mind on those happy memories, she thought as she drove east on U.S. Route 30. Then, her heart in her throat, she reached the turnoff to Old Leacock Road.

Seeing the neighbors' horse fence rimming the road, she recalled the time she'd taken off in the spring wagon, and a whole pile of pumpkins meant for market had fallen out. The load had splattered onto the narrow road near here, blocking passage. Dat had been forgiving of the expensive mistake, but Mandy had regretted not paying more attention and resolved to be more responsible in the future.

Mandy recalled all this in a flash as she passed by the Gordonville Book Store on the right, still heading toward the B and B. A ways up, the white clapboard homestead owned by Josiah's parents came into view, and she remembered the many times she'd gone with him to the fishing hole, carrying the pail of wiggling worms they'd dug together, and taking along peanut butter sandwiches with strawberry jam slathered on them—two sandwiches for Josiah Lantz, since he was a growing boy, his mother said. *Just a couple years older than me,* Mandy thought. From the start, the boy with only brothers had claimed her and Arie Mae as his so-called sisters. But Mandy had felt sure Josiah would be not just her inseparable childhood friend, but also her first beau . . . and her future husband.

········ ❀ ········

At the simple sign for The Butterfly Meadows Amish Bed-and-Breakfast, Mandy pulled into the lane and caught her first sight of the grand dame of a house—her childhood home—its rusty red brick still as striking as ever. The B and B was gracefully situated on a slight rise and surrounded by well-trimmed yards and gardens freshly tilled for the coming winter.

Am I ready for this?

She parked off to the side in the vacant guest parking lot and switched off the ignition, renewing her resolve. At least she'd thought to do up her hair in a formal bun and wear a modest top and skirt.

Pressing the release for the trunk, Mandy got out and went to retrieve two boxes, leaving her suitcase where it was. She would trust it was safe there for now and come back for it.

She made her way up the lane, thinking, *Under any other circumstances, I would never have come home.*

Mandy recalled one of her mother's letters, written three years ago. *Your sister is engaged to marry Josiah Lantz come fall.* Even though Mandy had known that day might come, she had taken the news hard and sent Mamma a note asking not to be informed of any further news on the subject.

In that particular letter, she had also written that nothing could induce her to return to Gordonville. To Mamma's credit, she had never stopped trying to connect with her, and Mandy had looked forward to the occasional letters, as well as the birthday and Christmas cards they'd exchanged over the years.

Mandy caught sight of one of her mother's several birdbaths and the perfectly trimmed hedges near the long paved walkway that led up to the front porch, which faced the east meadow, where the butterflies arrived in the first golden days of spring. The porch was not visible from the road, so guests had some privacy as they sat there. It had been the family's sanctuary, too, before the house was filled with tourists. *Before Mamma had to stretch to make ends meet.*

Mandy noticed the stone tablet set into the home's brick exterior at a grown man's eye level. *Built by William Dienner in the year of our Lord 1920.* She couldn't help wondering what her great-grandfather would think if he knew that one of his descendants was temporarily moving back onto his original property after five years of living in the world. Was this beautiful place truly going to belong to Mandy someday?

On the opposite side of the house, down near Mamma's rose garden, the old rope swing caught her eye, as well as the white trellis she and Arie had had fun painting every other year. In some respects, it seemed as if things had never changed.

Mandy's gaze lingered on the swing, where she and Arie had swung double and giggled till they were nearly hoarse, often with one of them standing and pumping extra hard while the other sat and squealed with glee.

On the front porch, she set down the boxes and took note of the blooming mums—purple, gold, and orange. Mamma had always loved making this porch a special spot, and Mandy and her sister had helped decorate for the seasons, with Mamma's vision in mind.

But now that she was here, Mandy began to dread even more the thought of seeing Arie again. *What will I even say to her?* She turned to walk the length of the porch, the same welcoming rockers lined up in their usual places. *The way Mamma wanted them.* Her mother had always been such a presence; it was hard to believe she was gone.

Reluctantly, Mandy meandered back to the front door and rang the bell, clenching her jaw at the sound of the battery-operated door chimes. It wasn't but a minute and here came pretty Sadie Kauffman to the door, clad all in black, her face solemn. Mandy was truly relieved to see Sadie first.

Sadie, however, didn't bother to conceal her shock at seeing Mandy and took an obvious step back. "Arie said you'd be comin', but we were thinkin' next week or even later."

"S'pose I should've called ahead." Mandy moved the boxes just inside the door as Betsy joined them in the hallway.

"Honestly, ya chose a *gut* time to arrive. Ain't any guests arriving today," Betsy told her. "Rare durin' wedding season."

Mandy was glad to hear she could catch her breath and get settled in a bit following the grueling drive.

"Are ya here to stay, then?" Like her older sister, Betsy looked mighty mournful in her black dress and full cape apron. Each sister had her dishwater blond hair parted down the center and pulled back properly, a dark bandanna tied tightly over the hair bun.

"You've prob'ly heard that I'm supposed to take my mother's place here," Mandy said, glancing back out the open door at her car. "*Ach*, my suitcase is still in the trunk."

"I'll go an' get it," Sadie said, giving Betsy a furtive look as she slipped out the door.

Mandy wondered why the young woman had seemed so eager to rush off. "Is Arie Mae around?" she asked Betsy, who was wringing her hands, looking for all the world like she didn't want to be left alone with Mandy.

"She's getting a few groceries over at the farm on Paradise Lane." Mandy could picture the small Amish-run store where Arie had gone. The delay in seeing her sister made her feel all the more rattled.

"*Willkumm Heem*," Betsy said, offering a small smile now as she picked up one of the boxes. The friendly *Deitsch* words sounded surprisingly good to Mandy.

Nodding and carrying the other box, Mandy let Betsy lead the way past the old rolltop desk, where Mamma had always kept the reservation book. They turned right toward the intersecting hallway to the back of the house, where three bedrooms and a small sitting room and bathroom were tucked away from the kitchen, breakfast room, and the common areas on the main level at the opposite end. Mamma had requested electricity be hooked up in the spaces for the paying guests back when she first had the idea to open their family home as an inn. Thankfully, their bishop had approved.

"Which room do ya want?" asked Betsy with a glance over her shoulder.

"Oh . . . my former bedroom's just fine, if it's available." She hadn't given much thought to this as they passed her mother's spacious room, where at first glance, the place looked unchanged. With Mamma's passing so recent, Arie and their sisters-in-law probably hadn't had time yet to go through her things.

"Arie Mae was real sure you'd choose your old room," Betsy said. "But there's also your Mamma's bedroom if you want to settle in there."

Mandy's heart ached at the thought.

Once in Mandy's old room, Betsy asked where to put the boxes, helpful as she'd always been.

"Over in the closet for now. *Denki.*" Mandy handed her the second box, then moved to the windows overlooking the famous butterfly meadow and the hay fields beyond. "Some of my brothers must still be farming Dat's old land," she stated absently.

"*Jah,* they pitch in when they can. The neighbor up the road, Karl Lantz, has been working here for some time now and comes every day to tend to the horses and clean the stable. He and his son moved here a year ago from Platteville, Wisconsin, after Karl lost his wife."

"Is Karl Amish?"

"Oh *jah.*" Betsy nodded. "And related to some of the oodles of Lantzes round here, though I'm not sure how closely. His little boy, Yonnie, tags along. Cute as a bug's ear."

"I'm glad to hear there's someone to look after the barn and the animals."

"No way we could do everything inside otherwise," Betsy said as she glanced around Mandy's room. "Well, I'll send Sadie back here with your suitcase. She'll go over the reservations with ya—three couples are scheduled to arrive tomorrow afternoon around three-thirty." Talkative Betsy motioned toward the upstairs. "All the guest rooms are ready 'cept one, since we had a late checkout

48

today—the woman didn't get going till two o'clock, but Sadie didn't charge her extra, since she's a regular."

Mandy nodded. "Of course." She noticed the sampler she and Arie had taken turns stitching together still hanging on the wall near the dresser. Mamma had been so pleased with their work. A lump rose in Mandy's throat. "Not havin' my mother around will take some getting used to."

"She was a *wunnerbaar-gut* woman," Betsy said softly just then, a catch in her voice. "I already miss her."

"She was so fond of you."

"I was blessed to know her," Betsy said, staring at Mandy as if wondering why her sensible mother would bestow the inn on the daughter who'd left them all scrambling when she'd run off without explanation.

Mandy drew a long breath; she needed to open some windows. Being back inside these familiar walls was nearly overwhelming.

She thanked Betsy, glad things had worked out to spend the first few moments back in this house with her.

Betsy went to the door. "Well, I'd best be finishing up, so I'll excuse myself now," she said.

Mandy turned back to the window and cracked it open, the weather too chilly to open it wider. There she stood, where as a child she'd watched rain droplets slide down the polished panes, or stared in wonder as thousands of snowflakes fluttered and drifted to the ground. And all the while, Arie Mae had leaned against her shoulder, chattering, or lounged on the bed doing her newest needlework project or reading a library book.

We shared everything back then. . . .

Straightening a bit, Mandy observed Sadie finally tottering up to the front porch with the heavy suitcase. *Oh dear,* Mandy thought. *She must think I packed rocks in there!*

The determined young woman had been a single grade behind

Mandy and Arie, and one of Arie's closest friends when they all attended the one-room schoolhouse.

Seeing Sadie perch herself on the bulky suitcase to catch her breath, Mandy was struck again by the Kauffman sisters' black mourning dresses and matching aprons. It was as though they considered themselves part of this family.

Chapter

6

With the supper hour approaching, Mandy wondered when Arie Mae was due back with the groceries. She headed down the hallway, then out to help Sadie with the suitcase.

"It's heavier than I expected," Sadie said, huffing as she heaved it in the door.

"Here, I'll take it to my room," Mandy said, reaching for the suitcase. "*Denki* . . . should've insisted on helping. Sorry."

Sadie straightened and placed her hands on her hips. "While I've got you alone, I'd best be tellin' ya . . . I'm just stayin' on till Monday afternoon. After that, I won't be workin' here."

Dismayed, Mandy took note of the young woman's deep frown. "Is it because of me?"

"I didn't wanna leave till you arrived," Sadie said. "Wasn't sure you'd really come back, to be honest."

"Well, just 'cause I'm here doesn't mean you can't stay, does it?" Mandy tried to smile.

Sadie shook her head. "It's just that . . . well, I realize that you weren't baptized, but the way you up and left so quickly . . ." She sighed. "My fiancé's concerned that by now you're thoroughly English." Sadie's gaze came to rest on Mandy's simple yet obviously not Amish clothes.

Answering to me as her boss is a problem for her. Mandy's standing among the community was definitely going to be a worry.

"If I can't persuade you otherwise, I won't stand in the way of your leavin'," Mandy said, her mind reeling with this setback.

Not waiting for Sadie to say more, Mandy lugged the suitcase back to her room at the far end of the house, then went back to have a look at the grand porch, having noticed earlier all the dead leaves scattered here and yon, something her mother would never have tolerated. *"First impressions are important,"* Mamma had always said, and Mandy went to tend to that immediately.

Hearing Sadie upstairs with Betsy, she went to the kitchen utility closet for the broom and made a beeline back to the porch, then swept it vigorously, attempting to quiet her frustration. Goodness, leaves even cluttered the seats of the rockers!

That task done, she wandered back to her room and unpacked, thinking ahead to what she might wear tomorrow to greet the afternoon guests. Slipping into the shower, she considered again how disheartening it was that Sadie was quitting; the People hadn't forgotten that Mandy had gone west with two rowdy girls from Ronks.

If so, it's no wonder Sadie's beau is worried, she thought as she toweled off. She towel-dried her damp hair and brushed it back on both sides, pinning a wide barrette on one side. Then she put on a long skirt and modest long-sleeved blouse and sweater.

Heading to her mother's room, Mandy crept to the foot of the double bed, uncertain why, really. Maybe it was curiosity. Taking in the roomy space, she saw little that personalized it other than the soft blue, green, and rose bed quilt. There were two freestanding oil lamps, one on the bedside table and one on the dresser—Mamma's favorite lighting for sewing or reading.

Lost in the moment, Mandy went to sit on the bed, gently tracing her fingers over the delicate stitches of the Whig Rose pattern she and Arie Mae had made for their mother's birthday the year following Dat's death. Such fun they'd had keeping their secret till the gift was given.

I loved Mamma, she thought sadly, *though we weren't very close.*

There were times when Mandy wished her mother's parting words might fade from her memory. Surely they would, given more time. But no matter Mamma's written apology, Mandy recalled them yet again as she sat there, and the intensity with which they had been said. *"If that's how you feel, Mandy, perhaps it would be best if you left for a while. It's none of your business who Josiah courts!"*

Even after Mandy's departure, she had hoped, even prayed, that Josiah might cast Arie aside and return to her, his first love. *Even as far away as I was in Kansas.*

But he hadn't.

And Mandy had never understood it. *Why?* she thought. *Josiah and I belonged together!*

She tried to shake off the rising sense of disappointment as she revisited the old emotions, as fresh as if she'd just left. *I had to leave. . . .*

Hearing footsteps in the hallway, Mandy stiffened.

"Anyone in there?" The voice Mandy least wanted to hear drifted into Mamma's room.

Inhaling quickly, Mandy felt reluctant to make herself known. "I'm here, Arie." She at last turned to see her sister, dressed in black. It felt uncommonly strange to see her in the flesh, as if they were both in a dream.

"When did ya get in?" Arie asked, her voice pinched as flat as her expression.

"Oh, just a while ago."

Arie didn't budge from the doorway. "How was your trip?"

"Longer than I remembered." Mandy grasped for something more to say. "I'm getting reacquainted with the house. Seems so empty without Mamma."

Arie nodded but remained stationed where she was.

Rising then, Mandy asked, "What else must be done for the guests arriving tomorrow? Is there coffee, tea . . . something sweet to offer?"

Arie said there was plenty of everything. "Betsy and Sadie are nearly finished upstairs, and I've put away the necessary groceries."

"*Gut* to know." Mandy supposed she should thank Arie for taking care of those details, but she didn't feel up to it. The truth was, Mandy's stomach hurt just breathing the same air as her sister. The painful past felt more alive now than it had in years.

"We have three couples comin' . . . some repeat guests," Arie Mae added, seemingly more calm now. "Two of the couples, the Hayeses and the Cohens, have been regulars for about four years now. Delighted with the inn and the area."

So I've never met them, Mandy thought. "And the other couple?"

"The Spencers are friends of the Cohens, from what I know. Patrick and Heather Cohen have been raving about Mamma's B and B to their acquaintances for quite a while now." Arie actually smiled, no doubt in an attempt to worm her way back into Mandy's good graces. "Now that they're all retired, the whole bunch of them will basically take over the upstairs for the weekend. Except for the large suite at the end of the hall."

Mandy jerked her head in a quick nod. "Is that booked, too?"

"It's empty till Monday and Tuesday—we have a two-night

minimum now, somethin' Mamma decided a few years ago. Makes for less stripping of beds and whatnot." Arie paused. "Would ya like to read through the guest list for the rest of the month?" she asked, running her fingers over her black apron waistband. Her tone had softened dramatically during this, their first encounter since that terrible day.

Mandy nodded. "Sure."

"I've made a few notes for you in the reservations book," Arie added. "Oh, and Mamma's favorite breakfast recipes are all in her thick notebook in the kitchen cupboard, far left side, where she always kept it." Arie's voice cracked, and she looked down for a moment, evidently composing herself before speaking again. "Coffee is available starting at six-thirty in the morning."

Same as before . . .

Mandy felt rooted at the foot of Mamma's bed. "I assume Betsy still feeds the chickens and gathers the eggs."

"*Jah*, she likes doin' those things." Arie bit her lower lip, unnecessarily silent for a time. "Mandy, all of Mamma's clothing and things are still here for you and me to sort through whenever you're ready."

Mandy's stomach was in knots. Arie had waited for her.

"Jerome said he talked with you by phone." Arie Mae eyed her curiously. "He didn't say how soon you'd be arrivin'."

"He didn't know . . . I wasn't sure when I could get away." Mandy wanted to blurt out the words her sister was surely thinking: No one had any idea why Mamma hadn't appointed *Arie* to inherit the B and B. Yet saying so would do nothing to improve this exceedingly difficult moment.

"You know, Mandy, I would've written to tell ya that Mamma died, but . . ." Arie stopped as if searching for the right words. Mandy could guess what she was about to say but did not. Maybe her sister didn't want to reignite their fiery past.

Still hugging the doorframe, Arie Mae sighed and glanced toward the windows, then back at Mandy. "There's food in the fridge for supper when you're hungry, and I'll be over early on Saturday morning to make breakfast, like I've been doin' since Mamma passed." Arie turned as if she was leaving.

"You're in a hurry?"

"I need to head home," Arie said softly. "Next farm over, so I'm close if you need anything after work hours." She pointed toward the north. "Dat's old cornfield nearly bumps up against my vegetable garden."

Next door! Truth be told, Mandy wasn't certain how she would handle them living so near. In spite of having read the telltale words in one of Mamma's letters, Mandy felt surprised. "Now that I'm here, it's hard to believe you went ahead and married Josiah . . . after everything that happened," she stated, but immediately regretted it.

"Please, Mandy . . . we're expecting our first baby next June," Arie said in a whisper.

Mandy recoiled at the news, and for a moment, she refused to look at her sister.

"I know Mamma told ya back when Josiah and I got engaged."

Mandy glanced up at Arie, who looked straight at her now, unflinching.

"*Jah*, she did." Mandy well remembered reading her mother's letter; it was the day she'd vowed never to return. "No doubt what you wanted all along."

Arie's face turned stony. And she remained silent, offering not a whit of an apology.

She must not be sorry, Mandy thought, wondering if her sister might make an attempt to come clean at long last. When she didn't, Mandy thought how awkward it would be, having to see Arie Mae on a daily basis, working together.

Unexpectedly, Arie's eyes seemed to soften, and she took a step forward. "Mandy Sue, I'm ever so glad you came home."

But Mandy was done with her sister's platitudes, not when she wanted—no, deserved—Arie's sincere apology.

This can't possibly work, Mandy thought, considering the challenges she faced, and something rose up in her. "Listen, don't bother comin' over to make breakfast on Saturday . . . or on any day after that," she said crossly. "I won't be needing your help."

Arie shook her head as if stunned. "What are you sayin'?"

"I'll run the place without you."

Arie's eyes widened, but she said nothing as she turned and fled down the long hall.

Trembling with anger, Mandy waited till her sister was surely gone, relieved she'd left without another word of protest.

Chapter 7

Upstairs, Mandy found Sadie and Betsy making up the queen-sized bed in the pleasant and airy Green Room, always a favorite of guests, with its expansive treed view from the tall windows. Mamma had named all four of the guest rooms for the jeweled hues of the featured bed quilts.

Still shaken, Mandy stood observing for a moment, trying to calm herself, yet unable to forget the time spent with Arie Mae in this pretty room, making up the bed, dusting, and sharing secrets as they worked.

"So Arie's gone for the day?" Sadie asked as she stood on one side of the bed while Betsy took care to tuck in the hem of the sheet.

Much as she wanted to, Mandy knew she couldn't put this off. "She won't be working here anymore."

Betsy's eyes fluttered wide, as if to say, *Are you* ferhoodled . . . *we need her!*

"Who's gonna make breakfast for the guests?" Sadie asked, frowning as she glanced at her sister.

"Well, as I recall, both of yous are fine cooks," Mandy said, which might have been stretching it a little. She smoothed out the coverlet folded at the foot of the bed.

The sisters exchanged looks.

"Sadie's the better one," Betsy said quickly, giving a shrug.

And the one who wants to quit, thought Mandy, groaning inwardly. She couldn't bear to lose Sadie, not with Arie out the door. But Sadie didn't seem willing to be convinced otherwise. "Would you mind showin' Betsy what you do in the kitchen, Sadie?"

But it was Betsy who shook her head. "Nobody would pay to eat my breakfasts!"

Taking stock of the situation, Mandy tried to soften her approach. She felt uncomfortable learning how to be a boss, especially to helpers whom she assumed had little respect for her. "Of course I'll do what I can, as well," Mandy said, her stomach sinking now at the thought of her own rusty culinary skills. Only Arie equaled Mamma in the kitchen.

"It's gonna be hard managing everything," Betsy pointed out.

"Well, don't fret 'bout breakfast," Mandy assured her. "Sadie and I will handle that."

Sadie nodded. "But only through Monday," she said, making it clear again.

Betsy's shoulders rose and fell, and she turned to look out the bedroom window. Mandy could well imagine Betsy must be thinking that someone who belonged here ought to be running the place. The fact that Mandy had once partnered with her mother and Arie Mae no longer seemed to matter.

Mandy followed Sadie out to the hallway. "If ya change your mind about stayin' on—"

"*Nee,*" Sadie said right quick. "My beau won't hear of it."

Mandy tried not to let the terse response jar her and went to check on the suite—the Blue Room—at the end of the hall. "Arie says this one's not booked till Monday night. Is that right?"

"Come on . . . I'll go over the reservations with you," Sadie offered, and Mandy hurried after her as the three of them descended the very stairs where, as a child, Mandy had slid down the bannister oodles of times, Mamma always calling after her, *"Careful you don't slip and break your neck!"*

Going to the oak rolltop desk in the entryway, Sadie pushed up the lid, removed the well-worn reservation book, and motioned for Mandy to go and sit with her in the bright commons area meant for guests, formerly the family's front room. It was the same room where Mandy's father had been laid out in his coffin as hundreds of relatives and neighbors filed past, she recalled with a sigh. Mamma's viewing and funeral, however, had been held at Jerome's, he'd told her.

A good daughter would've been present, Mandy thought gloomily.

Betsy followed them into the room and primly crossed her legs at the ankles as she and Mandy sat with Sadie between them, the book open on Sadie's lap.

"The inn is basically full through Thanksgiving," Sadie said as she went line by line, pointing out the regular guests and first timers, each listed with an address and a phone number. "Unfortunately, December through February look rather slow, as you prob'ly remember. . . . Things stay that way till the mud sales start in the spring."

Mandy hadn't forgotten and paid close attention to the tidbits of information Sadie was quickly sharing, including the special requests. Not all of it was in writing, however, and Mandy assumed that it was because Mamma knew the guests so well. "Here, let me get a pen and make some further notes," Mandy said, concerned that Sadie, who seemed to be the sister more familiar with everything, wouldn't be around for long.

"Betsy'll be here," Sadie reminded Mandy when she rose to go to the hall desk.

"I'm glad, but with only two of us, I'd rather not leave anything to chance," Mandy replied, recalling her brother's remark about the need to keep the B and B profitable. "I'm sure you understand."

"Honestly, I'm baffled why your Mamma dropped everything in *your* lap," Sadie said, holding the large book steady as Mandy wrote a few things next to various names.

"My mother's choices aren't for you to judge." Mandy wasn't about to admit to Sadie that she'd wondered the same.

Evident surprise flickered in Sadie's eyes. "Sorry," she whispered meekly.

"Now, getting back to the Blue Room—does the businessman from Baltimore still come for three weeks on the last day of November, like he used to?"

Betsy spoke. "*Jah*, he's one of our solid regulars."

Mandy snapped her fingers, trying to remember his name. "Gary, was it?"

"Gavin O'Connor," Sadie said, laughing a little now. "But you're close."

Mandy asked to go over the names of the guests coming in the next month a second time to double-check dietary issues and other needs.

"By the way, Mrs. Dobbins and her husband are comin' in a few weeks. Mrs. Dobbins can't sleep on our feather pillows, so your Mamma always kept a foam one for her in the linen closet. It's still there, last time I checked," Sadie said.

"I definitely want to keep track of details like that," Mandy said, jotting this down, as well. "And Jerome's droppin' by to have breakfast with me tomorrow. He wants to go over the current monthly budget then, too."

From what Jerome had said, Mandy had gleaned that her

other brothers weren't so knowledgeable about the details of the B and B—nor, perhaps, as interested. *Might be the reason Mamma didn't name one of them the heir—they didn't want the headache of running it.*

"Sounds like Jerome. We usually don't see much of your family. They're busy with their own farms," Betsy piped up, fidgeting with her black apron. "Arie and Josiah have always been the ones to help out."

"Josiah's handled whatever repairs are needed," Sadie added, flipping through reservations to the month of April, when the pages were once more filled with names.

Josiah's in charge of repairs?

Sadie closed the book and carried it back to the desk, then led the way into the kitchen. "Now let's have a look at the weekend menu options. We'll want a nice variety."

"Remember, Arie bought groceries today," Betsy said, pointing out that Arie evidently had a plan for that group of guests. "Maybe she left a note or two 'bout it. She usually has sticky notes all over the kitchen."

Sounds like her, thought Mandy, trying her best not to second-guess having sent her sister on her way. *I can't run this place with someone I don't trust. . . .*

Sadie searched and found nothing, so she opened Mamma's cupboard and reached for the famous recipe notebook.

"Maybe just go ahead and decide what you'd like to make for breakfast, based on the groceries on hand," Mandy encouraged Sadie, pleased to see a bowl of chocolate chip cookie dough in the fridge.

"Of course, your Mamma didn't serve hot meals on the Lord's Day." Sadie turned to glance at her. "Will you continue that tradition?"

Betsy spoke before Mandy could. "Well, this B and B has been advertised as *authentically* Amish," she said, catching Mandy's eye. "You don't mean to change that, do ya?"

"Not at all." Mandy exhaled. *Am I crazy to take this on?*

An awkward moment passed before Betsy spoke again. "There's never been any charge for guests stayin' Sunday night, either," Betsy reminded her, leaning against the long counter where Mandy had helped Mamma and Arie roll out dozens of pie crusts.

I could use the money, though, Mandy thought, knowing that every penny she earned could go toward meeting the goal of profitability. "Did my mother keep the books, or did Jerome?"

"Jerome," Betsy and Sadie said in unison.

"So he must be the one paying taxes to the county." Since the county used a portion of those taxes toward advertising, Mandy was all the more appreciative of her oldest brother's help. *Whatever keeps the inn booked.*

Betsy excused herself to go outdoors to gather the afternoon eggs, leaving Mandy alone with Sadie.

"I think I can still make a moist and delicious sweet bread," Mandy said, more to herself than to Sadie.

Sadie opened the apron drawer beneath the oven and put one on. "Better make a big batch so there's plenty, considering there are three men in this next bunch of guests," Sadie said.

"I'm glad you're stayin' on to help, at least for a couple more days," Mandy said.

"I'll make every minute count." Sadie nodded toward the fridge. "You've gotta be hungry. There's some sliced ham in there and goat cheese from the neighbors up the road."

"*Denki,*" Mandy said, suddenly realizing she was famished, considering how long the day had already been.

My first day out of three hundred and sixty-five!

Suppertime was unlike any Mandy had ever experienced here. And afterward, she did up the dishes quickly, thinking how, for all of the years she'd lived in this house, it was the only time she had ever been alone here come sundown. Mandy wondered if God had willed it that no guests had reserved a room for this particular night, so she could have the house to herself and get her bearings before embarking on such a challenging journey.

She swept the kitchen with her gaze, landing on the old wall hanging Mamma had made with Arie Mae's help. The verse had been one of their father's favorites. "'Let the children first show piety at home,'" she began to read, tears threatening. "'And to requite their parents; for that is good and acceptable before God.'"

"Please help me get through this year, Lord," she whispered, still bewildered that she and not Arie was the one on whom the business of the B and B now depended.

And to think I fired my sister flat out!

Chapter

8

Mandy settled into her room after supper and tried to read her Bible by gaslight but gave up, feeling out of sorts. Restless, she wandered out to the kitchen with the large flashlight, wearing her mother's white chenille bathrobe. There, she perused Sadie's Saturday breakfast menu on the counter, then crept into the well-appointed breakfast room that had once been part of the kitchen. She stared at the spacious room replete with an antique corner cupboard and sideboard to match. Her father had made the long table that could be enlarged to three times its present size, accommodating up to sixteen people, if necessary. At the time, they'd used it for extended family gatherings, not knowing that Mamma would need such a table to supplement her income as a widow.

Shining the light on the table's surface, Mandy was startled to see that Sadie or Betsy had changed out the placemats from earlier. These Mandy had sewn for her mother the first year they'd opened their home to overnight guests.

"She kept them," Mandy murmured, setting the flashlight sideways on the table. She went around adjusting each wooden chair, centering it with the pretty red-and-yellow placemats. That done, she moved to the stone fireplace and stood there, feeling the weight of responsibility, like a heavy quilt falling over her shoulders.

After a moment, she picked up the flashlight and made her way through the kitchen and back to her room. She pulled back the handmade quilt and bedding beneath and slipped in, still wearing the bathrobe.

Just then, her cell phone rang, and picking it up, she realized she would have to recharge it overnight on the other side of the house. Recognizing the number, she answered, "Hello, Winnie."

"I hope it's not too late to call."

"I'm heading to bed earlier than usual, so you caught me just in time. It's been a really long day."

"Are things going okay there?" Winnie asked, her voice a welcome sound.

Mandy said she was unpacked and getting accustomed to her former room again. "It feels odd bein' back, to tell you the truth."

"Well, you know the ropes. I'm sure it will come back quickly."

Mandy smiled at that. "Say, it just occurred to me that I might like to hire someone to set up a website—at least a home page—to help bring in extra business during the slow winter months. I know you've done that sort of thing for some of your friends and business colleagues. What do you think?"

"Sure." Winnie sounded delighted. "Will you be the one managing it?"

"Well, I hadn't thought of that." Mandy felt overwhelmed at the thought of adding one more thing to her to-do list. "Whether or not the site is interactive, I think it'd be wise to give the inn an online presence. Word of mouth is great, but it can't hurt to attract some new customers."

"Good thinking."

They discussed the cost to set it up and what Winnie would minimally need from her—a good digital photo of the inn, as well as photos of the guest rooms.

"Do you want people to be able to make reservations online?" Winnie asked.

Mandy didn't think so, suspecting Betsy, for one, would likely not approve. "It's better if they call directly," she said. "I'd like to just list the address and phone number."

"Whatever's most convenient for you."

She thanked Winnie and promised to take photos tomorrow and send them. After all, the rooms were unoccupied and spotless, so the timing was perfect.

They talked about the fact that she needed to hire more help right away. "At least an exceptional cook."

Winnie chuckled. "Yes, most definitely, since it's a bed-and-breakfast, after all."

"I can't just hope to get the right person," Mandy admitted.

"Do your brothers have any role at the inn?"

Mandy didn't reveal that she had yet to see any of her brothers or their families. *It's only my first day back.* "My oldest brother, Jerome, is coming for breakfast tomorrow," she said. "We'll discuss some things then."

"You must be relieved that he's involved," Winnie added. "If I lived closer, I'd be glad to help do something for you."

"You're so kind." She meant it, but she knew Winnie was very settled there in Scott City. "The website is a huge help."

"Call anytime, okay?"

"Thanks so much, Winnie."

"We'll talk again once I get the site set up."

They said good-bye and hung up, and Mandy smiled at how quickly Winnie had called to check on her. "A great friend," she whispered as she went to find the charger for her phone in the top dresser drawer. She carried the phone and charger all the way across the house and plugged them into a wall outlet in the common room, wondering how much she'd be using her phone now. *I'm going to be awfully busy.*

When she returned to the bedroom, Mandy opened the blanket chest at the foot of the bed and piled on two more warm quilts, recalling how chilly it could be this time of year. In another day or so, when the temperatures plummeted, she'd be carrying buckets of coal in for the stove to get that going over in the small sitting room not far from her room. Thankfully, the rest of the house would be plenty warm for guests.

Turning off her flashlight, she got back into bed and lay there. She couldn't help but remember the days when her family was in the other bedrooms, and how contented and safe she'd felt. Now all of those empty rooms made Mandy miss the ways things used to be, and she brought her knees up close to her chest and wept, missing Mamma. All those years before Mandy's leaving, there was a real comfort in knowing Mamma was just in the next room reading her Bible, doing some tatting, or at this time of night, sleeping soundly.

········ ❁ ········

Trina had pushed the speed limit to get to Gail Anderson's that evening, looking forward to spending time with the kind-hearted woman who'd recently told her, *"I can't imagine what I'd do without you."*

Gail needed extra attention as soon as Trina arrived, and she gave it willingly, relishing her role as caregiver. Tonight, though, when the dear woman was settled into bed, she surprised Trina by asking for a prayer.

Nodding, Trina closed her eyes and bowed her head. "Lord in

heaven, I ask that you bring peace to Gail. May her rest be sweet, and may she wake up feeling renewed. Amen."

"You are so good to me," Gail whispered, smiling up at her from the bed pillow. "Thank you."

Trina patted the woman's wrinkled hand and then, making sure the night-light was on, rose to turn out the lamp before she slipped into the nearby sitting room. She'd brought along a book but decided to read it later if she had trouble falling asleep, instead reaching for a travel magazine one of Gail's granddaughters must have left behind.

Paging through it, Trina kept her ears open for Gail's feeble call while enjoying the quiet house. *So unlike my former workplace,* she thought, counting her blessings. Losing her job only months after Shawn's passing had been upsetting, but she'd landed on her feet just fine.

A travel ad for mystery destination trips caught her eye. She perused the page, shaking her head. "Who'd be that crazy?" she murmured, dismissing the ad and turning the page to a woman's captivating account of a week-long visit to the small island of Bora-Bora, where she stayed in a tiki hut over the water, swam daily in the shining lagoon, and climbed the rocky slopes of Mount Otemanu.

"Now, *that* sounds wonderful!" Trina said, going on to another account of an exotic overseas adventure.

Eventually, though, she flipped back to the ad, and curious about the concept of a mystery vacation, she looked up the agency online. Such an idea was somewhat intriguing if you were inclined to permit someone else to decide your destination. *As if I could persuade myself to do that!* she thought, having always made her own vacation plans.

Reading on, she discovered that the prospective traveler set the parameters for budget, travel dates, length of time, and any kinds of vacation spots that were no-nos.

Trina scrolled to the endorsements and chuckled at the comments. Nope, this was definitely not for someone who didn't relish surprises. *Not my cup of tea.*

She set down her phone and finished looking through the magazine, then rose to check on Gail.

Chapter

9

Mandy was awakened by the bantam rooster before dawn the next day, and taking time to stretch, she knew this was her last morning with a somewhat relaxed schedule. Sitting up, she squinted into the dim room and got out of bed to reach for the light switch on the wall, then laughed at herself for having forgotten. She lit the gas lamp on the nightstand since the sun wouldn't be up for a while yet.

Going down the hall to the bathroom, she washed up and dressed before brushing her long dark hair and pulling it back into a tidy bun.

She made the bed, then afterward sat on the only chair in the room, unaccustomed to how uncomfortable it was, and read her morning devotions, something she had been taught to do as a small child. In fact, both she and Arie had often spent a few minutes on such early mornings reading aloud to each other from the Good Book. The memories tugged at her heart, so much so that it was hard to keep her mind on what she was reading.

········ ❀ ········

Once the sun rose, Mandy went outdoors and took pictures with her phone for Winnie, then returned inside to take advantage of the guest rooms being unoccupied and all made up pretty. She took numerous shots and various angles of each of the four rooms and promptly texted them and a brief description of each to Winnie. *She'll let me know if they aren't adequate.*

Mandy also sent Winnie seasonal rate information and the address and phone number for the inn, trusting her friend would contact her if she needed anything more to design the home page.

We'll keep it simple, Mandy thought. *Like the Plain life.*

········ ✥ ········

Jerome arrived in the horse-drawn two-wheel cart he'd always used to shuttle back and forth between relatives' farms. Mandy noticed he let himself in the back way, just as he and the rest of their siblings always had, and she hurried to greet him.

He removed his black work coat and black felt hat first thing, hanging them on the wooden coat-tree he'd made years ago, and without saying a word, headed straight to the sink. He pulled up his sleeves and washed his hands vigorously before drying them on the kitchen towel lapped over the cupboard door below.

Putting his nose in the air, he sniffed. "Somethin' burning?"

"Oh!" Mandy hollered, rushing to the stove to turn off the gas and move the frying pan from the burner. "It's been a while since I've had a kitchen to use, but I thought for sure I could make eggs over easy without a speck of trouble." At least there were sticky buns, yogurt, and some red grapes . . . as well as toast and jam.

"Is there coffee?" Jerome asked, pulling out a chair and sitting down at the table. "You can't burn that, *jah*?" He chuckled, setting the tone for their breakfast meeting.

"Watch me," she joked, glad something might be to his liking as she poured the steaming coffee into a good-sized mug, remembering he took his black. She carried the mug over to the table and set it down in front of him.

"Might need to brush up on your cookin', ain't? The guests will be disappointed with eggs and toast, I'm sure you know." He reached for the mug and took a sip. "Arie Mae can give ya pointers."

"She could have," Mandy said sheepishly.

"*Was is letz do?*"

Mandy sighed. "I fired her yesterday."

"You did *what?*" His frown was fierce and he groaned, shaking his head. "That's a mistake, Mandy."

"I'm tellin' ya straight out, she cannot work here—and it's my decision to make, right?"

Jerome pressed his lips together. "Well, it ain't smart, nor is it the Christian way. And you'll have trouble replacing her, once the word's out. Folks will think you're *ferhoodled.*"

She had expected to be preached to, so she was surprised when he let it go with that and a disgusted shake of his head. *Surely he knows something about our rift,* Mandy thought.

"Did you two have a chance to start goin' through Mamma's clothing before you showed Arie Mae the door?" Jerome asked.

"Didn't have time," she said. "I'll ponder what to do with the clothes," she said, knowing they would typically be given away. Mandy scooped a good portion of peach yogurt into a dish and placed it on his plate next to two pieces of toast smothered with strawberry jam. "I don't want you to go hungry."

Jerome glanced at the stove. "Bring those eggs over," he said, "and a bottle of catsup, too. Wouldn't be the first time I've doctored up eggs."

"Well, surely not from Hannah's kitchen." Mandy had eaten his wife's delicious meals enough times to know he'd married a wonderful cook.

Jerome was grinning now. "I do remember your first attempt at cookin' back when. Who could forget that?"

"Oh, but I was only eight when Mamma said she wanted more help in the kitchen."

"*Jah*, but it didn't take, did it? Not like with Arie Mae." She knew he meant it in a good-natured sort of way. Even so, Dat never had pointed out her cooking snags.

She gave him the burnt eggs and catsup, and joined him at the table. "Some people are just born *gut* cooks."

Jerome bowed his head, and she did the same, praying the silent rote prayer they'd both learned as youngsters. As was their tradition, he cleared his throat, said amen, and then started into the eggs and toast on his plate.

It felt strange to sit there with her brother taking Mamma's old spot. Mandy looked at her own plate—the toast and yogurt and fruit—and realized she'd lost her appetite.

He glanced at her across the table. "Better eat something that sticks to your gizzard."

"Oh, don't mind me," she said. "You came by to talk about the finances, right? You've been handling the books?"

He nodded his head, and she noticed his brown beard was a shade or two darker than his light brown hair. "Mamma was slowin' down some," he began. "She just wasn't as strong as she'd always been, yet she didn't want the family to know. But her keepin' the Kauffman girls on here . . . and Arie Mae, too, should have provided an inkling that she needed plenty of help."

Mandy took a sip of coffee. "Did she see a doctor?" she asked, spreading jam on her single piece of toast.

"Mamma did things her way, ya know."

"Was she still taking all those minerals and herbs?"

Jerome nodded quickly. "Far as I'm concerned, she took too many. And she was always goin' over to see that herbalist . . .

not a medical doctor, really, just someone to fork out a pile of money to, I daresay. Mamma once suggested Hannah go and see that there fella, too, but I put my foot down on that right quick."

"Hannah was feelin' poorly?"

"Oh, a while back . . . she's fine now." Jerome finished his burnt eggs and catsup and asked for another piece of toast.

Mandy had practically forgotten how the menfolk here expected to be served at the drop of a hat, but she rose and went to do his bidding. Meanwhile, she took a look at the egg pan and decided it needed a good soaking, so she placed it in the deep sink and ran water over it. "Why on earth did Mamma name me as heir for the inn?" she blurted, returning to the table with the toast. "I mean, she knew I couldn't cook worth anything."

Jerome reached for his coffee mug. "'Tis a mystery."

"She never said why, then?"

Jerome folded his hands on the table and gazed at her. "Why not just look on this as a blessing, Mandy."

She should have known he'd say that. "I may not deserve it, but I'll sure do my best to earn it." *I'll prove myself worthy.*

"Attagirl."

She speared a piece of fruit. "I haven't done any bookkeeping outside of my personal finances, but I'm a fast learner."

"You're right frugal, ain't so?" He removed the keys to the inn from his work pants and put them on the table. "And I'll continue to help with the books, at least for the year. Which reminds me: You won't have any legal paperwork to sign till after the full term's up."

"Once the place is mine," she said softly, studying him. "If all goes well, *jah?*"

He nodded.

"You're welcome to look over my shoulder. . . . I won't mind one bit," she added. "Or Hannah, if she has time to drop by."

Mandy ate another piece of fruit. "Have *you* wondered why Arie Mae wasn't Mamma's choice? Or one of you boys?"

Jerome wiped his mouth with the back of his hand. "If I wanted to spin my wheels on somethin', it wouldn't be this. No point in it."

"*Puh!*" she teased, shaking her head at him.

"At least you still have a sense of humor, even if you *are* lookin' mighty English."

Mandy decided now was the right moment to make her plan clear. "You know there's only one reason I've come back. I was pretty content living out there in the world . . . though I'm not really very fancy." She lightly touched her hair bun and smiled, hoping he noticed she'd worn a conservative skirt and blouse. "I've never owned high heels or yoga pants."

At that, he smiled. "I think you're gonna do just fine here."

Won't be forever, she thought.

Jerome got up and went to the drawer where Mamma kept the ledger, and carried it back to the table, where he opened it to the present month, explaining that she would be expected to pay herself each week, just as she would the Kauffman girls and the stable hand, Karl Lantz. "You'll have more money to go around if you don't ask Arie Mae back to help, but more of the work will fall on your shoulders."

"I intend to hire more help," she said. "Mind if I call you if I need advice?"

"Well, you can ring up the barn phone, but I'm not that far away, even on foot." He paused, eyes blinking. "Do ya plan to keep your car?"

"I hadn't considered selling it. Why?"

A pained look crossed his face. "Just wondered."

"I might need it to run errands." Truthfully, there was no way on earth she would give up her car now. Having wheels saved so much time.

"Don't forget Ol' Tulip and Gertie are out yonder, and the family carriage is in fine workin' order . . . if you're so inclined."

It was more than a suggestion; it was a blatant hint.

"And I'll drop in now and then to see how things are goin'," he said. "Early Monday mornings work well for me."

"Sounds fine to me," she agreed. She was glad he lived but a half mile away. "Tell Hannah and the children hullo. I sure hope to see all of yous sometime. That goes for Danny, Joseph, and Sammy and their families, too," she added, wondering when she might see her other brothers.

"Church is bein' held just up the road this Sunday," he said. "They'll *all* be there."

She was surprised he'd bring this up. "I really haven't thought that far yet."

"Might want to make it your priority, Mandy, since ya need *gut* help to replace Arie Mae." His words were pointed.

"I'll think on it," she said, unable to commit to going back to the Amish church. She had been attending more relaxed worship services for so long now, and besides that, based on how Sadie had reacted, she didn't think the People would receive her with open arms. *Especially since firing Arie Mae. . .*

"*Denki* for breakfast," Jerome said.

"Such as it was."

"Maybe I should visit just so you can practice on me out here in the kitchen while the guests enjoy Sadie's delicious cookin'," he said. "Better be stocked up on plenty-a catsup, though." He grinned at her.

Did she dare tell him?

"What's the matter?" he asked. "You look pale."

"Sadie's quitting after Monday. I hope she'll change her mind, but I really doubt it."

He looked alarmed. "Sadie *and* Arie?" His eyes pierced hers.

"Best be lookin' for someone to fill their shoes right away. You can't run this place with just Betsy." Jerome reached for his hat and placed it on his head, down over his bangs.

She knew as much. Feeling very much alone, Mandy watched him mosey to the back door and head out.

Chapter 10

The door chimes rang at three-thirty sharp that afternoon. Mandy hurried to greet the expected guests, keen on fulfilling her obligation. Sadie had already left for the day, but Betsy lingered near the kitchen doorway as Mandy had requested of her. Having someone in sight who looked properly Amish seemed like a good idea.

"*Willkumm*," Mandy said as she opened the door to the two couples.

The taller of the two men took one look at her, frowned, and turned to study the house number on the exterior. "Did we come to the wrong place?"

His wife poked him. "We've been coming here for years, dear."

The man straightened a bit, and with a glint in his eye, offered Mandy a handshake and introduced himself as Patrick Cohen, and his wife as Heather. "Did Saloma sell the place to Englishers?" he asked, adjusting the leather luggage strap on his right shoulder.

"Please come in, and I'll explain." Mandy stepped back to usher them inside. "My mother passed away unexpectedly last week."

"Saloma?" Heather clasped her throat. "Oh . . . but she was so lively the last time we were here."

Patrick looked grim. "Your mother was going to grow old with us—that was our little joke. We've been longtime guests."

Mandy quickly mentioned the stroke. "It was a shock, to be sure."

"She was such a darling woman," Heather Cohen said, shaking her head. "You must be terribly sad."

Awkwardly, Heather's husband stepped forward to introduce Gene and Nadia Hayes, who had lingered behind the Cohens. Both shook Mandy's hand. "They're just as fond of your mother's place as we are," Patrick said, evidently trying to lighten things up again.

Nadia Hayes eyed Mandy curiously. "You know, you really look a lot like your sister. Arie Mae, is it?"

"Yes . . . we're twins—but I'm brunette and she's a strawberry blonde." Mandy offered her best smile, but she could tell by their expressions that they were puzzled, no doubt by her attire.

"Oh, so *you're* the twin," Nadia said, glancing at her husband. "Arie mentioned you lived out west."

"*Jah*, for a while," Mandy volunteered.

The room fell silent, and Mandy could almost predict the next question. *You're not Amish, are you?*

Quickly, lest they pepper her with more uncomfortable questions, she offered them some coffee and treats.

Before anyone could reply, Nadia spotted Betsy and waved to her, looking somewhat relieved. "Hello again . . . it's nice to see you," she said, and Betsy smiled back but stayed put, letting Mandy take the lead.

"Is Arie Mae around?" Nadia asked, looking about. "We'd like to express our condolences." She turned to her husband, who had gently nudged her arm. "Oh, and I have a surprise for her."

"Well, she's not workin'," Mandy said, pushing the words out.

"Her day off?" Heather asked.

"*Nee.*" Mandy shook her head.

All four simply stared at her, as if waiting for more.

Mandy took a deep breath. "She doesn't work here now."

More frowns. Heather stepped forward, clearly troubled. "Is she okay? I mean, she's not sick, is she?"

"Not at all," Mandy said. "In fact, if you'd like to visit her, she lives right across that field." Mandy added that she was sure her sister would enjoy that.

"I certainly will," Heather said, her eyes fixed now on Mandy's skirt. Finally, she addressed the elephant in the room. "And . . . I take it you're no longer Amish."

Oh dear, Mandy thought. "*Jah,* I was. But really . . . nothing's changed for the B and B," she replied, her heart in her throat.

"Well, as I recall, your mother's breakfasts were heavenly," Nadia said, forcing a smile, as if to ask who was cooking now.

Needing to reassure the guests, Mandy motioned toward Betsy. "Betsy over there, and her sister Sadie—remember her?—still work here. In fact, Sadie's planning a *wunnerbaar-gut* breakfast for all of you tomorrow." She was tempted to add, "*You'll see.*"

Before things went further downhill, she asked Betsy to show the couples to their rooms, then thought to ask about the Spencers. "Did they mention when they expect to arrive?"

Patrick nodded. "They stopped off at Kauffman's Fruit Farm and Market to pick up some apple butter to give to your mother . . . and some apple schnitz for themselves."

"Apple butter was Mamma's favorite," Mandy said.

"And they didn't even know her . . . other than what we've told them," Nadia said, shifting her purse to her other hand. "A truly beautiful woman, inside and out." She said it almost reverently.

"Mamma would've been so pleased," Mandy managed to say,

increasingly worried that these couples might not want to stay now that they were aware of Mamma's passing. Mandy had always respected her mother's ability to make guests feel at home, but until now, she hadn't taken into account how vital her mother was to the very fabric of the place.

A half hour later, Mandy sat alone at the kitchen table, concerned about the reaction of the two couples, wondering how she was going to manage future arrivals and how best to respond to their queries. Not being Amish was turning out to be an unexpected challenge.

Mandy recalled the wooden plaque she'd seen at the florist shop in Scott City. *Home is where your mom is.*

Now that she was here, everywhere she looked, various things reminded her of growing up in this house. Mamma's kitchen in particular—all the times Mandy had scrubbed this floor and the baseboards, down on her knees, content to clean up after her mother and sister, who did all the cooking and baking. As best as she could remember, that's how it had always been. *I came in behind them and put things back to order.* She recalled how badly things had just gone with the first batch of guests and leaned her head into her hands. *How will I make this work without Arie Mae?*

············ ❀ ············

When they finally arrived, Kyle and Roberta Spencer were less abrupt and more pleasant than the first two couples. Even Betsy, who'd helped to greet them at the door, mentioned this to Mandy once the Spencers were getting situated in their room.

Thankfully, Mandy thought while finishing her solo supper. She'd tried to relax in the light of the gas lamp overhead as she heard the three couples move about upstairs. *Tomorrow will be better . . . I hope.*

Later, in her bedroom, she stretched out on top of the bed quilt and relived the latter afternoon hours and her discussion with Betsy. The two of them had gone over every detail in preparation for tomorrow morning, as well as set the table for six in the large breakfast room.

Betsy had suggested using the best white dishware in the china closet, since it was Mandy's first morning in charge of the inn. At first, Mandy had thought there was no need, but Betsy said she'd overheard the tentative responses by the Cohens and the Hayeses upon their arrival and was concerned they might turn tail and head elsewhere for the weekend. Reluctantly, Mandy agreed to use Mamma's nicest china, after all.

I shouldn't let the guests' reaction to my being here make me feel blue, Mandy thought. *After all, it's only natural they'd miss their former hostess.*

She opened her Bible, remembering that Dat liked to read from the Psalms at the end of a trying day. *Like this day,* she thought. One of the horses neighed loudly in the stable, and she wondered how early the rooster might start crowing tomorrow. Their small but sturdily built barn held so many stories from her growing-up years—like an old diary recording family events and secrets.

Mandy felt a sudden wave of sadness mixed with sheer frustration, knowing she was stuck here for a full year. *Memories are lurking in every corner. Memories . . . and plentiful obstacles.*

Brushing her own thoughts aside, she began to read silently.

After a time, she rose and walked over to what had once been Arie Mae's bedroom, and going to stand at one of the windows, she could see golden flecks of light reflected in the windows of Josiah's great-uncle's old house across the cornfield. *Next farm over, of all things. Yet Arie is still so far away.*

Chapter
11

Even before the windup alarm clock sounded, the pesky rooster began to crow, and lest the guests come down for early coffee or tea, Mandy darted out of bed even before offering a prayer.

Going to the dresser, she picked up her brush and began pushing her hair back into the expected bun, feeling an air of anticipation as she started her first full day with guests. *Running the place,* she reminded herself, wondering how on earth she could ever live up to Mamma's reputation.

Mandy hurried to the closet, glad her father had added one to this room and to the other bedrooms clustered on the Amish side of the house. Standing there, she took stock of her few choices, realizing that, aside from one other long skirt, all the clean clothes left were jeans and pants. Sighing, she removed the skirt from the hanger and slipped it on. Sometime today, she would have to do laundry for herself if she was to fit in as a somewhat Plain woman around here. After last night's fiasco, it would never do to parade around in anything but skirts and dresses, as much as she'd come to appreciate her jeans. As it was, yesterday's guests had looked on her with suspicion. What could she possibly do to convince them, or future guests, that the place was still an Amish establishment?

Listening for the creaking floorboards overhead that indicated the early risers were up and moving about, Mandy took a few moments to read from where she'd left off yesterday in the Psalms, then did her best to eke out a prayer for the day, also daring to ask for guidance and wisdom from above, especially in regard to Sadie, whom she prayed might have a change of heart and stay on.

Rising from the cane-backed chair, she went to the window and purposely looked toward the south, avoiding the direction of her sister's—and Josiah's—farmhouse. Several market wagons rumbled by at this predawn hour, their battery-operated lights twinkling at her through the dim morning, and she remembered riding to market as a little girl with Dat, who'd once permitted young Josiah to go along, too. They'd ridden in the back with boxes and boxes of freshly picked vegetables. She still recalled Josiah's apple red cheeks. Just a second-grader then, he had seemed shy about being back there with her alone.

Let it go, she thought, seeing a large gray bench wagon rumble this way up Old Leacock Road. It was most likely headed toward the farm of the family hosting Preaching service tomorrow. *Jerome urged me to go*, she remembered, but it was enough of a jolt to be back on Lancaster County soil again, and she certainly was not prepared to go full-scale Amish. It was better for her to simply slip into the back of the community church down the road, where she wouldn't run into Arie Mae or anyone else who might recognize her and question her choices.

When she entered the kitchen to get things rolling, Mandy lit the gas lamp hanging over the table, then set the flame under the stove-top coffeemaker. Then, pulling out the apron drawer, she put on one of her mother's white half aprons before filling the teakettle with water and turning the range knob to high.

She sliced the sweet bread that Sadie had made yesterday, arranged the pieces on a pretty rose-colored plate, and placed it out in the breakfast room, opposite the kitchen. There, she heard the familiar squeaks of the floorboards and assumed the guests would appear soon, at least those looking for coffee.

Aware the clock was ticking, Mandy bustled back to the kitchen, now brightened by the sun. She put out the lamp, grateful for the glory of the sunrise flooding her favorite room in this old house.

Back in the breakfast room, Mandy did the same, letting the sun shine in through the open green shades, then struck a match from the mantel to light a line of block candles. Mamma's guests had always enjoyed having breakfast near the hearth in a room lit with only gas lamps or candlelight; it allowed them to experience Amish life for a moment in time.

Just then, she heard Sadie and Betsy arrive by way of the back door and went to meet them. Sadie carried a loaf of bread that she mentioned having made last evening at home. Though they had bread enough on hand, there was nothing quite like the smell and taste of freshly made, Mandy knew. The apple butter the Spencers had brought for Mamma was on the counter to be placed on the breakfast room table, along with some homemade grape jelly and peach preserves, put up last summer. Considering all of this, Mandy tried to convince herself that the place was still as Amish as anyone could possibly want.

"How'd ya sleep last night?" Betsy asked kindly as she went to the sink to lather up her hands. After drying them, she took the bread over to the large wooden cutting board and removed the long knife from its wooden block.

"I slept all right," Mandy said. *But I kept thinkin' that Mamma*

89

was just in the next room over, she thought, missing her mother with everything in her. "How 'bout you?" Mandy asked, including Sadie in the question.

Turning, Sadie shrugged. "Honestly, I stayed up too late talkin' to my *Mamm,* who had plenty to say."

Betsy looked at her sister and turned red-faced, then seemed to hide her fluster by beginning to cut the bread into near-perfect slices.

Sadie got busy preparing the oven egg casserole Mamma had often made through the years. "Could ya boil some water for the oatmeal, Mandy?" Sadie asked in a somewhat sharp tone. "There's plenty-a raisins to put in it, and some English walnuts, too. I think it's *schmaert* to have something other than eggs."

"Sure," Mandy said, overlooking Sadie's attitude as she brought up a medium-sized saucepan from the lower cupboard.

"Your Mamma always wanted the guests to be well satisfied at her table," Betsy observed softly. "I'm sure you remember."

Mandy silently thanked Betsy for her peace-making ways.

"Right from the start, when we first opened the inn, Mamma was keen on offering a generous breakfast. I don't want that to change."

Betsy glanced at her and nodded. "I can't imagine how hard losing her must be for you," she said, eyes glistening. "I'm so sorry."

Swallowing the lump in her throat, all Mandy could say was *"Denki."*

.... ❀ ....

The phone rang while they prepared breakfast, and Mandy called to Sadie and Betsy, "I'll get it." Swiftly, she went to the small walnut phone table and chair against the kitchen wall. "Butterfly Meadows Amish Bed-and-Breakfast," she answered.

"May I please speak to Saloma Dienner?" a woman asked.

"This is her daughter. May I help you?"

"Oh, of course. How are you, Arie?" asked the woman. "I almost didn't recognize your voice."

Mandy made herself smile. *I'll have to get used to this,* she thought. "I'm Arie's sister, Mandy . . . but what can I do for you?"

There was a lengthy pause. "Ah, I see. Come to think of it, you don't sound as Dutchy as your mother or sister."

Mandy laughed lightly. "That's not somethin' I hear too often," she said, hoping to keep things pleasant.

"It's late notice, but I'm wondering if you have any rooms available for tonight."

"I do," Mandy said. "There's one available—a lovely suite."

"The Blue Room?"

"That's right. Would you like to book it?"

"Yes. It will be for my mother and me. We've stayed in the suite before—ideal for relaxing. My mother likes to sit in the separate room facing the road to watch the buggies go by."

Mandy took the woman's name and her mother's—Kristen Turner and Helene Carson—as well as their contact information. She reminded Kristen of the three-thirty check-in time, as well as the required two-night stay. "There is no charge for Sunday, as you may recall."

"That's one of the nicest things we've encountered at the Amish inns in Lancaster County," Kristen said. "What a wonderful way to honor the Lord's Day."

"*Jah,* that's always been my family's wish," Mandy replied. "We'll see you this afternoon, then."

"I look forward to meeting Arie's sound-alike sister!" Kristen laughed softly.

Mandy thanked her and hung up. *Just not so look-alike,* she thought as she went to get the coffeemaker and carried it into the breakfast room, where she set it on the sideboard covered by

Mamma's handmade crocheted runner. Then, before the guests came downstairs, she returned with a tray of coffee cups, sugar, and creamer, and set it on the sideboard, as well.

Opening the hutch, she removed some teacups and saucers and a small basket with an assortment of tea bags. "*Guder Mariye*," she greeted Patrick Cohen as he entered. The man looked bright-eyed even before caffeine. "Just make yourself at home," she said, pointing to the items on the sideboard. "And if something's missin', I'll be in the kitchen with Betsy and Sadie."

"Thank you," he said, glancing at her curiously as he went straight for a coffee mug.

She made her exit and noticed that Betsy must have gone to get the coal bucket for the stove. When she asked Sadie what she could do to help, Sadie literally waved her away. "Everything's under control," she replied. "Breakfast will be family style. The guests will dish it up themselves—no special orders."

Mandy nodded, pleased they were still doing things the way Mamma had established a decade ago.

When Heather Cohen joined her husband and the other two couples also gathered at the table, Mandy went in and offered the silent table blessing, just as Mamma had always done.

At her amen, several of the guests glanced at one another, seemingly pleased.

After making sure everyone had coffee or tea, Mandy excused herself, and she and Sadie returned immediately with the baked egg casserole and the raisin-walnut oatmeal, along with the homemade bread and a bowl of cinnamon applesauce.

Mandy didn't stay to listen in on what the women were saying to Sadie, but they sounded content enough as they engaged the *real* Amishwoman in conversation. Oh, she hoped Sadie wouldn't spoil things and reveal that she was quitting.

Having forgotten to put the jams and the apple butter on the table, Mandy placed those items on a tray and carried them into the breakfast room, where the pleasant clink of utensils against the plates and the gentle hum of amiable chatter made her feel like this day was going to turn out just fine.

Nothing to stew about, she told herself, not wanting to think ahead to Tuesday's breakfast and onward. She would definitely ask around that afternoon about getting another Amishwoman to help, particularly a good cook. But first, Mandy was desperate for clean clothes. *Maybe I'll just use the laundromat in town,* she thought suddenly, knowing how long it would take to use the wringer washer and hang everything out on the line.

Sadie reappeared in the kitchen and put her thumbs up, bobbing her head toward the breakfast room.

Mandy smiled. "They're too busy eating to talk much, so it must be tasty."

Sadie suggested Mandy go in and pour more coffee and tea. "*Ach,* we forgot the juice."

"My fault." Mandy shook her head. "I'll get it."

Sadie looked befuddled. "How'd we overlook that?"

"Well, you're not used to doin' Mamma's work," Mandy said, opening the fridge and reaching for the orange juice. "And I hope ya know I'm grateful for your help today . . . very grateful."

Ducking her head a bit, Sadie made her way over to the back door and looked out for the longest time. Then she said, "The stable hand is here to feed the horses. Your Mamma used to call him a godsend."

"Karl Lantz?" Mandy said, busy pouring juice into small glasses. "I'll run out to meet him sometime later today. Oh, by the way, the suite is now booked for tonight and Sunday," she told Sadie. "A woman and her mother—they're repeat guests, too."

Sadie turned and smiled. "Anyone I know?" When Mandy told her, Sadie brightened. "I remember Kristen Turner and her mother, sure. Kristen calls herself an Amish buff—even speaks *Deitsch* for fun." Sadie looked sad all of a sudden, and Mandy wondered if she really wanted to quit or if it was more her fiancé's idea.

Mandy left to carry the tray of juice glasses into the breakfast room, where she placed a glass on each placemat. "Better late than never, *jah?*" she said, allowing herself to once again throw in a word or two of her first language. Perhaps doing so would reassure the guests that she truly belonged here.

"Maybe you're new to this?" Nadia Mayes commented, looking relaxed this morning in her jeans and burgundy sweater.

"Not at all." Mandy explained that she'd worked alongside her mother and Arie Mae when they'd first started the B and B together. But Mandy left out that she had been away for five years.

"But you don't dress like your mother or sister . . . or Sadie and Betsy," Heather spoke up. "Are you a Mennonite?"

"Well—"

Just then, something in the kitchen crashed to the floor, and horrified, Mandy quickly excused herself. *Oh dear! This won't inspire confidence in my guests!*

Chapter 12

Sadie repeatedly apologized for breaking the pitcher, but Mandy told her not to fret and stooped to help Sadie pick up the largest pieces of glass. "It wasn't intentional, I'm sure."

Sadie hurried to get the broom and dustpan, still fussing about it, and when she returned, she swept up the shards. "I'll definitely pay ya," Sadie said, her voice quavering.

"Don't worry about it," Mandy insisted. "Let's just be glad it wasn't the crystal one."

Mandy returned a bit later to clear the breakfast room table and ask the lingering guests about their plans for the day, wishing them well just as Mamma always liked to do. Mamma, however, would sit with them and have coffee while Mandy and Arie Mae cleaned up the kitchen.

When the last guest had left the room, Mandy wiped down the table and paused when she heard someone talking in the hall near the stairs.

"Don't get me wrong, the baked egg dish was all right, but it didn't compare with Saloma's fare," Heather was saying.

"Breakfast *was* a letdown compared to what we're used to," Nadia agreed. "I hope we don't find other unpleasant changes. Saloma's B and B has always been such a unique Amish experience. I really wonder if her daughter is up to the task. I mean, she doesn't even *look* Amish!"

The voices faded away.

I'll work at making the breakfasts better, Mandy thought, but then glanced down at her clothes and realized that improving the menu might not be enough. *I need to look the part.* She certainly didn't have time to sew any Amish dresses and aprons and was quite sure Sadie, who was roughly her size, wouldn't want to loan any of hers. Besides, Mandy wasn't about to ask.

Discouraged, she carried the large tray of dirty dishes and utensils into the kitchen and set them on the counter near the sink, noticing through the window that Betsy was leaving the henhouse with the egg basket and returning this way. "I thought things were off to a *gut* start this morning," she told Sadie as she picked up a tea towel. "But I was quite mistaken."

Sadie stopped running the dishwater and glanced at her with a frown. "Somethin' the matter with the guests?"

"Not the guests, *nee.*"

.... ⚘ ....

Trina Sutton traipsed around her kitchen, still in her warm bathrobe and cozy slippers. She poured a second cup of coffee and sat down at the table to look at digital photos of herself and Shawn. She was especially interested in two of their weekend adventures in the Twin Cities. They had once spent an entire day sailing with the Lake Calhoun Yacht Club, then returned another time, months later, to go to the Minneapolis Sculpture Garden at the Walker Art Center. *I wanted to have our outdoor wedding there,* she thought, recalling the lively discussion she'd had with Shawn, who was too practical to want to deal with the risk of poor weather marring such a special day.

"But Shawn let me win," she whispered, "like always." In the end, they had planned to go ahead with an outdoor wedding. Selecting the photos, she moved them to a designated folder, freeing up space on her phone.

Then Trina called her sister. "I really just had to tell someone," she blurted when Janna answered.

"And that happens to be me, right?" Janna laughed. "Nice to hear from you, sis."

Trina took a breath. "My engagement ring is now officially tucked away in a drawer."

"Congratulations. This is a big deal for you, Trina."

"And now that it's done, it feels right, even though I thought it wouldn't."

"So . . . dare I ask if this means you're ready to get yourself out there?"

Out there? Trina gulped. *You mean . . . dating?* "I don't know. I'm moving on, whatever that means."

"Well, it's an answer to prayer to see you take this step," Janna said.

Trina agreed. "I should let you go—I know you're up to your eyebrows there."

Her sister laughed. "What's new? But I'm glad you called."

"You know what? So am I," Trina replied, grinning now.

Yet when she hung up, it was all she could do not to retrieve her ring and put it on again. *One step at a time,* she told herself.

.... ❀ ....

After the kitchen was put back in order and the dishes done, Mandy thoroughly swept the floor to get any remaining shards of glass. Then she washed the floor, her old favorite chore, while

Sadie and Betsy hurried to tidy the empty guest rooms, as well as clean the common areas. Everything needed to be polished to a good shine.

While the floor was drying, Mandy stepped out to introduce herself to the stable hand. The barn was as tidy as when Dat was living—the walkway to the horses' boxed stalls had been newly swept, and on the low shelf, all the grooming brushes and tools had been placed neatly in the large bucket. Even the mane comb was free of horsehair.

She saw a tall man scooping up feed for the trough. "Hullo, you must be Karl Lantz." She offered a smile.

"And you're Arie's twin sister, I assume." He wiped his hand on his shirt, then shook her hand, his eyes appearing to take quick notice of her modern clothing.

She nodded. "Amanda Dienner." She felt a bit flustered, expecting a much older man. "But everyone calls me Mandy." She paused a moment. "I understand my Mamma hired you some time ago."

"That's right," Karl said, his blue eyes turning sad. "I'm mighty sorry 'bout her passing. She reminded me of one of my dear aunts back in Wisconsin, where I'm from." He suddenly gave a warm chuckle. "I still claim that state as my home, I'll admit. Have you ever had the opportunity to visit?"

"*Nee*. Do you miss it?"

He mentioned that his parents and siblings were all still there, so he was glad when he could get back for a visit. "And my wife, Waneta, is buried there."

Mandy expressed her condolences, and Karl thanked her, saying then that his move to Lancaster County had been "just what the doctor ordered."

They talked a while more, and Karl brought her up-to-date on the health of the horses, before she excused herself to go back to the house.

Inside again, she made a bologna and cheese sandwich and told Betsy she had an errand to run. She slipped out with her dirty laundry in a pillow slip and saw that Sadie was hitching up Ol' Tulip to the Dienner family buggy, still insisting on buying a new water pitcher, even though Mandy said it wasn't at all necessary.

Mandy hurried to her car and started toward town, hoping she wouldn't be spotted by any of the People. Once there, she got her two loads of clothes going right quick in the laundromat, then sat and read the local newspaper, surrounded by the din of dryers and several other customers discussing politics. She shut out the noise by putting in her earbuds to listen to music, deciding to email Karyn Fry at the florist shop to say she had arrived safely. That done, she ate her sandwich.

When her clothes were ready for the dryer, Mandy loaded them immediately, thankful for the time savings. *If only I could install a washer and dryer at the inn*, she thought momentarily, but she knew the bishop would never give permission for that. *And it would be another strike against giving guests an authentic Amish experience!*

She considered emailing Eilene Bradley, too, then decided to give her a call after supper tonight. *But first, I'd better take Jerome's advice and practice my cooking. Guess it'll be a ham and cheese omelet tonight*, Mandy thought, not exactly salivating at the thought.

········ ❀ ········

A bank of dark clouds had muted the noontime sun, and just as Mandy finished folding her clothes at the laundromat, a light rain began to fall. The sudden change of weather made her feel she had been sensible to choose the modern conveniences.

Even so, she ducked her head as she made her way to the car, not wanting to be seen. Placing the clean clothes in the back seat, she closed the door just as she spotted Gene and Nadia Mayes pull into the parking spot next to her.

What lousy timing!

Nadia's hand flew to her mouth when she saw Mandy, though just as quickly, she seemed to compose herself and managed a wave.

Mandy waved back and pushed forth a smile as she opened the driver's-side door and slipped in behind the wheel. She still felt Nadia's disapproving gaze as Mandy backed out of the parking spot.

.... ✿ ....

Back at the B and B, Mandy skedaddled to her room and put her clean clothes away. The blouses would have to be touched up with an iron later.

Going to the kitchen, she could see Betsy through the back door window, sweeping the walkway and stoop. With the guests out and about and Betsy occupied, now was a good time to go around to visit a few of her close-in-age cousins, especially those who might still be single and interested in earning some extra money.

She drove to her aunt Suzy's house and knocked on the door, feeling unexpectedly nervous about this first encounter with extended family. When Suzy came, she seemed a bit startled, her eyes blinking too fast as she swung open the screen door, not inviting Mandy inside. Not wanting to make too much of the lack of a welcome, Mandy told her she was looking for her cousin Rachel. "I hoped she might be interested in working at the inn."

"Oh, she wouldn't be," Aunt Suzy said right quick. "She's got plenty to do as it is."

"All right, then," Mandy said, saying good-bye and returning to the car, which she'd parked clear out on the road, so as not to offend. *Not that it made much difference,* she thought wryly.

The response was much the same at the next farmhouse, and the next, as her relatives offered a similarly tepid response, not inviting her in and saying that her cousins were either employed elsewhere or simply not interested.

Determined to fit in at least one more stop, Mandy approached Uncle Dave Dienner's place, where her cousin Kate was on the back porch shaking rugs. Mandy hoped this might be her chance. "Hullo, cousin!" she called, going over to greet her. "*Wie geht's?*"

Kate's eyes widened. "Mandy! Wasn't expectin' ya."

"Well, it's *wunnerbaar-gut* to see you," Mandy said.

Kate nodded, her attention still devoted more to the rug than to Mandy.

For goodness' sake! Mandy thought, realizing that this visit wasn't going well, either. Yet she needed to at least ask. "Would ya like to work with me at the inn? You could cook like I know ya love to do."

Kate stopped shaking the rug and looked directly at her. "To fill Arie's spot?"

Feeling more awkward now, Mandy nodded.

"Maybe ya should've thought before you fired her. After all she's done!"

Mandy knew there was no way to explain herself to Kate, so she simply tried again. "Would you at least consider the job, cousin?"

Kate grimaced and shook her head. "I doubt you'll find anyone willing to help, either. Your Mamma would be awful disappointed." With that, she headed into the house, leaving the rug hanging over the railing.

Disheartened, Mandy realized that further searching would likely end in more rejection. *Looks like I may have to do this alone.*

Sighing, she walked back to her car while two barn cats meowed loudly at her, as if scolding her.

Instead of heading home, Mandy chose the opposite way, driving toward the Amish schoolhouse where she had attended all eight grades. When she came up on it, she pulled onto the shoulder and sat there, staring at the school through the windshield, memories washing over her.

A wave of melancholy overtook her. Mandy and Arie Mae had always walked to school together, and Mamma sometimes surprised them by waiting at the end of the stone path to greet them at the end of the day.

Mandy remembered, too, the creaky oak floor and all the lunches lined up at attention on the shelf behind Josiah's wooden desk . . . with their initials concealed just under the lid.

The small white building looked like it had a fresh coat of paint, and she recalled Dat and her older brothers helping with that chore before the school year began back when she was twelve. *Eleven years ago,* she thought. *The year Josiah fell and broke his wrist chasing a fly ball at recess.*

Pondering those early days, Mandy recalled that Josiah's mother and Mamma had thought nothing of their close friendship. *They seemed to think we were like brother and sister, but I never saw us that way.* And now, there was no point in dwelling on any of her long walks with Josiah during their teens . . . or the things he'd ultimately declared to her the year they'd courted.

········ ❁ ········

When Mandy returned to the house, Sadie was preparing to bake some pumpkin nut bread for tomorrow's breakfast. "Can ya handle things on your own in the mornin', Mandy?" Sadie asked. "My mother and I will be taking twenty snitz pies to church for the shared meal, and she needs my help to haul them to Preacher Lapp's house before the service."

Mandy glanced at Betsy, who was wiping down the cupboard doors. "Betsy's needed, too?"

"That's up to her," Sadie said, opening the oven door and sliding the loaf pan inside.

Since Betsy had overheard the conversation and hadn't responded, Mandy guessed that a Sunday morning breakfast, easy as that was, might be a good time for her to learn to manage on her own. "Well, I can—"

"*Jah*, I'll be over to help," Betsy interrupted.

Mandy drew a deep sigh of relief. "*Denki*."

.... ❀ ....

Around four o'clock, Kristen Turner arrived with her mother. Mandy saw them drive up the lane and park, and wiser now, she sent Betsy to the door to greet them and sign them in. Mandy couldn't risk any further upsets. The idea of going through the same rigmarole as she had with the first group of guests made her stomach churn. Feeling anxious, she took herself outdoors briefly to calm her nerves, glad the rain shower was past. The sky had cleared a bit, and she breathed in the lingering freshness as she walked through the backyard and over toward the butterfly-shaped garden, all trimmed back for the coming winter.

Then, glancing over toward the house where her sister and Josiah lived, she noticed Jerome's two-wheeled cart parked in the lane. She wondered what he was doing there. *Comparing notes, perhaps. . . .*

She walked to the henhouse. *Arie and I loved to gather eggs here*, she thought as she stepped inside, remembering the nonstop giggles.

Struggling with the memory, she left the henhouse and headed back to the house.

.... ❀ ....

An hour or so later, when Mandy happened to glance out the kitchen window, she noticed Josiah on a ladder against the far side of the stable, hammer in hand. He was as tall and lanky as he'd always been, his light brown hair and beard noticeable against the white clapboard stable exterior.

She observed him for a moment, glad she hadn't run into him outdoors earlier and wondering if the old feelings would stir. But they didn't, and a comfortable realization pervaded. *I'm over him,* she thought, something she'd hoped for for years. Yet that fact didn't undo the hurt of that terrible day five years ago.

The fact that Josiah was still coming over to repair things occasionally, as Jerome had mentioned, was between Josiah and Arie. Mandy would just let that be.

.... ❀ ....

Supper that night consisted of an overcooked omelet. Not to be wasteful, she ate it anyway. Still hungry, she went to the basement and chose a pint of her mother's canned tomato soup and brought it upstairs to heat, adding milk. Sprinkled with crushed crackers, the familiar taste reminded her of sitting there at mealtime with her parents and siblings, and she could almost hear their merry chatter.

She felt wistful, knowing Mamma wouldn't be making more soup for her . . . no more of her delicious stew or chow chow, either. *No one but Arie Mae can mimic Mamma's way with food,* she thought sadly.

When she finished eating, Mandy went to the breakfast room and saw that Sadie and Betsy had already set the table for eight. *So helpful*, she thought, returning to the kitchen, where she made a checklist for tomorrow morning. At the top, *Pour orange juice first!*

Mandy was happy for the large quantity of homemade granola ready for tomorrow, as well as the pumpkin bread that had already cooled and been placed on the counter covered in plastic wrap. Tomorrow she would slice the bread before setting out the cold milk for the granola, then cut up bananas and cantaloupe for the breakfast table. *I'll let Betsy serve everything*, she decided.

After a shower, Mandy dialed Eilene's number, and when it went to voice mail, she left a message that probably sounded much more cheerful than she felt. "I'll call you another time to chat," she said. "Miss you, Eilene, and tell Don hi."

Mandy ironed her blouses in the kitchen with her mother's old gas iron, glad the second full day was behind her. She folded up the ironing board and put it away, and again considered the possibility of making herself some Amish clothes. Had Mamma even kept Mandy's old dress pattern?

There were times, she recalled, when she would come home from the florist shop and just sit in her quiet bedroom, high in the Bradleys' house, trying to imagine what her family was doing back here in Gordonville. As each year passed, she wondered if they missed her, or if Mamma kept praying she would return, as she'd written in her letters. Had Arie Mae ever hoped Mandy might come home?

Mandy grimaced at the way her cousin Kate had treated her today. And in that moment, she felt justified in not darkening the door of tomorrow's Preaching service. It was merely a way of protecting herself . . . and a way of avoiding an encounter with either her sister or Josiah.

Surely if Jerome knew much at all about the past, he would understand.

Chapter 13

Early Sunday morning it started to rain, coming in sheets, wave after wave. The low gray clouds had covered the sunrise, causing the house to be dark when earlier it had been brilliant with light. After starting a small fire in the hearth, Mandy went around and lit all the gas lamps, including the ones in the breakfast room, trying to cheer up the place.

From what Mandy could hear from the kitchen, all went well while Betsy served breakfast to the guests, even when Kristen Turner, one of yesterday's new arrivals, asked if Betsy might have a recipe for wedding tapioca, remarking how delicious it was.

"Saloma used to offer a candlelight supper three evenings a week for an extra fee," Kristen added.

One of the men mentioned that he had been to such a supper himself. "The tapioca was only one of the delicious desserts she served."

"Oh yes," Betsy replied, "Saloma used to love to do those meals, though it's been some months since we've hosted one. Still, I'm sure that recipe is in her notebook," Betsy told them.

"I'll jot it down and leave it on the desk in the entryway for ya, if that's all right."

"Oh, would you? How nice," Kristen thanked her.

Mandy hoped an evening meal wasn't something guests would start pressing her to provide. Goodness, first she had to learn to cook breakfast!

········ ❁ ········

The service at the community church was inspiring, though punctuated by the heavy rain on the roof, and Mandy wondered if the weather would keep her houseful of guests indoors on this Lord's Day. If so, there might be more tricky encounters to navigate, especially with Betsy having the rest of the day off, since there was no housekeeping today.

After the closing hymn, "Jesus, Keep Me Near the Cross," Mandy waited in the line to exit the sanctuary, the melody continuing in her mind. She noticed the minister standing at the doorway to the lobby to shake hands with each person. Every time the outer doors opened, people opened umbrellas as they stepped out, pausing under the overhang, then making a dash to the parking lot through the rain, which was still making down.

"Lord bless you," the pastor said as she approached, smiling as he took her hand. "Are you new to the area?"

She shook her head, not wanting to hold up the line. "I enjoyed your sermon very much."

He nodded. "We hope you'll join us again."

She thanked him. "I'll be back next week," she said, glad she had chosen this small fellowship of believers.

········ ❁ ········

Even though it was Sunday, Mandy went upstairs to Mamma's sewing room after a simple lunch to see if she might put her hands on the old dress pattern she'd once used. She was formulating a plan, although with Betsy around to interact with the guests, there was no hurry to move forward quite yet.

The room afforded a center table for cutting out patterns and laying out piecework for quilts and whatnot, as well as a treadle sewing machine against one wall and a hutchlike cabinet with fabric and sewing notions.

Poking through the shelves of fabric, Mandy found nothing that would suffice for more than an apron or a child's garment. But just being in the room again somehow made her feel closer to her mother than she had in years. And she pressed her hand to her quivering lips, again wishing with all of her heart she could have talked to Mamma once more before she died.

When she returned downstairs, a quick rap at the back door startled Mandy from her reverie. She went to answer it and found Deacon Ed Yoder and his wife, Rhoda, dressed in their black Sunday best.

Mandy had wondered when she might be paid such a visit and put on a smile when she opened the door to welcome them inside. She asked if they'd like some coffee, but both shook their heads.

"We're here to check in on ya," the deacon said, glancing at his wife as they stood just inside the doorway.

"*Kumme*, have a seat in the sitting room," Mandy urged, trying to be as hospitable as Mamma would have been, though her mother would never have needed such scrutiny. And scrutinized she felt as Rhoda gave Mandy's fancy clothing a quick once-over.

"That gully washer was really somethin', ain't!" Deacon Ed remarked as they followed Mandy through the kitchen to the family's private sitting room. "Nearly blew us off the road when we went visiting Rhoda's sister and family earlier."

"It's nice out now, though," Mandy said, on edge as she took

a seat across from them. "Are ya sure I can't pour ya some coffee
. . . or make some tea?"

Rhoda was quick to decline. "But that's ever so kind."

"How can I help you?" Mandy said, anxious to get to the crux
of their visit.

Deacon Ed nodded slowly and folded his bony hands together.
"Your mother depended heavily upon your sister for the years you
were away, Mandy," he began.

At this, Rhoda emphatically nodded, and Mandy waited, think-
ing Rhoda might speak next, but it was the deacon who continued.
"We've heard from others in the community that you've let Arie
Mae go." He sighed. "It's hard to understand, really."

"'Specially since Arie basically ran the inn with your Mamma,"
Rhoda added.

"Honestly, folk are scratchin' their heads, wondering why you
returned, if not to engage with your family . . . and the People,"
Deacon said.

Mandy listened and wondered if she should attempt to explain
that she'd only returned for her inheritance, despite the difficult
conditions. But as she tried on the words in her mind, she realized
they would never win favor with the deacon.

"What with your hastiness toward your sister, seems you're
more English than Amish anymore," Deacon Ed said, eyes moist-
ening. "Mighty sad to think that of one of Saloma and Ephraim's
daughters . . ."

If she hadn't felt entirely guilty already, Mandy certainly did
now. True, she had been hasty, but she doubted the deacon was
privy to the circumstances between her and Arie Mae.

"We'd sure like to see ya at Preachin' services, Mandy," Rhoda
said, as if to back her husband up in this.

"Jerome has invited me," Mandy said, knowing they likely
hoped for some kind of commitment.

"Well, then, that's three of us opening the door for ya," the deacon said, standing just then and offering his hand to his wife to assist her from her chair. "And you'll find many more behind that door."

"*Denki* for your visit," Mandy said. It still felt a little odd to be able to speak *Deitsch* again. And while she felt chastened, she did not see herself going back to church with the People. How could she when she was merely biding time?

········ ✿ ········

At a few minutes to four, Mandy's friend Winnie called, eager to describe what she'd accomplished for the basic layout of the website.

"You're that far already?" Mandy was so pleased, and the call was a nice distraction from the deacon's unsettling visit, to be sure.

"I'll send you the link so that you can request changes or make suggestions before it goes live."

"Sounds great."

Winnie laughed heartily. "One more thing: You might want to consider contacting some travel agents and travel websites to get referrals. I bet there are a few who provide expertise to travelers headed to Lancaster County. Just a thought."

"I'll get right on it," Mandy said, thanking her.

Thinking that Eilene Bradley would surely be home at this hour, Mandy placed another call to her and couldn't help but smile when Eilene answered on the third ring.

"We were happy to get your voice mail, Mandy. Thanks for keeping in touch."

They talked a bit more, Mandy asking about Eilene's husband, Don. "And I'm curious . . . have you rented my old room yet?"

"Well, just today, in fact." Eilene went on to say that the new boarder was an older gentleman. "He seems to want a family setting, so Don and I are tickled pink to be able to bless him this way." Eilene also mentioned that she and her husband were praying for Mandy every morning during their joint devotional time.

"That means a lot. I need all the prayers anyone wants to give these days." She thanked Eilene and gave her the mailing address for the inn before saying a fond good-bye.

With a new spring in her step, Mandy made a double-decker ham and turkey sandwich for her supper, following in the People's tradition of not cooking on Sunday. And she thought more about possibly creating a dress pattern and going to Good's Store to purchase black fabric to make a proper mourning dress to wear around the guests. Would doing so improve her standing among the People?

She had just finished her sandwich when Mandy heard male voices in the breakfast room. Assuming they were looking for more hot coffee to accompany the cookies Sadie had baked yesterday, she went in to check and found Patrick and Gene sitting at the table with their coffee mugs full and the plate of cookies centered between them.

Patrick looked up and asked if she might recommend a good place to dine. "Specifically an Amish buffet."

She mentioned Fisher's Amish Restaurant over on Harvest Drive, but then remembered it wasn't open on Sundays. "If it's Amish owned, it won't be," she said, giving other options close by.

Patrick nodded and thanked her, then glanced at Gene, who looked downright embarrassed just then. "We were surprised to see you at church this morning," Gene said. "My wife and I slipped in the side, so you probably didn't notice us."

"No," she said, feeling awkward.

"We were under the impression that Amish only attended their own services."

"'Tis true," Mandy said, second-guessing her decision to attend worship so close to the B and B.

Patrick seemed to ponder that as Gene stared hard at what little was left of his cookie. "So then, I guess you don't consider yourself Amish."

Mandy disliked being cornered like this. "I'm here to oversee things at the request of my deceased mother," she said firmly, but when she didn't bother to elaborate, an uncomfortable silence seemed to fall over the room.

Chapter 14

Sadie's last day at work came and went, and the rest of the week was a flurry of activity, with Amish folk pouring in from Ohio and elsewhere for the local weddings. Mandy still kept herself hidden away in the kitchen as much as possible, putting Betsy out in front with the guests. Having gotten her scrambled eggs with various mix-ins down to a science, or so Betsy had stated, Mandy cooked those, changing things a bit with things like purchased donuts and coffee cake. But breakfasts were still not up to par, considering Mandy's attempt at omelets was nothing short of a calamity one morning. She'd had to jump in the car and run up to the grocery store to get a few premade quiches.

Each afternoon, when Betsy left for home, Mandy finished up odds and ends, bringing in more wood for the fireplace, and then carrying the coal for the stove in buckets from the shed. There were occasional visits from her sisters-in-law, as well, but they never stayed long, nor did they offer to help or seem to know what to talk about.

With what little time was left before and after supper, Mandy sewed like there was no tomorrow. Without telling a soul of her decision, she had been altering her mother's black dresses and cape and aprons to fit her. It seemed like a necessary shortcut, and she was quite certain none of her siblings would mind.

By that Friday morning, she slipped into her fully altered clothing, ready to be more visible around guests. She looked at herself, running her hands down over the bodice and around her waist, feeling oddly at home in the familiar attire. Then, going to the dresser mirror, she glimpsed the old, yet new, Mandy Dienner and sighed. *So much the same, yet so much different.* Still, there was something comforting about wearing Mamma's dress, she thought as she headed to the kitchen.

When she saw Mandy wearing proper mourning attire, Betsy stumbled all over herself, like she didn't know what to say. "Ach, you look . . . it's so *gut* to see ya wearin' . . ."

"I want to honor Mamma," Mandy explained as Betsy got out the skillet to make griddle cakes.

Mandy smiled weakly as she put on her mother's work apron, then set about making scrambled eggs mixed with spinach and goat cheese, which she knew for a fact were tasty because it had been her supper a couple nights this past week.

Even Jerome would like them, she thought, hoping so.

········ ❀ ········

When the guests checked in that afternoon, Mandy immediately noticed they greeted her with much more enthusiasm. *It's a good choice to dress Plain again.*

But another problem had arisen. For some odd reason, four calls in a row came in on Saturday morning, three canceling reservations for that very day. Mandy wondered what was happening. Particularly this time of year, Mamma'd never had so many rooms sitting vacant.

She brought it up to Betsy, who said she had a theory. "Well, knowin' how connected so many of our guests are, I wonder if word has spread of the changes here. Some of the guests have seemed rather disgruntled. After all, the breakfasts here were a pretty big draw, and folks were loyal to your Mamma . . . and Arie Mae."

Mandy frowned, finding this hard to believe. "So that many of the inn's guests are related or know each other?"

"They either knew each other before comin' here, or met here over the years, *jah*. And considering wedding season, that's especially true. Lots of the usual guests have Gordonville connections, ya know."

What's our cancellation policy? Mandy wondered, but she knew Mamma would never have held someone to a reservation.

All the same, Mandy worried aloud about this to Jerome the following Monday morning. "We had another couple of cancelation calls yesterday for dates further out, too. Word of mouth is powerful," she said, showing him the emptying reservation book while he ate her pancakes and scrambled eggs. She also described the completed website which, in her opinion, looked quite professional and inviting, despite not having any bells and whistles.

"I went to see Arie more than a week ago," Jerome told her. "We talked about—"

"That's all right. . . . I really don't need to know," Mandy said, recalling seeing his two-wheeled cart parked over there.

"*Nee*, hear me out, *Schweschder*." He continued, "Puttin' it mildly, Arie was taken aback at your firing her."

"Truth be told, I really doubt she wants to be around me, either."

He inhaled audibly and shook his head. "*Ach*, Mandy . . . at the very least, I'm glad to see you've decided to dress Plain."

"Tryin' to fit in," she was quick to explain. "And maybe, to save the inn."

He pushed his empty plate aside and folded his callused hands on the table. "Then maybe ya should think on this: Very few Amish establishments have websites, 'least round here. Makes it look like the inn's not really authentic."

"I've seen plenty online, though," she contradicted him and reached for her phone on the counter. "If ya want proof, I'll show ya."

"*Nee.*" Jerome shook his head. "If you ask me, things should've been left like they were." He glanced at her. "It was prob'ly hard for folk to believe this was a genuine Amish inn, the way you were dressed an' all." Then he smiled. "I'm glad you've decided to wear Plain clothes now, but I truly wish it meant a change of heart."

Jerome smoothed his beard and rose from the table, wandering over to the sink to wash his hands while Mandy sat there, willing herself to say no more.

.... ✿ ....

First thing Thursday, Betsy dropped some very unexpected news. "I'm sorry, Mandy," she told her, looking pink in the face, "but I just don't feel right staying on and workin' here."

Mandy shook her head in disbelief. *Betsy's quitting, too?*

She rubbed her neck and sighed. "To be honest, I was so happy when you started dressing Plain again, 'cause the fact you didn't was something of a stumbling block. But honestly I was disappointed when I realized you're doin' it just to keep customers. And there's no talk of inviting Arie back . . . and you're still driving your car."

Mandy could see how difficult this was for Betsy.

"I'll go ahead and work the rest of today, but then you'll need to find other help," Betsy said.

Mandy bit her lip, frustrated. "No one's interested in helpin' here as long as I'm in charge, though. Isn't that true?"

Looking sheepish, Betsy nodded. "I daresay it's more than that."

If I'd just go to church again with the People . . .

"Oh, Betsy, I really can't do this myself." Mandy knew she had come to her wit's end. "Don't ya see?"

Hanging her head for a time, then slowly lifting her eyes, Betsy answered, "I'm sorry . . . but it has to be this way."

Mandy felt as upset as Betsy looked and wondered if Sadie had encouraged Betsy to quit, as well. And yet Mandy couldn't blame either of them, really—everything Betsy had just said made good sense to Old Order church members.

Mandy let the room fill up with the silence. At last, she said, "I'm here to keep the inn running . . . profitably. One way or another."

Betsy's gaze met hers. "And you'll inherit it, right?" Her eyes welled up with tears. "Isn't *that* why you came home?"

Seeing her like this, Mandy felt a twinge of guilt. Even so, she dared not admit that it was the *only* reason.

.... ⚘ ....

Ironically, without Betsy working at Butterfly Meadows, Mandy could not afford to take the time to look for a replacement—the work was all on her shoulders. So she quickly outlined her day on paper, marking out time for every aspect of running the place, no matter how trivial. In her scant spare time, she continued to practice cooking, still falling short of her mother's elaborate spreads, though she'd put together a farmer's skillet breakfast—a recipe she'd found in the back of Mamma's notebook—and the guests seemed to be enjoying it.

And there were now plenty of guests. By the following Tuesday, reservations had miraculously begun to stabilize, possibly because of the small ad Mandy had run. Surprisingly, folk were booking clear up through New Year's, many of whom had never before stayed at Butterfly Meadows. And when she inquired of the new guests, the big draw seemed to be the free buggy ride with a two-night stay, something she had managed to handle at first but with which she was now seriously thinking of asking for Karl Lantz's assistance. Of course, if he was too busy at his woodworking shop, Karl could always decline.

So, at noon that day, in the midst of a sudden cold snap, Mandy decided to go out and talk it over with him. She found Karl watering the horses, his back to her, and went over to Gertie's stall to stroke her mane.

Karl turned and smiled, removing his straw hat and revealing his full head of blond hair. "Hullo again, Mandy."

She wondered why *he* was still working here when the Kauffman sisters had quit on her. But on second thought, maybe Karl wasn't one to pay much attention to gossip. "So tell me, what's it like in Wisconsin?" she said, making small talk.

"I thought you'd never ask," he said lightheartedly, returning his hat to his head. He rubbed his hands together, then blew his breath into them before rubbing them together yet again. "During a Wisconsin winter, a wise farmer would never leave the house without his work gloves, for one thing. If folk think it's chilly here, well, let me tell ya right now . . . your breath would freeze in midair in Wisconsin, and right before your eyes."

She was captivated by the way his hands moved as he talked. "*Ach*, that's mighty cold."

"Everyone carries a winter emergency kit in their buggy, which is heated, otherwise a body could freeze to death." He grinned, bringing a liveliness to his face as he continued to rave about his native state. "By the way, if you ever get the chance, you must take a tour of the Cave of the Mounds . . . not too far from my former home. There are honest-to-goodness lighted walkways inside the cave and even some butterfly gardens outside . . . but nothin' like the thousands of butterflies you have here in the spring and summer."

She couldn't help but smile at that. "Sounds like a *wunnerbaar-gut* place."

Karl reached over to rub Gertie's forehead. "This is one special horse, I'm sure you know." He nodded at Ol' Tulip, whose nose was clear out of the stall as she whinnied over at them. "Her too."

In the middle of this hectic day, Mandy let herself soak in the peace of the stable. "I agree wholeheartedly. Reliable as driving horses, but as dear as any pets."

"Not to embarrass you, but I couldn't help noticing you're dressin' Plain now."

She glanced down at the black coat over her black mourning dress and long apron, and nodded. "Thought it was 'bout time, ya know."

After another exchange about the animals, Karl said, "Well, it's been nice talkin' to ya, Mandy."

"You too." She turned to hurry back across the yard, not realizing until she was in the house again that she'd forgotten to ask him about taking the guests for buggy rides. *Puh!* she thought, aggravated. *I don't have time today to hitch up Gertie, take guests around for a half-hour ride, and have the banana nut bread and the hot spiced cider ready to serve, too,* she fretted, then remembered she'd forgotten to include gathering the afternoon eggs.

All this work is making me ferhoodled!

She looked out the kitchen window back at the stable but figured it would seem odd for her to run out there again to ask just now. She would simply have to continue to do her best. *I'll ask him another time, maybe.*

"There's a full house again tonight," she murmured, thinking of all she had to do yet today. Tucking a stray hair behind her ear, she rushed to the basement to check on the bedsheets, hoping they were dry—if not, it might be useful to purchase some gas-powered fans. If Mamma hadn't purchased multiple sets of sheets for each bed, Mandy would be in a jam, for sure!

Chapter

15

Trina Sutton settled in for a quiet evening with Gail Anderson, her ear tuned toward the sleeping woman's bedroom while Trina scrolled through the news headlines on her phone. Earlier that Tuesday, she had enjoyed listening to the jovial woman tell about the *MythBusters* reruns she'd watched on the Discovery Channel. It was reassuring evidence that Gail's mind was clear and readily processing new information.

I hope I'm that sharp at her age, Trina thought, deciding to text an old friend from high school, now a new mom. *If you ever need to get out of the house, let me know, Lainey,* Trina offered. *I'm free during the day and on weekends, since I'm working weeknights. Keep me in mind, OK? I'd love to help.*

More than a half hour passed before the phone chirped to signal a message. Lainey thanked her for the offer but politely declined.

We really must get together soon, Trina texted back. *It's been forever.*

Baby's crying . . . GTG! came the near-instant reply.

No worries, Trina thought, not particularly surprised. In the past year, almost everyone she'd known had run to the nearest exit.

All but Janna and Gail, she thought, looking over at the built-in bookshelf on one side of the fireplace, where a golden-framed photograph commemorated Gail and her late husband's fiftieth wedding anniversary. Gail had worn her candlelight-white wedding gown for the picture, though she'd asked her granddaughter to pin it in back for the pose, she confessed to Trina a couple of nights ago as they sat there in the comfortable room. Gail had gone on to reminisce about other happy moments of her life. *She's become my closest friend*, Trina thought. *And she's old enough to be my grandmother!*

Trina was paging through a dessert cookbook packed with scrumptious options—cream cheese pecan pie and apple sugar-plum pie among them—when she heard a thump, the sound of a bird hitting the window, perhaps.

Surely not this time of night.

Getting up from the cushy chair, she hurried toward Gail's bedroom, where the door was always kept open. "Are you all right?" she called. "Gail?"

A slight whimper came in response. Worried, Trina darted into the dimly lit room and found the poor woman lying on the floor on her left side. "Oh, you've fallen," she said, aghast yet trying to remain calm.

"Thank the Good Lord you heard me," Gail whispered, her wrinkled hands covering her face suddenly as she moaned.

"Where do you hurt?" Trina asked, turning on the bedside lamp and then sitting on the floor beside her.

"My right hip," she cried, reaching for Trina's hand. "Is it broken? Oh, please don't leave me . . . please."

"I'm right here," she said gently, pulling out her phone to call 9-1-1. "I'm not going anywhere." Immediately after ensuring emergency responders were on their way, she called Gail's oldest son.

Gail must have feared a scenario like this when she insisted on hiring a night nurse. She hadn't used her walker, which was still parked near the bed. *All this on my watch,* thought Trina miserably.

When the call went to voice mail on the fifth ring, Trina left a brief message to let Bill Anderson know that his mother had fallen and the paramedics were on the way. Then, hanging up, she returned her full attention to Gail.

"I feel like an old woman." Gail gave her a faint smile.

"You'll be fine."

Gail's eyes were pleading. "Promise?"

Trina reached to caress her furrowed brow. "I'll take care of you."

.... ❀ ....

Mandy fell exhausted into bed that night, thinking how she had gone from relatively confident that she could run the inn for a year to feeling like a one-woman band, so to speak, and worried sick she might actually fail.

I could lose this whole thing, she realized, pushing panic away.

As she was drifting off toward dreamland, she wondered how her family could sit idly by and let this happen. Why did everyone seem so aloof? Did it all come back to her firing Arie Mae?

.... ❀ ....

Trina stepped out of the elevator onto the eighth floor of the hospital where Gail Anderson was resting, waiting for the swelling in her hip to subside so that surgery could take place to repair it. She had inquired about Gail's room number at the information desk upon first arriving late that afternoon, anxious to see how the woman was doing.

She found her in room 807, lying flat on her back on the hospital bed. Seeing Gail was alone, Trina pulled a chair away from the window and moved it next to the bed, where she sat down to wait for Gail's eyes to open. The call button had slipped out of reach, and Trina clipped it to a pillowcase.

After a time, she walked to the window and adjusted the flower arrangements lined up there, and looked at the small cards attached—one each from Gail's children and their families, as well as a white blooming cyclamen from her church. According to the greeting attached, the largest bouquet had been sent by Gail's son, Bill.

Smiling, Trina was glad the family had stepped up and demonstrated their care, at least with flowers.

"Is that you, Trina, dear?"

Hearing the feeble voice, Trina hurried back to Gail's bedside. "How's my favorite patient?" she asked, accepting the woman's bony hand.

"Alive, apparently," Gail said, her eyes blinking, then closing again.

Trina gently squeezed her hand. "You'll be as good as new after surgery."

Gail smiled weakly. "The nurses here . . ." She shook her head as if refusing to speak ill of them. "You've spoiled me, Trina," she whispered.

"What do you need most?" she asked, tucking Gail's hand back under the sheet.

Gail murmured about how she felt stiff, even numb. "They don't move me enough."

She must be worried about blood clots, Trina thought.

"I'll look into that," she told her, making a mental note to stop at the nurses' station to ask for air compression leg massagers. "What else can I do?"

"Well"—and tears sprang to the woman's eyes—"they had an awful time getting the IV needle in my arm when I arrived."

Trina moved to the other side of the bed and inspected the

back of Gail's lean hand, where the needle had been inserted into a bulging vein. "If you need another poke, I'll request a small butterfly needle," she said, wondering why someone hadn't ordered one from pediatrics. It was common practice for elderly patients.

Gail reached for Trina's hand again. "Something else," she said.

Trina leaned closer.

"You promised to look after me."

Trina nodded. "And I will."

"You'll be my nurse when I get out of here . . . full time?" the woman's voice was a near whisper.

Sighing, Trina assumed future arrangements for Gail's care were out of her hands. "Have you talked with your family about where you want to be once you're finished with rehab?"

Gail's eyes shot open wide. "That's a given—I want to go *home*."

Most people wish for that.

Gail's hand shook and her lower lip quivered. "Please talk to my children. They're coming back to visit tomorrow evening."

Realizing the frail woman was likely depressed, given the circumstances, Trina stayed past the dinner hour, during which time she offered Gail some food when the tray came around.

While she tended to the dear, helpless woman, Trina felt sad where Gail's future care was concerned. And later, when talking firmly with the head nurse to address the patient's complaints, she felt all the worse when the nurse seemed distracted and raised her eyebrows. "I expect these matters to be taken care of," Trina emphasized. "And I'll check back tomorrow to make sure they are," she added before leaving, barely suppressing her anger.

········ ✾ ········

At home, Trina decided to warm up yesterday's leftovers, unable to get Gail out of her mind. Eager to nose around a bit, she gave one of the daughters a call. After exchanging a few niceties, Trina asked if the family had talked about plans for Gail after transitional care. "I'm sure you know she's hoping to return home when she's able."

Fifty-something Kathy Anderson sounded thoughtful as she replied, "I'm sure she'd rather die at home than around strangers."

Who said anything about dying? Trina thought, taken aback. She chose her next words carefully. "Understandable, but your mother is hardly terminal."

"Well, her balance is off—she shouldn't be home alone anymore."

"The family should jump through hoops for her," Trina wanted to say. Surely all of them cared as much about Gail's wish to return home as the woman herself did.

Instead, she replied, "I agree she needs more care." Trina didn't say that Gail had asked her to be a full-time nurse.

Kathy paused, then said, "We don't have many options, quite frankly, because Mom can't afford twenty-four-hour nursing care."

"Not many people can." Again, Trina badly wanted to suggest the family help out more, but she really shouldn't stick her nose in any further. "I'm planning to visit her again tomorrow . . . see how she's doing."

"She'll be thrilled. She talks about you all the time, Trina."

Trina grinned into the phone. "I think the world of her, too."

They talked a bit more and then hung up.

Gail won't be going home, Trina realized, a painful lump in her throat.

She lightly salted her reheated vegetables and removed the food from the burner, hoping the Anderson family would pay close attention to their loved one's needs. The truth of the matter was that Gail would undoubtedly go from rehab to assisted living . . . and Trina would miss her terribly.

Fighting tears now, Trina hugged herself. *Get ahold of yourself. You're taking this too hard.*

But she couldn't help it. *What am I going to do?*

She took a few deep breaths, letting them out slowly, and little by little, pulled herself together.

When at last she felt calmer, she sat down to eat and decided to keep in touch with Gail regardless of whether she remained her patient or not. Trina prayed the blessing over the food, tucking in one for Gail, too. "Dear Lord, my friend needs Your comfort tonight. Please be with her as she looks ahead to the coming surgery. I ask this in Christ's name. Amen."

For dessert, which she rarely ate, she had a thin slice of peach pie with a cup of coffee. Savoring the pie, which she'd made yesterday to share with Gail, she was overcome with discouragement again, even loneliness, the kind that was sure to engulf her once Trina's responsibilities to the woman were a thing of the past. And yet, despite that, she hoped she might not be reassigned a new evening patient, not yet. *I need some space,* she thought. *Some time away . . .*

Time to grieve losing Gail, she thought while carrying her dishes to the sink. There, she rinsed them before loading them into the dishwasher, and as she did, the idea of getting out of town for a couple weeks crossed her mind. *Somewhere warm and unpopulated,* she thought, relishing the impulsive notion. *And away from difficult people.*

She recalled the magazine ad she'd seen and opened her laptop, deciding to sign up for a mystery trip before she changed her mind.

Laughing at what she'd done, she dialed Janna's number to tell her. "I threw caution to the wind! Can you imagine me doing something so spur-of-the-moment?"

Her sister was chuckling, too. "What did you tell your boss?"

"I haven't yet. Actually, I'm planning to take a leave of absence."

"If anyone can manage it financially, it's you."

Trina nodded at the phone. "I make penny pinchers look like impulsive spenders!"

Janna laughed, and Trina promised to let her know where the trip took her. "As crazy as this sounds, I'm actually excited."

"You need something to look forward to, I think."

"Totally agree."

"I hope you can relax while you're gone. Most days, you prefer to go ninety miles an hour."

I do need a break, Trina thought. But her sister was right. *How will I manage nearly two weeks of doing nothing?*

Chapter

16

That Sunday morning, after serving the guests a simple breakfast, Mandy attended the community church, but this time she decided to wear her Amish clothing, having become quite comfortable in it again. This elicited more than a few head scratches and stares as she took her seat in the padded church pew with a few other single women.

Reaching for the hymnal, she waited for the minister to take his seat on the platform while a family of nine filed in reverently and sat down, taking up the long pew in front of her. Two of the younger sisters, both brunettes, seemed especially affectionate, one whispering something to the other and receiving a sweet smile in return.

Arie Mae and I were once that close, Mandy thought, tears welling up.

After the service, instead of making something to eat at home, Mandy stoked the black coal stove and walked straight to her room, where she fell asleep on the bed while still wearing her black woolen shawl. This being her only day to catch her breath, she slept for two solid hours before waking with a start. Seeing what time it was, she shook her head in surprise, then, hungry, she went to the kitchen and made a generous salad with tomato, cucumbers, and avocado, and added some leftover chicken strips from last evening, when she'd baked several chicken breasts.

Lunch finished, she decided she'd like to visit her Dienner grandparents down in Paradise, so she got in her car and headed that way. *How will they receive me?* she wondered, hoping for the best from her only remaining grandparents.

As it turned out, *Dawdi* and *Mammi* Dienner were gone from their house, undoubtedly out visiting this no-Preaching Sunday, since the gray family carriage was nowhere to be seen. So Mandy left a note saying she would drop by to see them another time, signing off *With love, your granddaughter, Amanda Sue,* and headed back to Gordonville, feeling blue.

The gray sky threatened snow, and she shivered as, before going inside the house, she gathered a bucket of coal to bring to life the smoldering fire in the stove. While outside, she had noticed that someone had stacked more firewood near the back door. Karl, perhaps?

Moments later, she heard a timid knock and hurried to open the back door. She peered down at the most striking little blond boy, his cheeks rosy with cold. "You must be Yonnie Lantz," she said, immediately seeing the resemblance to his father.

Shyly, he bobbed his head.

"*Kumme* in an' get *waerme,*" she said, introducing herself in *Deitsch,* since she knew he was too young to understand English. "I'd be glad to make some hot cocoa. All right?"

Timidly, he stepped into the house and, as if on cue, removed his little black felt hat and hung it on the back corner of the nearest kitchen chair. "Dat'll hitch up for the buggy ride today," he announced in a husky little voice.

"Ol' Tulip, then?" she replied in kind.

Yonnie's big blue eyes smiled as he nodded.

"Such a help." She smiled to herself as she made her way to the pantry, where she took down a canister of Mamma's homemade cocoa mix. "This won't take but a minute," she said, asking if he'd like to sit at the table to wait. "I'll have some coffee with you, how's that?"

Bless his heart, Yonnie beamed at her.

Once the hot drinks were ready, they sat across from each other at the kitchen table, blowing gently, then sipping. The boy was silent all the while as he seemed to take in the expansive room with his inquisitive gaze. Mandy did the talking, letting him know that if he ever wanted to get warmed up, or wanted something to drink or eat, he could just open the back door and walk right in. "If I'm here in the kitchen, I'll see ya. If not, do ya see that cowbell on the counter over yonder? Well, just ring it."

Yonnie seemed to like her plan, his eyes sparkling as he peeked over the top of his cup of hot cocoa.

Mandy also offered him a cookie, which he eagerly accepted. "Be sure to thank your father for me," she said, wondering if she dared hope that Karl might even offer to take the guests for a ride, too. But she wouldn't ask for that favor. After all, it was *her* inheritance she was attempting to earn. Challenging though it was!

.... ❀ ....

Once Mandy had taken the guests on the buggy ride down to Irishtown Road and back, Janice Hart—who'd earlier told Mandy she had been a close friend of her mother's in recent years—asked if she and Mandy might sit and have tea by the fireplace sometime later today.

"Sure, but I have to get the horse back to the stable first,"

Mandy said as she halted Ol' Tulip to let her guests out near the front walkway.

"That's perfectly fine," the woman agreed as Mandy headed around the back of the house, where right away she spotted Karl's fair hair peeking out of his hat. He waved her forward.

"Yonnie really enjoyed the hot cocoa—the special attention, too," Karl said with a grin. "If ya'd like, I'll go ahead and unhitch for ya."

Mandy thanked him while stepping out of the carriage. "Yonnie's welcome anytime."

"Well, it was kind. You must be tuckered out, considering all you're doin'," he said, taking the driving lines from her.

"You have no idea . . . well, *jah*, s'pose you might." She felt silly, stumbling over her words like that.

"Listen, if it's all right, Mandy, I'd be more than happy to take your guests out ridin' each afternoon, if that'd help."

She couldn't have been more pleased. *Somehow he guessed what I wished I could ask*, she thought, remembering how Betsy said Mamma had called Karl a godsend.

"I appreciate it more than you know . . . and everything else you're doin' round here. Now, if I could just get some *gut* help inside the house," she said, immediately wondering why she'd opened her mouth.

"Your sister used to—"

"Well, she's not helpin' anymore," Mandy interrupted, then realized how she must sound. "*Ach*, I . . ." She didn't know how to begin to explain herself, or if she should even attempt it.

Karl nodded, but his expression was puzzled. "I've noticed Josiah and your brother Sammy comin' by to see about things from time to time."

"*Denki* again, Karl." Mandy wished this conversation hadn't taken such a disquieting turn.

He nodded slowly, his face ever so serious now. "Glad to do what I can."

.... �֍ ....

Daylight had begun to fade as Mandy walked toward the house. The smell of woodsmoke filled the air, and blackbirds cawed to one another where they sat atop the corncrib.

Back inside, she removed her mother's candlesnuffer bonnet and warmest wool coat and hung them up on the wooden wall pegs along the far wall of the kitchen. Catching her breath, she made her way around to the breakfast room and found Janice Hart seated at the table closest to the hearth, two steaming cups of hot water already poured.

"I heard you come inside and took the liberty of getting you set up," the woman said, pointing to the teacups and the basket of tea bags. "Hope it's all right."

"Thank you—such a treat," Mandy said, soaking in the warmth of the fire as she pulled out a chair next to Janice, who looked close in age to Mamma.

"I'd like to get to know you." The woman's smile was contagious. "You see, your mother was more than my acquaintance; she was a wonderful friend . . . wrote numerous letters and cards of encouragement after my daughter, Candace, was diagnosed with leukemia, three years ago."

Janice continued sharing, saying she might never have yearned for a relationship with the Lord if she hadn't come to this inn. "Your mother was a guiding light in so many ways . . . truly a spiritual sister to me."

This warmed Mandy's heart.

"She kept in close touch throughout the years between my husband's and my visits." Janice dabbed a tissue at her eyes. "I was so despondent after Candace died, I scarcely wanted to live anymore. She was our only child . . . we were so very close."

Mandy felt moved by the woman's emotion.

"Your mother's faith and dependence upon God gave me the courage I needed. And not just for myself, but to reach out to other grieving mothers." Janice gently tapped the tabletop. "In fact, she and I sometimes spent an hour right here sipping tea."

"I'm glad Mamma cared so deeply for you," Mandy said. "I can't imagine your loss."

"When I first met Saloma, I just felt I could openly share my heart with her. I became envious of her joyful nature and the sense of peace she seemed to have found even as a widow. Eventually, her Lord and Savior became mine . . . but it all started because she was such a consistently dear friend to me."

"You must miss her terribly." Mandy was surprised at the depth of caring Mamma had shown for an *Englischer*.

"I cried when my husband and I learned that she'd passed away. Regrettably, we heard too late to attend the funeral—that's one of the reasons we're here now." Janice touched Mandy's hand. "Your mother talked of you often, Mandy. She loved you dearly . . . confided she prayed for you every day."

Mandy resisted the inclination to frown, taking Janice's words at face value. It seemed odd to hear this from a stranger. And she couldn't help wondering whether Mamma had also told Janice why Mandy had left home.

"It's obvious so many people loved her," Mandy said quietly.

Janice nodded slowly, eyes locked on Mandy. "She asked God to bring people her way—here to the B and B—those who needed Him most."

Mandy pondered that, wondering if that was also the reason her mother had left the inn to her . . . Mamma's way of asking God to bring her home again. "I'm glad you shared that with me . . . and I hope you enjoy your stay here, even though my cookin' can't hold a candle to Mamma's."

Janice shook her head but didn't refute Mandy's comment. "It can't be easy running the place by yourself."

"It certainly gives me a *gut* reason to get up in the morning!"

Pouring more hot water into her cup, Janice smiled. "You have some of your mother's spunk."

"I'll take that as a compliment." Enlightening as it had been, Mandy felt honored that Janice had sought her out for tea and a chat.

Later, when it was way past her bedtime and she had finally accomplished everything on her must-do list, Mandy had much to be thankful for, including the delightful visit with little Yonnie and the openhearted talk with Janice.

Chapter

17

Thankful for a sunny *Weschdaag* morning, Mandy got up as soon as the clock alarm sounded at four-thirty. She managed to scatter feed to the chickens and gather the morning eggs . . . then ran back inside to get coffee on and start the daily routine for the guests all over again. And as she started making breakfast, she realized that even if she'd felt called to sit and visit with guests as Mamma had done, there was simply no time with the way things were now.

Would Betsy return if I offered more pay? she allowed herself to ponder.

But no, the hardworking young woman had not left because of low wages; she'd seemed quite offended that Mandy was dressing Amish without really *being* Amish.

· · · · · · · · ❀ · · · · · · · ·

At breakfast, Janice Hart's husband, Theodore, asked Mandy about Zook's Homemade Chicken Pies. "Do you recommend the shop?"

"Most definitely. They have delicious meat pies—beef, chicken, and sausage—and a few other items. It's just over on Harvest Drive," Mandy said.

"Thanks, we'll stop by today," Theodore replied, glancing fondly at his wife.

As the guests resumed eating and talking among themselves, Mandy excused herself, knowing she must get back to the kitchen to brew more coffee and retrieve the fresh fruit, which she had forgotten. She simply must do something, and quick, to get help.

I'm not going to make it another week, much less twelve consecutive months! she thought, out of breath.

.... ❁ ....

Longtime guest Gavin O'Connor checked in just a little after four o'clock on Wednesday afternoon. Though she remembered him from prior to her moving to Kansas, weary Mandy welcomed him less enthusiastically than she should have. Gavin was a businessman who enjoyed the peace of the place and came every year around the same time to write business-related articles and sometimes even poetry—although he steadfastly maintained the latter was just for fun.

Mandy stepped aside as he brought in his bags and laptop. Glancing through the open door over at the farmhouse where Arie Mae lived, she saw several buggies parked in the side yard.

She directed Gavin to sign in to the inn's registry for his stay. "There's fresh coffee and some cookies, too, as always," she told him after reintroducing herself.

Tall with hazel eyes, Gavin had a pleasing smile as he, like so many others had upon their arrival, inquired about her mother, no doubt surprised not to see her answer the door.

Mandy repeated the sad news, and the realization that her

mother was gone and never coming back struck her anew. The awareness made her feel even more worn out.

"You have my deepest condolences, Mandy," Gavin said, his expression as sympathetic as his words.

"You're very kind," Mandy said. *"Denki."*

"Your mother taught me many things about life," Gavin said after signing his name in the registry. "One that I try to remember every day is that God's ways are beyond my understanding." Gavin ran a hand through his thick reddish brown hair. "Sometimes I forget I don't need all the answers."

"S'pose we all tend to forget that," Mandy said, nodding.

"Your mother wasn't shy about sharing her joy for life."

If only I could've known more of that side of her, Mandy thought regretfully.

She waited for Gavin to gather his bags, then encouraged him to make himself at home upstairs in his usual suite.

Back in the kitchen, Mandy prepared to bake a pan of corn bread for her supper, along with Mamma's beef stew recipe, thinking that even though it was a chore to prepare, she could enjoy it for several days. She recalled Janice's comments about how Mamma had prayed for the guests God would send her way, and Mandy hoped with all of her heart that someone was praying for *her.*

.... ❁ ....

Trina was tired of traveling by plane and then limousine from Harrisburg, Pennsylvania. But when the limo driver pulled into a narrow country lane just off the two-lane road, she was also confused. The driver said to leave her bags in his care. "They'll magically appear at the entrance to the inn," he assured her, giving a wink.

"It's a *farmhouse,*" she protested. *Albeit a very large one.*

But the limo driver had already gotten out.

Trina took another look at her surroundings. *Like going to visit Grandma's house . . . if Grandma was from the last century,* she thought.

"This is a joke, right?" she said, stepping out of the passenger's compartment while the driver held open the door. "Or are we just stopping for tea and scones?"

"Ah, Miss Sutton, you forget . . . it's a mystery trip. Welcome to Butterfly Meadows Amish Bed-and-Breakfast." He tipped his dapper black hat. "In the heart of Lancaster County farmland."

Such a quaint little stopover on the way to my final destination, she thought. Feeling relieved, she stood there gazing up at the picturesque redbrick house as the driver gathered up her bags. "What a place," she whispered, conscious of the tranquil setting as a light snow began to fall. "So quiet."

She made her way across the lane toward the sidewalk and noticed a number of cars parked off to the side. "Must be popular," she said, making small talk with the limo driver behind her.

"According to my mom, who lives near a large community of Amish in Conewango Valley, New York, Amish inns are popular right now. Eat fried cornmeal mush and sticky bun breakfasts by lantern light. . . . An authentic Amish inn gives guests a real interesting experience."

"Well, if your *mom* says so," Trina joked. "But I wouldn't have listed anyplace like this as one of my desired destinations."

When they reached the front porch, he set her bags down and stood there with his arms folded.

"Oh, you want a tip, don't you?" She fished in her purse and pulled out a five-dollar bill. "Are you sure this is where I'm supposed to be?"

Glancing at the address near the door, he opened his long black coat and pulled out his phone, scrolling on it for a moment. He nodded. "Yes, Butterfly Meadows in Gordonville, Pennsylvania. Location confirmed."

"Only for the night and then off to the Bahamas, right?"

"Not sure, but I believe this is your *final* destination." The driver shrugged. "Why not just go with the flow—that's what trips like these are about. Besides, there must be some reason you're here."

A dog barked in the nearby field, and a cold wind rattled through the bare trees overhead. Trina shivered in her down jacket. "This can't be correct," she murmured as the driver turned and headed back toward the limo.

She watched him go, feeling abandoned. *Don't leave me here. . . .*

The cold getting to her, she pressed the doorbell, and hearing chimes, she laughed under her breath. "If only Janna could see me now." Soon, a young woman came to the door wearing a long, plain black dress with an apron over the top, her dark hair parted down the middle and pulled back on the sides and tucked under a black bandanna.

Have I fallen through a time warp? Trina wondered, wishing she could run down and catch the driver, who'd already driven away.

Chapter

18

Mandy wondered who this young *Englischer* with big brown eyes and a puffy blue jacket was, since all the guests were already checked in for the night. She'd left the thick beef and vegetable stew simmering on the burner to answer the door. "Hullo?" she said.

"I'm Catrina Sutton, here for the night, I suppose."

She supposes? Mandy merely shook her head. "The inn is already filled. I'm real sorry, miss."

"Please, could you check your reservations?" the woman asked. She appeared to be in her midtwenties.

"I'll look, but there's really no need. Every room in the house is full."

"Well, I'm supposed to have a room tonight. You see, I signed up for a mystery trip, and this is where the driver dropped me off." Catrina Sutton looked as dog tired as Mandy felt.

"A mystery trip, ya say?" Mandy eyed the pretty woman, wondering whether this was some kind of trick.

"I'll show you my trip reservation—that is, if I don't freeze to death first."

145

"Come in. *Ach,* what was I thinkin'." Mandy ushered her inside. "Please warm yourself by the hearth." She led her into the breakfast room, aglow with gaslight and the flickering fire. "By the way, I'm Mandy Dienner, the innkeeper."

"Thanks for saving my life," the young woman said, shivering as she glanced toward the window. "Could it be any colder?"

Mandy grimaced, wondering what to do with her now that she was inside.

"Here, have a look." Catrina Sutton shoved her phone with the pertinent information under Mandy's nose.

Mandy noticed the name on the screen was Trina Sutton . . . then saw the name of the travel company, too. Suddenly, the details came back to her, and she felt terrible. "Goodness. I *do* remember getting a call now from your travel company. For two weeks, I think it was." Truth be known, Mandy had blundered and double-booked one of the rooms in the wake of Betsy's leaving. *What an embarrassing mistake!*

"So I'm supposed to be here the *whole* time? This inn is what they came up with after reading my preferences?" Trina looked incredulous.

Mandy forced a smile. "I'm awful sorry," she said. "Unfortunately, I still have no place to put you up."

"Well, as far as I'm concerned, it's for only *one* night. This isn't at all what I had in mind."

Mandy would have liked to send Trina on her way, but to where? The woman had said she'd been dropped off by her driver. . . .

"And I've paid good money for this trip, so I demand a room," Trina said.

Mandy shook her head, at her wits' end. "I simply don't have any more rooms designed for guests."

"Look, I'm tired—just give me a sofa somewhere, and I'll be out of your hair by tomorrow. I'll use a camping mat on the floor . . . anything." Trina motioned to the fireplace. "Right here would be great, in fact."

"I'm not permitted to—"

"Forget it. I'll get the driver to come back!" Trina suddenly punched some numbers on her phone. "I'm calling the travel company."

Mandy could hear a ringing in the background as the young woman waited and then listened to some sort of recorded message. Scowling, Trina clicked off her phone. "They're referring me to their website. Can you believe it? Who cares if their client is stranded in the middle of nowhere!"

In a huff, Trina went to sit on one of the chairs at the breakfast table and leaned her head against her hand, elbow on the table. "Guess I'll sit up all night and rest my head right here." She sighed and looked like she might either break down or have a fit. "I should've known this was a lousy idea."

Wracking her brain for a solution, a thought occurred to Mandy. "Well, there are two vacant family bedrooms, but—"

Trina's eyebrows shot up. "Why didn't you say so? All I need is one, thank you."

"But . . . you don't understand," Mandy said. "Those rooms are on the Amish side of the house—so no electricity or baseboard heat."

"Excuse me? How do you sleep without getting frostbite?" Trina's eyebrows rose higher on her forehead.

Mandy smiled. "There are heat vents into each room from the coal stove . . . and plenty-a quilts." She didn't admit to having failed to stoke the stove hours earlier, due to all the work swirling about her.

"I suppose you also bundle up to go to the outhouse in the middle of the night?" Trina asked.

This struck Mandy as funny. "Listen, we're both tired." She motioned for Trina to follow her through to the kitchen and back to Arie's old room, where she showed her inside. "You can sleep in here for the time being."

"One night. No longer."

Mandy stood in the doorway watching her haul her pieces of luggage inside and set them on the floor. "So this is supposed to be a two-week trip?"

"Yes, but not to Amish land."

"Well, it might not be as unpleasant here as you think."

Trina frowned. "Did I miss something, perhaps a beach around here with an ocean?"

"*Nee.*"

"Well then."

Mandy smelled the stew's aroma, and her stomach rumbled. "Say, might ya be hungry? I made a pot of stew."

Trina's face brightened for the first time since her arrival. "Stew? I'm totally in."

"You're welcome to join me in the kitchen once you're ready. And please, try to make yourself at home."

"Is the kitchen heated?" Trina asked, a smirk on her face as she unzipped her jacket.

"Oh, just come an' see." Mandy headed back to stir her supper, hoping that it hadn't scorched.

Such a lippy one!

Mandy served Trina a generous bowl of the stew, along with a large square of fresh-baked corn bread and some homemade butter from the Amish grocery store on Paradise Lane. "There's plenty of jam, too, if you'd like. Just name your flavor and I'm sure we have it."

"Butter is fine," Trina said, sighing, her wavy brown hair falling over her shoulders.

Mandy sat across from her in the spot where Jerome preferred to sit for their breakfast meetings. "Amish pray silent table blessings," she said, bowing her head.

"No, *I'll* pray," Trina piped up. And she did so, right out loud, too.

At first, the two of them ate without speaking; then Mandy thought it wise to let her unexpected guest know when breakfast would be served.

Trina frowned at her bowl and set down her spoon. "Listen, I'm not a morning person, so I'll probably just sleep in and grab something to eat after I'm out of here."

"Did your travel company give ya *any* clue 'bout where you'd end up?" Mandy was curious.

Trina grimaced and folded her arms. "It was all supposed to be a surprise."

"Well, I hope you can get ahold of them."

"Oh, don't worry—someone is going to get an earful," Trina assured her.

"I 'spect you'll feel better tomorrow, once you're rested."

Trina laughed and sat up straight in her chair. "You really think so? I guess you've never met anyone who works nights. Mornings are absolutely the worst for me."

Mandy shook her head. "Round here, we tend to go to bed with the chickens . . . at least the farmers do." Though since Betsy left, Mandy's bedtime had been well past midnight.

Trina sliced through her corn bread and buttered both sides. "So, Mandy, were you raised Amish?"

"In this very house, *jah*." She didn't feel like revealing that her mother had died in October. There was no need for Trina Sutton to know that.

Trina picked up her spoon and took another bite of her stew, then stared at her bowl. "Listen, I wasn't going to say anything, but . . ."

Now what? Mandy braced herself.

"Something's missing," Trina said, spooning up some more.

Par for the course with my crummy cooking, Mandy thought.

"I'll figure it out." Trina chewed thoughtfully, as if evaluating it.

Mandy wracked her tired brain, going over the ingredients in her mind, all from Mamma's recipe book. Beef, potatoes, shredded cabbage, string beans . . .

Trina glanced now at the ceiling. Then, strangely, a smile broke across her face. "Oh, it needs some seasoning, right?"

Mandy was embarrassed. She *had* forgotten to put in the homemade seasonings Mamma always made each summer—drying parsley, celery, and onion in the oven, and then grinding all of it up. "*Ach,* don't know how I failed to add that."

The young woman simply picked at her stew, which Mandy actually thought was quite delicious—with or without the seasoning.

"And while we're talking about cooking, how much salt did you put in the corn bread?" Trina asked now.

Mandy stared at her, wondering what to say.

"Is it possible you doubled the amount called for?"

Instead of putting others in their place, Mandy thought of the Amish proverb *Put yourself in their place.* Even so, Mandy couldn't imagine being so critical at someone else's table.

Now Trina was staring at her. "You know what . . . you look tired. Just forget I said anything about the meal. You should go to bed."

Shaking her head, Mandy said she still had things to do.

"Well, you can't sleepwalk through the rest of the evening, can you?" Trina pushed her corn bread aside. "Thanks for the supper. Like I said, I'll clear out of here tomorrow . . . once I get things sorted out."

"No matter what you find out, tonight's stay is on me," she offered. "Sweet dreams," she said, relieved to see Trina rise and push in her chair.

"My mother always tucked us in with that and a prayer." Trina Sutton chuckled and reached for the half-eaten bowl of stew and the plate with the leftover corn bread and carried them to the sink. "Good night. And thanks."

"*Gut Nacht*," Mandy said softly, leaning her chin on her hands. *She's a tough one to figure out—curt one moment, then kind the next.*

Mandy stopped herself—it wasn't her place to judge. She could just imagine the way some of the People, her relatives included, talked about *her* even now.

Who's to say what this woman's going through?

It was dark in the room Trina had claimed as her own, and when she found the flashlight that Mandy had said was on the bedside table, Trina switched it on, sighing at the state she was in. *I was too rough on her,* she thought, frustrated still more when she realized her phone wouldn't last the night on the present charge. And she'd need a *full* charge before she could do anything about this mystery trip disaster. Too upset now, though, Trina decided to turn off her phone for the night. She would shower in the morning, as well, since there might be a chance the house would be warmer once the sun was shining. *And once Mandy remembers to fuel the stove in the next room, too.*

Trina got ready for bed by the light of the powerful flashlight and shook her head at her bad fortune. Going across the hall to the small bathroom, she took the flashlight with her to brush her teeth and comb through her hair.

She remembered just then to contact her sister, but that, too, would have to wait. Gail would also want to hear from her by phone tomorrow, eager to know where she ended up. The dear woman had taken some pleasure in Trina's adventuresome spirit. *"A mystery trip sounds splendid!"* she'd said, patting her hand after their temporary good-bye, Trina assuring her that she would not be forgotten.

In bed, she ran her foot across the cool sheets, feeling the stiff texture—not smooth and silky like at home. The quilts weighed her down, yet she was too chilly to sleep, so she got up and shone the flashlight into her suitcase and found her white hoodie and a pair of clean socks to put on.

Where have you brought me, Lord? she prayed, her teeth chattering as she headed back to the bed.

Then she remembered what the driver had said before he left: *"There must be some reason you're here."*

Maybe, maybe not, Trina thought.

Chapter

19

The next morning Trina woke with a jolt. Someone's chicken was carrying on. Or was she merely dreaming? Stretching, she looked around the stark room, marginally furnished with a small dresser and scant mirror over it, plus a single chair. She remembered where she was and groaned. *Oh yeah . . . the mystery vacation without the white sand and palm trees.* She laughed at the absurdity of ending up here. She never, ever would have paid money to come to a backwoodsy place like this!

Trina pushed away the blankets and realized the room was much more pleasant in temperature than it had been last night. Nevertheless, she recalled the online mystery trip questionnaire and wondered how the travel company could have messed up like this. For the life of her, she couldn't fathom which of the answers she'd given had pointed to an Amish farmstead in the middle of barren cornfields and meadows.

The *clip-clop-clip* of a horse's hooves drew her attention, and she scooted to the edge of the warm nest of a bed and stepped onto the rag rug beneath her stockinged feet. Moving to the frosted window, she rubbed a circle with her fist, then peeked through at a landscape so white with snow she could scarcely make out the shapes of things. "Oh," she groaned. *Not snowed in!*

"Please, Lord, get me out of here," she whispered before heading over to the shared bathroom to take a shower.

———

Mandy had something of an undeclared competition going with the rooster, and though she would have liked to doze a few minutes longer, she had gotten out of bed before the annoying crowing began that morning. She'd gotten the coal stove going again last night, so this side of the house was warmer this morning, and there was no reason for the unexpected guest—Trina Sutton—to complain about that. Then Mandy built a roaring fire in the hearth, on this, the coldest day since her return.

Having had five hours of sleep—more than most nights lately—she felt somewhat renewed and resumed her mundane yet hectic ritual, wondering how any of the guests would manage to get out of the lane and on their way. She also wondered if Jerome or Karl might come to shovel them out, not wanting to ask any of the male guests to assist. Mandy estimated a good foot or more had piled up against the stable.

There'll be no buggy rides today, she thought with relief. And when she looked out the kitchen window later, she could see heavy, fast-falling flakes.

Miss Sutton might just be stuck here, Mandy thought grimly.

———

Mandy ventured out of her comfort zone and decided to make Mamma's baked egg dish, the same one Sadie had made on Mandy's first morning as the innkeeper. She felt sure that she had practiced enough to attempt it for the guests, so she placed the egg casserole in the oven and almost prayed that all would go well.

While pouring apple juice into all the small glasses, she remembered her father coming through the back door on such a cold and snowy day years ago. He'd picked her up in his strong arms and carried her to the window to show her the long, pointy icicles hanging off the porch roof. The lovely memory made the ache of his and Mamma's absence from her childhood home more tolerable today.

Going to the sink, Mandy looked out that same window, and there, near the stable, stood Josiah Lantz with his big snow blower. Karl was there, too, both of them bundled up in scarves and knit hats, talking, their breath making thin white columns in the air. After a few minutes, they started up the noisy snow removers and set to work.

Mandy slipped away from the window, curious if the two men had become friends. Then again, Betsy had mentioned that Karl was related to some of the Lantzes here locally. Could it be Josiah was a cousin?

When Gavin O'Connor poked his head into the kitchen to say good morning, Mandy went right over to him, wanting to make up for her halfhearted greeting yesterday. "I hope ya slept all right," she said, offering a smile.

Gavin waved it away. "Oh, that's never a problem here—it feels like a second home to me."

This surprised her, coming from an *Englischer*, although perhaps it shouldn't have, considering how many years he'd been staying at Butterfly Meadows.

"I especially enjoy how quiet it is around here at night," Gavin added.

But surely not the noisy rooster in the early morning hours, she thought, motioning around the corner. "The coffee's *gut* and hot," she said, going into the breakfast room with him to check on the table. She added an eighth place setting for Trina, just in case she showed up for breakfast.

Gavin glanced out the windows, where the sun was trying to peek out of heavy clouds. "It's the perfect sort of day," he commented.

"Oh?"

"A wintry day like this works best for writing—seems to encourage the muse in me. And I need all the creativity I can muster considering the article I'm writing." He chuckled, and just then, Trina appeared in gray yoga pants and an oversized pink sweater, heading straight for the coffeepot, her eyes bleary.

"*Guder Mariye*, Trina," said Mandy, hoping she might be more pleasant, at least around Gavin, who'd spied her and was walking over to the sideboard.

"English?" Trina shot back.

Gavin spoke up. "That's good morning in Amish . . . well, *Deitsch*." He introduced himself and smiled warmly. "You must be new here. I hope you enjoy this place as much as I do."

Trina glanced Mandy's way and grimaced in an approximation of a smile. "Nice to meet you, Gavin. I'm Trina Sutton from . . . well, civilization," she said with a straight face.

Mandy cringed and held her breath.

"Sounds like you've found the ideal place to get away," Gavin said, smiling over at Mandy now. "The peace here gives you a chance to focus on what's most important. Get grounded in nature, if you will. Or whatever you enjoy doing."

Trina merely went to stand with her back to the fireplace, her hands encircling the coffee mug. "I'm always chilly first thing in the morning," she said. "Especially when snowbound."

Gavin looked puzzled. "You can adjust the thermostat if your room's too cold."

"*Some* people can, true," Trina said, raising an eyebrow at Mandy.

"Well, it's a long story—and entirely my fault," Mandy said, giving Trina the opportunity to fill Gavin in on the unfortunate trip—and double-booking—that had landed her in Arie's room. "Excuse me while I see about breakfast," Mandy said and slipped out to the kitchen.

Though Mandy wished it were otherwise, there were no enthusiastic remarks about the egg dish, except that Gavin and another man did have seconds of the angel biscuits Mandy had made late last night and refrigerated, then baked this morning. No rising required.

Thankfully, there were no outright complaints today, either, though Mandy honestly wondered if she would ever reach Mamma's level of proficiency in the kitchen.

After a few of the guests had gone upstairs, others lingered in the nearby sitting room to plan their day. Mandy noticed that Karl and Josiah were nearly finished clearing the walkways and the lane out to Old Leacock Road. Grateful for the help, she was relieved that her next batch of guests could easily get their cars in and parked later that afternoon, and those scheduled to leave after breakfast would have no trouble—assuming the main roads were plowed. Two of the couples were staying for another night, and thus far, there had been no cancelations, so even if Trina did decide to stay around, she was stuck in Arie Mae's room.

Going in to clear the breakfast table, she found Gavin and Trina sitting there talking quietly. But then Trina frowned as Gavin removed a small tablet from his shirt pocket and began to write. He glanced out the windows as if attempting to ignore her.

Meanwhile, Trina turned to ask if Mandy needed some help, which took Mandy off guard, as she'd never had a guest offer, least of all someone as prickly as Trina.

Mandy almost said, *"I thought you were leaving,"* but then scolded herself for even considering mimicking the young woman's rudeness. "If you'd like to help out, sure," she surprised herself by saying. "That's kind of you, but I should be doin' more for you, considering your plight."

Trina shook her head. "It won't take long to get things straightened out with my travel company and find out where they *really* planned for me to be."

"You should stay around," Gavin spoke up. "Give it more time here."

"I'd really like to enjoy my vacation," she retorted. Then, grinning at him, she added, "And, to be clear, in my opinion, free verse is *not* poetry. It is merely prose."

"Merely . . . is that right?" Gavin said, eyebrow raised before he returned his attention to his little notebook.

Trina turned away, shaking her head as if she'd just dealt with a difficult child.

In the kitchen, as Trina set down the stack of plates near the sink, she said quietly, "I'm not sure how to take him."

"Who?" Mandy said, blinking her eyes.

Trina huffed. "That guy in there from Baltimore."

"What about him?"

Trina huffed a bit more. "He's way too serious . . . thinks the free verse he's writing is poetry, but anyone knows the difference between what rhymes and has a meter . . . and, well, *prose*."

Mandy would not stand for this tone, nor this ridiculous hairsplitting over poetry. "Gavin O'Connor was one of my mother's favorite guests. And she was a very *gut* judge of character," Mandy said, attempting to set Trina straight. "Not to mention fond of his beautiful poetry."

"*Was?* You said she *was* a good judge of character." Trina's eyes softened as she stared at Mandy. "Did something happen to your mom?"

Mandy paused for a moment, reluctant to say much about her

family to this woman, of all people. "She died suddenly . . . quite recently, in fact."

"Oh, I'm so sorry." Trina took a step backward. "So is that why you do all this? In memory of her?"

Mandy wanted to shoo her out of the kitchen with a tea towel. "*Nee*, that's not the reason," Mandy said, motioning her out of the room with her hands. "Maybe you'd be happier if you were just on your way."

"Well, first where can I plug in my phone charger?" Trina asked, ignoring her comment. "I can't go anywhere without a ride. I need to straighten out this mess first."

"*Ach*, I'll show ya."

While Trina waited for her phone to charge, she returned to the breakfast room, where Gavin still sat writing in his notepad near the windows. Taking a seat herself, she stared at the fireplace, surprised that any guy would want to spend his annual vacation at an Amish inn. *What sort of person does that?*

She absorbed the warmth from the fire and considered where her life might have been at this moment. If Shawn hadn't died, she would be married to him, traveling with him to some warm and romantic getaway, maybe even expecting their first child. *I would have been an amazing wife . . . and mom!* she thought, convinced of it. *Above all, I would have been needed. . . .*

Thinking of Gail Anderson just then, Trina reminded herself to call the woman as soon as things with the incompetent travel company were straightened out. She knew one thing for sure: She had better get rerouted to another location. *And soon!*

"Is that steam coming out your ears?" Gavin said, interrupting her thoughts.

"Very funny." She glanced at his little notepad, smiled, and left the room to pack her suitcase.

Chapter

20

Mandy dry mopped the vacant sitting area, then moved around the corner to the breakfast room, where she noticed Gavin O'Connor chuckling to himself as he rose and made his way toward the stairs. *At least someone's in fine humor today*, she thought, working quickly.

There were groceries to purchase and a long list of things to do. Coupled with all of that, she was on edge not knowing when Trina Sutton was going to be leaving the house. Truth be known, the young woman had thoroughly frazzled her nerves. *So direct!*

The door chimes rang, and Mandy found the postman there with the mail, as well as an envelope too large for the mailbox. "It's real nippy out here, Miss Dienner. Stay warm."

"*Denki*," she said, quickly closing the door and carrying the mail into the kitchen, where she dropped it on the table and returned to her mopping.

Only after she'd hung the second batch of washing in the basement did she take a breather and sit to investigate the mail. One envelope had come from her mother's cousins in Dover, Delaware—

to Mandy's surprise, they hadn't heard about Mamma's passing. The other piece of mail was from the Bradleys in Scott City.

But the large envelope had *Mystery Trips Travel Company* as its return address, so she started with that. Inside, Mandy found the reservation confirmation along with a list of planned events and tickets with accompanying brochures. *Looks like fun.* There was also a check on behalf of Trina Sutton of Rochester, Minnesota, paying in full for two weeks at the Butterfly Meadows Amish Bed-and-Breakfast. *Everything Trina needs for her trip. . . .* She searched for a phone number and jotted it down.

Mandy sighed, contemplating the unpleasant future. *What if Trina decides to stay?* Ultimately, this meant that the young woman needed accommodations for thirteen more nights—accommodations the inn simply didn't have. Arie's sparsely furnished room was hardly worth the same price as a full-price guest room. If it came to it, Mandy supposed she should offer Trina a discount for staying there and not in a bona fide guest room. Then again, Mandy had no idea what to expect from the testy young woman.

········ ❀ ········

Later, when she saw Trina heading into the kitchen, Mandy showed her the package of information from Mystery Trips Travel. "Looks like this is, in fact, where they chose for you to be," she said as politely as she could manage.

Trina puffed out her cheeks like a chipmunk and blew the air out hard. "Please tell me you're joking," she said, but when Mandy didn't respond, she added, "I'd better not say what I'm thinking."

Wise, jah, Mandy thought, pressing her lips together. *For both of us.*

Trina flipped through the planned excursions and tickets,

giving them only a cursory glance before tossing them on the counter. "So what do your usual guests do when they stay here?"

"Well, it looks like you've already paid for some real nice events," Mandy said, showing her the tickets for the Sight and Sound Millennium Theatre and American Music Theatre, as well as the site brochures. "I'll be glad to give you additional recommendations, if that'd suit ya more."

"Nothing here suits me." Trina sighed and went over to the stairs. "And I sure won't be sitting around here writing poetry, or whatever you want to call it all day, either." She said this quite loudly, which struck Mandy as odd.

"What do you usually like to do on vacation?" Mandy asked, thinking that might be a good starting point.

"Walk along the beach, go swimming in a lagoon . . . eat at outdoor cafés while roving musicians serenade me and the other tourists. You get the picture."

Befuddled, Mandy led her to the brochure rack. "Well, swimming obviously isn't an option this time of year, but there's somethin' for everyone in Lancaster County. The Mennonite Information Center would be a *gut* place to start." She pointed out several brochures for tourist attractions that other guests had enjoyed. "I'll let you decide."

Trina shivered. "And I'm stuck in that bedroom again tonight . . . that is, if I decide to stay."

"*Jah*, and till I have an opening—which, to tell the truth, is unlikely," Mandy sputtered. "I'm real sorry about that. It's all my fault that this happened, and I'd be more than happy to charge one-fourth of what I usually get for a real guest room. And you can eat your noon meal and supper with me, if you'd like," Mandy quickly added before she could regret it.

"What a nightmare," Trina murmured, seemingly mulling over her options.

"I can see you're unhappy. . . . If you'd be more comfortable with a free stay, that's fine, too."

Trina turned and stared into the breakfast room. "I didn't mean that I wanted a free vacation."

"Just let me know what you want to do," Mandy said. "In the meantime, I can call for a driver if you'd like to go sightseeing. You could even take an Amish sleigh ride up to Bird-in-Hand."

"Thanks, but never mind. I can always call a cab."

Thank heavens! Mandy thought. With all she had to get done today, she couldn't spare more time to discern what, if anything, might appeal to Trina Sutton.

It took only minutes for Trina to file her online complaint to the worst travel company on the planet. Since no one was answering her call, she assumed they were avoiding her—perhaps based on her earlier voice mail.

Next, she texted Janna, fuming as she did. *You'll never guess where I am. Think road apples and people dressed like they're straight out of the Colonial era.*

In a few minutes, her sister's answering text appeared: *Wait . . . are you signed up for an Amish tour?*

Trina didn't laugh, but she could easily imagine Janna doing so. And her co-workers, if they knew.

I never actually signed up for this place, Trina replied. *Who would?*

It took a while for the next message to ping through. *You wanted surprise and mystery, right? Try to make the most of it, Trina. And while you're there, would you mind picking up a hand-stitched quilt for me?* Janna wrote.

Sounds like you're the one who should be on this trip! Trina texted, thinking she'd happily give ten quilts for one fluffy, down-filled comforter.

They exchanged a few more comments; then Trina said she

164

was glad she'd contacted her. *You always know how to calm me down, don't you? Thanks, sis.*

Afterward, Trina called Gail and was delighted to hear the woman's voice. She told her about her travel snafu and that she'd made her grievances known.

"Well now, you just never know about these sorts of things, my dear," Gail said. "Maybe it can all work out. With every situation, there's always a chance for new discovery—that's certainly been true of the start of my rehabilitation experience. I'm relearning this very thing every day . . . but I so want to be mobile again."

"I'm glad you have a positive outlook, Gail. You'll heal more quickly."

"Ah yes, there's the nurse I know and love!" Gail paused a moment. "The Trina I know relishes adventure."

"Well, sure . . . but on a tropical island somewhere."

"That's easy," Gail remarked. "Anyone can find adventure in the tropics, but you like challenges, don't you?"

"I've had enough of that lately."

"Do you have any other options?"

"I'm waiting to hear from the company. It's clear they got their wires crossed—this trip can't be based on my list of preferences. Makes me wonder where the person who wanted this backroads experience ended up—probably having a spa day or sunbathing in Cancun. Where *I* should be."

Gail laughed softly. "There's no one quite like you, Trina. Rain or shine."

This warmed her heart. "Well, you take care, Gail, and don't flirt too much with the rehab technician, okay? I'll keep in touch."

.... ⚘ ....

Trina enjoyed the warmth of the taxicab as she traversed the snow-packed roads of rural Lancaster County, seeing one Amish buggy after another. Passing through Bird-in-Hand, she noticed the Bird-in-Hand Bakery and Café, as well as the Plain and Fancy Country Store, both mentioned in the inn's brochures. She was tempted to stop for a pastry but knew from eating junk food during her days at the nursing home that the sugary treat would just stir up more hunger pangs later.

Everywhere she looked, there were bearded men, or women wearing black bonnets. She lost count of the Amish stores and Amish children, all looking like miniatures of their parents.

She thought of Gail. *"Anyone can find adventure in the tropics,"* she'd said. And Trina blew out a breath, trying to somehow look on the bright side.

When the driver asked if she'd like to stop somewhere, Trina said she wanted to keep heading east on Route 340, and soon she was on the outskirts of a village named Intercourse, surrounded by vast snow-covered fields, silos, and windmills scattered here and there. She assumed this farmland must be owned by Amish, too. *Where does it end?*

She'd thought that by now there would surely be some semblance of civilization—fewer quaint towns, more city-like places. Wasn't the Big Apple only an hour or two away? She imagined going there instead, hitting a Broadway show, ice-skating at Rockefeller Center, seeing the Empire State Building, but her bags were back at the Amish inn.

Spotting a sign for White Horse Luncheonette, Trina asked the cabbie to pull into the parking lot. "Thanks," she said. "The ride was interesting, but I can't imagine wanting to live around here."

"Well, lots of fine folk do," he said. "It's the world's largest Plain settlement, as you probably noticed."

"Plain is right." She paid him and headed into the restaurant, where she was seated quickly, despite the crowd. She ordered a fish sandwich with lettuce and tartar sauce, nearly elbow to elbow with Amish. The woman next to her looked remarkably similar to the young innkeeper, who it seemed to Trina was running the place by herself. Seeing some of the waitresses wearing small white heart-shaped head coverings, she realized that Mandy didn't wear one, which made her wonder why not.

While waiting for her order, Trina scanned through her phone to see if the travel company had responded. But there was nothing, and in spite of the delicious sandwich—easily the best food she'd eaten since arriving—her sense of annoyance crept back.

········ ❀ ········

"Do you ever offer evening meals like your mother used to?" Gavin asked Mandy when he came downstairs for coffee that afternoon.

"You're not the first guest to ask, but the truth is, I'm shorthanded at present. But it's something I'm thinking 'bout once I hire some help."

Gavin nodded as he poured his coffee. "What happened to those young women—what were their names? Sadie and . . ."

"Betsy," she said, mentioning both had chosen to move on since her arrival.

"I'd think any Amishwoman would enjoy working here."

"Honestly, I had hoped so, too." She knew she'd better not say more. "Is there anything else I can get you?"

"Coffee's all I need, thanks. I have a few energy bars in my room. For some reason, eating less helps when I'm writing." He headed toward the stairs and paused to look outside. "Say, isn't that your sister, Arie, walking down the road there?"

Mandy went to look. "*Jah*, 'tis." Arie was bundled up in a black wool coat and candlesnuffer bonnet.

"Out there on such a cold and snowy day?" Gavin asked with a glance at Mandy.

"Might be walkin' over to Jerome's place, not far from here."

"Your eldest brother?"

Mandy smiled. "Have ya met him?"

"Several times, in fact. He's dropped by to see your mother during most of my stays here."

"Jerome's been a real help to me." Considering how that one conversation had ended, Mandy was glad Jerome hadn't held it against her, instead coming over a few days afterward to make sure she was faring all right.

"It's good to have someone in our corner, isn't it?" Gavin smiled and mentioned that he'd first stayed at the inn after hearing about it from a friend in Baltimore, who had been burned out from overwork. "He advised me to start taking a yearly break like this to recharge. Good advice!"

"I'm glad you did," she said. "And to think ya keep comin' back."

"The writerly side of my brain works well here," Gavin replied. "Don't ask me why. Speaking of which, I should get back to my work now."

"Another poem, maybe?" she asked, enjoying his congenial manner.

Gavin brightened. "A *poem* it is."

Mandy grinned as she went back to grab a quick snack for herself. Yet thinking of sitting alone at the kitchen table where she and Arie Mae had once sat side by side, she found herself returning to the front entrance. There, she peered out the window where Gavin had spotted Arie earlier, but there was no sign of her sister.

Chapter 21

An early December cloud cover foretold more moisture the next morning, and Mandy rose to do the same thing she did each and every day—tend to the needs of her guests, as well as make sure that breakfast was palatable and the inn was spotlessly clean.

As determined as Trina Sutton had been to leave, Mandy was rather surprised that she stayed over another night after returning from sightseeing yesterday afternoon. Trina hadn't said why, and Mandy wondered if it might have given her an opportunity to make other arrangements. Mandy hoped she would also use the opportunity to make peace with Gavin, though the man had seemed to take Trina's somewhat snarky attitude in stride.

Yet as Mandy rushed back and forth between the kitchen and the breakfast room, she soon realized how futile her hopes were. Alas, Trina was bickering yet again with Gavin.

Goodness, disrespect isn't the best way to get a man's attention . . . if that's what she's after.

········ ✿ ········

"What would *you* choose?" Trina decided to ask Gavin there in the common room after returning from her room, where she had hidden away to take a call from her sister.

"Between touring Wheatland and Lancaster Central Market?" Gavin asked. "That's easy."

"For you, perhaps," Trina said, showing him the listing of specific outings and dated tickets she'd received in yesterday's mail. "Hmm . . . ancient history versus living history."

Gavin looked at her, as if confused, his eyes seeming to say, *"Why ask my opinion, if you've already made up your mind?"*

"It's a slam dunk for Wheatland," she told him.

"So your mystery trip is a package deal?" he asked.

"Right. And this morning I woke up to an email informing me there's no chance of a refund for dissatisfied customers. Apparently, I signed a waiver." She paused to shake her head at her own stupidity. "And whoever contacted me indicated that 'an open-minded traveler can always find something to enjoy.' Isn't that a hoot?"

"I take it you don't agree?" The look Gavin gave her was somewhat amused.

"Have you seen where I'm staying?"

"Oh, c'mon . . . it's all about perspective, right?"

"No." Trina shook her head. "It's more about *expectations*." And she proceeded to share with him some of the wonderful locations where she had *hoped* to spend these fourteen days.

Gavin listened quite patiently. "That's all great sounding, but have you considered looking at the bright side of things?" he asked. "To begin with, how about deciding to just enjoy where you are?"

"If only! But it's not that easy . . . at least not for me," Trina protested. The fact that Gail and her sister had said much the same bothered Trina more than she cared to admit.

He seemed to contemplate that. "I'm simply saying that you could just as easily decide to be happy."

"Sounds like prose to me," she said, smiling a little at his persistence.

He laughed, then asked, "So what's on tap for today per your trip itinerary?" he asked.

"*Mystery* trip," she said, correcting him. "Dinner at Miller's Smorgasbord, after a tour of the Amish Farm and House in Lancaster. Tomorrow, it's the matinee at the American Music Theatre, and Sunday and Monday are free days. And on Tuesday, a driver will pick me up for *The Miracle of Christmas* at the Sight and Sound Millennium Theatre."

"Any other events?" asked Gavin, seemingly enjoying her recitation of upcoming happenings.

"According to the initial package, in a few days, I'll receive more information. They're keeping me on a short rope. Very mysterious, right?" She grinned at him. "Well, I wanted a surprise, and I sure got one. But, wow, I should have known better than to jump on the mystery vacation train."

Gavin took a sip of his coffee and set it down slowly. "In the meantime, why not enjoy the company of new acquaintances. You never know what fascinating people you might meet." He raised his eyebrows as if to indicate his own fine company.

She considered that, trying to decide if Gavin was just debating her for the fun of it or if he believed what he was saying. Trina really wasn't sure how to read this man.

At that moment, Mandy rushed down the hallway that led to the kitchen, the poor woman looking as frazzled as ever. "This is my first time staying in a B and B," Trina said to Gavin. "I always had the impression that the breakfasts were supposed to be something really special, but these . . . Do they measure up to what you're used to?"

"They're not so bad."

She gave him an eye. Was he serious?

"Are you saying you could do better?" Gavin smiled now.

"Definitely," she bragged. "Cooking is one of my skill sets."

They talked awhile longer; then he asked if she had plans for lunch.

Trina wondered why he was asking. "I think Mandy offered to heat up some of her leftover stew for me."

"Mandy has enough to do," Gavin said. "How about we go out somewhere to eat?"

The sincerity of his expression took her by surprise. "You mean, have lunch . . . together?"

"Yes, if you can handle more time with a man who writes free verse." Gavin chuckled.

It was her turn to smile. "Well, there is that." Gavin was the first man who'd shown any interest in her since Shawn died, and she realized his teasing had something of a calming effect on her. Trina liked how it felt.

"There might be more to me than meets the eye," he added.

Despite the disappointments of the last day and a half, she couldn't help but be intrigued. "Okay, I'll go—if you let me drive."

"My car?"

"Sure, why not?"

He shook his head. "Not happening. Not when I know the area like the back of my hand," he said, getting up and walking toward the door. "Well, I'm hungry. Are you coming or not?"

She stared at this man, and for a moment, she was speechless. "I guess I *am* hungry. But we're going Dutch."

He nodded. "I'm cool with that."

Trina's stomach growled. "Okay," she said, surprising even herself.

.... ✿ ....

Mandy initially wondered if Gavin had taken Trina out for a meal just to get her out of Mandy's way. But it honestly seemed like Gavin and Trina had gone from seeming completely incompatible to flirting. *None of my business,* Mandy thought.

Before she had her leftover stew—now with added seasoning—she tidied Arie's room, making up the bed without changing the sheets, something generally scheduled for every fourth day of a stay. She also brought in a basket of special homemade soaps and other local toiletries, just like ones the other guests received, as well as a freshly laundered cushy white robe. The room wasn't up to the standards of the regular guest rooms, but hopefully Trina would notice and appreciate these little touches.

Mandy found it ironic that someone like Trina Sutton had to resort to sleeping in a family bedroom. Arie Mae's room was nearly the last one Mandy would choose to accommodate such a picky guest, and she wondered what her twin sister might think of the pickle Mandy now found herself in. Would she have handled anything differently?

After the noon meal, Mandy headed down to the basement and discovered that the clean sheets were dry at last. She folded them carefully, remembering the days when Mamma had insisted on ironing the ones for guests, which Arie had discouraged, but Mamma did anyway. *"You mustn't wear yourself out,"* Arie would say as a young teen, worried Mamma was trying to bury her grief in work. And Mandy had agreed.

She and Arie hadn't necessarily always agreed on other things following the death of their father, but until Josiah, everything had been minor.

.... ✿ ....

Tuckered out as she was all the time now, Mandy was looking forward to the day of worship and rest. The somewhat milder winter temperatures were also welcome, as was the sunshine . . . and the sight of the little community church down the way.

After giving it some serious thought, she decided to try again, knowing she was putting herself at risk for rejection. So following the later church service and a bite to eat at a coffee shop, Mandy drove to Paradise, hoping she might catch Dawdi and Mammi Dienner at home after Preaching.

Stomach churning, she knocked on the back door and could hear a dog barking—possibly the cocker spaniel her brother Danny had given them some years ago, a cuddly pooch named Rex that Mammi Dienner had liked to sit and pet after supper every night.

After a few minutes, during which Mandy heard snippets of discussion, her grandfather came to the door and stood there a moment, as if appraising her.

"Hullo," she said softly, wondering if he would turn her away.

"We'd heard you were back," he said stiffly, glancing over his shoulder. "It's taken ya a while to drop by to visit." Her Dawdi looked a lot grayer than the last time Mandy had seen him, and his once powerful shoulders had begun to stoop.

"Well, she's here now, so let her in, Reuben," Mammi called as she came from the kitchen, little Rex still yipping loudly as he followed behind.

"Did ya see the note I left ya when I stopped by last Sunday?" Mandy asked, wanting to reach out and hug him, but he seemed so different—so distant.

Mammi nodded her head and wiped her hands on her apron, then came over to greet Mandy, taking both of her hands, tears welling up in her brown eyes. "Ain't you a sight. We'd nearly given up on ya, I daresay."

"I've missed ya so," Mandy said, reaching up to brush away a tear of her own.

"Seems like a miracle to have you here," Mammi said while Rex quit his barking and began to wag his fluffy tail near the hem of Mammi's blue dress. With a glance at Dawdi, Mammi led her to the table. "Sit yourself down and have a treat. We need to catch up."

"There's your Mammi's wonderful snitz pie," Dawdi said as he took the spot at the head of the table. "She baked a bunch for church today. . . . Ya might remember the shared meal we have after Preaching."

"Now, Reuben," Mammi gently scolded as she sat to his right. "No need to poke."

"She's been gone awhile. It's possible she might've forgotten," he said, not looking at Mandy.

"Dawdi, you can talk directly to me, you know," Mandy said. "I know I was wrong not to stay in touch with you and Mammi . . . but please don't pretend I'm somewhere else."

Dawdi looked at her and sighed, then bowed his head for the silent prayer.

"Your mother loved ya so," Mammi said as she began to serve coffee and pie. "You were at the tip-top of her prayer list, for sure and for certain."

Mandy recalled the similar remark Janice Hart had made. "I prayed for her, too. And for you and Dawdi."

Dawdi spooned some sugar into his coffee and then took a bite of the pie, smacking his lips as the menfolk did to show their satisfaction as they ate. "Wish ya could've been here when she died, 'stead of clear out west," he remarked. "It was so sudden . . . you leavin' like that." He shook his head.

"I wish I'd been here, too," Mandy replied softly, meaning it with all of her heart.

Dawdi gave a little grunt and nodded, seemingly mollified.

"Let's just eat and leave Amanda be, dear." Mammi smiled kindly at her from across the table.

So they ate silently, and despite the somewhat rocky start to her visit, Mandy was glad to be seated at the table with her father's parents again. It had been much too long.

It was after his second cup of coffee that Dawdi Dienner asked how her mother's bed-and-breakfast was coming along, his eyes trained on the last bite of his pie.

"The inn is plenty busy, and it's all I can do to keep up." Mandy was embarrassed to admit it. "And I haven't been able to hire any new help. It seems the People want nothin' to do with me."

A sudden hush came over the kitchen, and Mandy dreaded what either of them might say. *Likely they're as upset as everyone else that I fired Arie Mae.*

At last, Dawdi set down his fork on his empty plate. "You left your widowed Mamma without explanation," he said solemnly. "She had enough on her—she didn't need to grieve your leavin', too."

The depth of sorrow her mother must have experienced hit Mandy's heart anew. "I wish I hadn't handled things thataway," she admitted, not saying what had caused her to rush away so awful quick. "At the time, I felt I had no other choice."

"*Ach,* there's always a choice," Dawdi said, folding his hands for the after-eating prayer, "if we look for it."

Chastened, Mandy folded her hands and bowed her head.

Chapter

22

On the way back toward Gordonville, Mandy stopped at the Amish cemetery where her parents were buried. Up till now, she hadn't felt ready to see their gravesites side by side, but after the visit with Dat's parents, she knew it was time.

Getting out of the car, she picked her way over the encrusted snow to the fenced-in graveyard, where she opened the wide gate she and her family had filed through numerous times. There, she studied the neat rows of graves, some of the older markers more gray now than pure white when accented by the snow.

She walked reverently past her mother's parents' graves—Dawdi Benjamin and Mammi Sarah Hostetler—and several great-uncles' and aunts', too, before coming upon her father's small white grave marker, unadorned as was customary.

Mandy stepped to the side, respecting the snowy ground where his coffin lay. For the longest time, she stood there, aware of a quiet so profound it was broken only by her own breaths. "Would Dat have intervened 'tween Arie and me?" she whispered into the frosty air.

Warm tears ran down her cheeks, stinging her cold face. *If he'd lived, would I be married to Josiah?* she permitted herself to ponder, then realized that the answer to that no longer mattered.

After a while, she folded her gloved hands and focused on the unmarked plot next to her father's. It would be some time before the gravestone would be set in place. Mandy bowed her head, wishing again she had been present for the funeral and burial service. She uttered not a word as she silently thanked God for giving her such a hardworking and faithful mother.

A breeze stirred the stark tree branches, and Mandy shivered as the cold seeped through her coat and scarf, the wind turning sharp since this morning. Her nose and face began to feel numb.

At least Mamma was able to witness Arie's wedding. . . .

The thought still hurt.

With a sigh, Mandy turned to walk back toward her car parked at the bottom of the hill.

········ ❀ ········

On the drive home, Mandy considered the fact that Dawdi and Mammi Dienner had invited her in to eat with them, and was heartened by it. She considered Jerome's weekly visits, as well as those of her other brothers and sisters-in-law who had dropped by to say hullo, though none of them had lingered or brought their children. Jerome *had* been clear, though, about being able to see all of their extended family at church. Mandy wondered if she would find any real opportunities for fellowship with them if she never once went to Preaching service during this year of proving herself. As busy as she was, how would she find the time to visit them all?

Back at Butterfly Meadows, Mandy parked her car and, out of habit, walked around the back way, preferring not to track snow and dirt into the entry. She would leave her shoes just inside the kitchen till they were dry enough to clean up. Thinking of the warm kitchen, she longed to rest like she had been doing each Sunday afternoon since returning home.

Making the bend toward the sidewalk that led up to the back door, she spotted Karl just a few yards from the stable.

She hastened her pace. "Hullo," she called, her steps sinking into the snow.

"Blessed Lord's Day to ya, Mandy."

Instinctively, she wiped her cheeks with her scarf, wondering if it was obvious she'd been crying. "Might Yonnie be with ya today?" she asked.

"He's in with the horses," Karl said, his smile widening as she came near. "And still talkin' about your delicious hot cocoa."

"My Mamma's recipe," she said, looking toward the stable and wondering if Yonnie might hear them talking and come out. "A real sweet treat, my father liked to say." It crossed her mind that Karl might be hinting at having a cup for himself, but she didn't want to make a fool of herself by offering some if he was merely being polite.

"Say, I can get a sleigh and bring it over later, if ya think your guests would enjoy that instead of a buggy ride today."

"Oh, that'd be perfect," she said, quickly adding, "but only if it's not too much bother."

"None at all."

"I'll tell the guests to dress warmly."

"*Gut* idea," he said, practically grinning. "And if you'd like to come along, Yonnie might wanna go, too."

This perked her up. "Well, how can I say no to that!"

"I shouldn't have said anything in front of him, but when I suggested the idea earlier, he begged to go ridin' in Josiah's sleigh."

Josiah's? Mandy tried not to let on how surprised she was.

"Hope it's all right. It was Arie Mae's idea," Karl explained. "She thought it would be extra special for the inn guests."

Arie's idea? Mandy was truly dumbfounded now. "I'd forgotten 'bout that sleigh."

"Well, if I understand correctly, it's been in the family for several generations."

Mandy knew more about it than she cared to let on. She briefly recalled one long-ago December day, close to Christmas, when Josiah had hitched up the horse and sleigh to take her skating on the frozen fishing hole. "Well, I'd better go inside before I turn into an ice cube."

He nodded. "*Jah*, go in an' warm up. Ya don't want to start off cold."

Turning, she went to the house and let herself in, then sat down in one of the kitchen chairs to catch her breath. *Arie wants to treat the inn guests to a sleigh ride? Why would she even bother suggesting such a thing?*

········ ❀ ········

Trina still found it hard to believe she had accepted a lunch date Friday. It had gone incredibly well, so much so that she had reluctantly agreed to attend church with Gavin O'Connor. *We actually have a lot in common*, she realized. And because Gavin had proposed they drive up to Reading for lunch at Anthony's Trattoria, here she was spending even more time with him.

I must be out of my mind, she thought as they drove back from a leisurely meal at the charming restaurant, wondering, as well, why Gavin seemed drawn to her.

He's lonely; that's all, she decided. *Maybe it isn't as much fun to sit around writing as he claims.*

But Trina had to admit that she was very glad to escape the

touristy restaurants in Lancaster County, especially the Amish buffets and smorgasbords, particularly after her experience at Miller's, where she had unwisely dished up a spoonful of practically everything offered.

"I'm going on a starvation diet when I get home," she declared now.

"Sounds like the lyrics to a lousy country song," he replied, laughing.

She couldn't help chuckling along with him. "Is writing all you ever think about?"

"Well, that and my work."

She asked about his job, and he described his booming consulting firm in Maryland, which provided human resources for start-up businesses.

"Oh, so you own the place?"

"That's right. And I have some terrific employees who make it possible for me to get away every now and then."

"Which makes it possible for you to get lost in Amish farmland." She looked at him. "I'm still not sure what you see in Butterfly Meadows. Why there?"

He shrugged. "Well, I think I must have Plain in my blood." At her look of surprise, he grinned. "Not seriously, of course. But it's a great place to decompress. No meetings, no emails piling up or phones constantly ringing. What's not to like?"

Trina tried to imagine staying at the Amish inn for the duration of her vacation. Would the place grow on her eventually? She doubted it, and if she hadn't already paid for her activities and accommodations—deeply discounted by Mandy Dienner as they were—she would be flying home to Minnesota immediately.

Back to civilization, she thought.

⚛

As it turned out, Mandy slept right through the time when her guests left for the sleigh ride with Karl. Disappointed, she spotted Trina's note in the kitchen, saying Yonnie had come looking for her earlier.

Trina left me a note? she thought. *Who's running this place?*

"I guess I was tuckered out," Mandy murmured, deciding she would try to make it up to the boy somehow.

Then an idea came to her, and she hurried to make her Mamma's hot cocoa recipe for everyone, including Yonnie and his father, once they were all back from the sleigh ride. She got the fire going strong in the breakfast room and made sure the table would accommodate all who wanted to sit and visit over cookies and hot chocolate.

She enjoyed preparing for the gathering, recalling Karl's generous manner and his son's endearing smile. And, odd as it seemed, Mandy no longer regretted missing out on the sleigh ride. In fact, she had a feeling the afternoon was supposed to end up just this way.

Chapter

23

Mandy kept watch for the sleigh filled with guests, and quickly pulled on a coat and her mother's black candlesnuffer bonnet when Karl Lantz stopped the horses. She hurried out to invite everyone inside for hot cocoa, including little Yonnie and Karl.

Yonnie had ridden up front with his father, and she apologized to the boy for missing the ride. "I'll go with ya another time," she told him, and he seemed to take his disappointment in stride, his blue eyes brightening at her invitation for hot cocoa and cookies.

The gathering for afternoon refreshments seemed to go better than those for the daily breakfasts. Several guests commented to Mandy about their delight at the unexpected treat. Even Trina was cordial to those around her—especially to Gavin. The two sounded as if they had been spending a fair amount of time together.

Mandy gave Yonnie special attention, offering him another cookie when he seemed too bashful to ask for the cookie plate to be passed his way. Meanwhile, Karl was visiting with Harold and Elaine Garfield from Connecticut, an older couple who'd known Mamma for a number of years.

When the overall conversation grew quieter, Harold told of Mandy's mother once giving them a week's free lodging "for a sanity break." He stopped to look thoughtfully at his petite wife. "Saloma had learned from another regular guest that my father had died of cancer, and because Elaine and I had been his sole caregivers, Saloma wanted to provide a respite for us."

Elaine nodded her head and smiled at her husband. "She made it possible for us to rest in this tranquil setting just as the butterflies returned in the spring. What a blessing that was!"

"Saloma was an angel of mercy in more ways than I can say," Karl agreed, looking now at Mandy.

Hearing the Garfields and Karl speak so fondly of her mother touched Mandy deeply. She supposed her mother had been particularly understanding of Karl's loss of his bride and thus taken him under her wing. Had she helped give him his start in Gordonville by hiring him at the B and B, perhaps? That would explain his hard work in the stable and elsewhere around the inn—all things that would have made life easier for Mamma. At least this was what crossed Mandy's mind as she sat there, enjoying the company of her guests.

When Mandy offered seconds on the cocoa, the response was so enthusiastic—a first!—she rushed out to the kitchen to make another batch. *At long last, they're truly enjoying something I make,* she thought.

Of course, she couldn't just serve hot cocoa for breakfast, but she knew that if she could pull off such a well-received afternoon get-together, maybe she could improve her breakfasts, as well.

Oh, if only that were so! she thought, stirring the milk over a low heat, lest it scald.

⁂

Monday heralded the start of Mandy's weekly routine, and she tried to encourage herself by remembering the guests' positive comments about what the inn had meant for them over the years. She knew that she was unlikely to ever match Mamma's abilities as a hostess, but it was heartening to realize that all the work she was doing to keep the inn humming might not go unnoticed—at least not by *all* the guests.

As for Trina, she had ceased threatening to leave and instead chose to stay on. Over the next few days, Mandy noticed that she and Gavin made a habit of talking together in the sitting room. Apparently, they were getting along quite well now. Trina even seemed more pleasant around the man.

Trina had just returned from a tour of the famous Ephrata Cloister that Thursday when Mandy asked if she'd like to have a grilled cheese sandwich for supper with her. "You must be tired from the long day, *jah?*"

Trina said that it would be nice to stay in on such a cold and windy night. "But let me make some soup to go with it, okay?"

"Well, you don't have to," Mandy said, wondering why she couldn't simply accept the invitation.

"I *want* to," Trina said, but it sounded like she meant to say she *needed* to—at least, that's how it came across to Mandy. "Why don't you just show me what you have on hand, and I'll figure out something from there?"

The house was all theirs, since the rest of the guests had gone out for supper, Gavin included. Mandy wondered why he hadn't taken Trina along, as he had at least twice now that she knew of.

After a quick investigation of the refrigerator and pantry, Trina decided on a cauliflower soup and made quick work of chopping the vegetables, which were soon on the stove simmering in some canned chicken broth.

"How was your tour today?" Mandy asked, bracing herself for a critical reply about the once flourishing church community of eighty celibate members.

"Really fascinating," Trina said as she finished whisking some half-and-half into the white sauce for the soup. "Did you know they composed a cappella music and practiced Germanic calligraphy? They were remarkably talented." She briefly described the primitive publishing center, which consisted in part of a paper mill, a printing office, and a bookbindery.

"I've heard 'bout it but have never gone there," Mandy said, buttering both sides of the bread for the sandwiches. "A very popular place with tourists."

"It's a national historic landmark, and I brought back a handful of brochures if you want some for guests."

"*Denki.*" At this kind gesture, Mandy glanced at Trina, who carefully stirred the white sauce into the tender vegetables, then seasoned the soup.

"Oh, does that ever smell delicious," Mandy said. Trina clearly had a knack in the kitchen. "It's too bad you're aren't Amish, or you'd be the perfect cook for this place!"

"What a nice thing to say." Trina smiled. "Just wait till you taste it!"

Then, just as Mandy had begun to warm to the young woman a bit, Trina said, "You're not *really* Amish, are you?"

Mandy's mouth dropped open. "What makes ya say that?"

"Let's see . . . you drive a car. You don't wear the white head covering like other Amishwomen." She paused, her hand still holding the wooden spoon. "And to be honest, your cooking leaves something to be desired."

Peeved, Mandy said, "Listen, I was born and raised Amish, just like the rest of my family."

"Right, but something must have happened, because despite your dresses and buns, you don't seem like you belong here."

Mandy felt cornered.

"And Gavin remembers you were once a full-fledged Amishwoman, back when he first started coming to this place. Then one year, you just weren't here anymore."

"Why does this concern you, Trina?"

"It just seems to me that you're killing yourself trying to keep the place running when you don't really want to be here." Trina tilted her head and frowned. "Why is that, Mandy?"

At that, Mandy lost her will to remain cordial. "Why not live *your* life, Trina? And I'll live mine."

"You know what—maybe I should just take my supper to my room and get out of your hair," Trina announced.

Mandy bit her lip, knowing nothing would be accomplished by arguing with her. Oh, how she wished Gavin had taken Trina with him!

"No need for that," she said more gently now.

Once the soup was ready, Mandy removed the skillet from the gas burner and placed the grilled cheese sandwiches on a platter, then carried it to the table.

Joining Trina there, Mandy folded her hands. "Should I say the blessing?" she asked, hoping that might get Trina's mind off their previous exchange.

Trina gave her a long look. "I understand that *real* Amish pray silently. You know, like you do at breakfast with the guests."

This irked Mandy all the more. "Then let's both bow our heads in *silent* prayer."

"Oh, for heaven's sake, I'll pray!" Trina said.

Unbelievable, thought Mandy. *How will I survive the rest of her stay?*

········ ❀ ········

By Saturday, Mandy found herself bending over backward to placate Trina after their spat. If the woman was so unhappy being at Butterfly Meadows, why didn't she just go back to Rochester?

Mandy was cleaning the breakfast room when she happened to look out the windows, and found herself gazing over at Arie's house, remembering the days when they teamed up together so efficiently, making short work of endless tasks.

I'm going to fail on my own, she thought, kneeling down on all fours to scrub the kitchen floor yet again, no longer relishing this chore. *After only a month.*

She recalled Trina's harsh words to her, and truth be known, Trina was right, to a degree. Mandy disliked everything about keeping the inn clean on her own, disliked going to get firewood and carrying buckets of coal to the house in the bitter cold, disliked cooking breakfast for unsatisfied guests, disliked reporting every red cent to Jerome. She felt completely overwhelmed.

Mandy knew it was pointless to go door to door again looking for help, and thus far, the help-wanted signs she'd put up in a few local businesses hadn't netted any interested Amish.

She questioned why she continued on when the situation seemed so hopeless. *And I'm so isolated here,* she thought, frustrated as she realized it was largely her own doing.

Maybe I should just throw in the towel come Monday when Jerome drops by, she thought, ready to return to civilization, as Trina called the English world. And the more she thought of it, the better she liked the idea. *I won't have to weed Mamma's perennial garden come spring!*

But then she remembered the astonishing beauty of the butterflies' mass arrival, a yearly reminder of nature's rebirth and the Lord's resurrection. Sighing, Mandy knew she would miss witnessing it, especially after so many years.

I'll give it more time, she decided.

.... ✿ ....

It was Trina's idea to play a game of checkers with Gavin in the breakfast room, where a roaring fire made the place particularly appealing this chilly day. Trina couldn't prevent the smile that came to her face when Gavin immediately brightened at the invitation and said he'd take her on.

She placed her red checkers on the board and let Gavin make the first play. The only thing missing was some soft music in the background, but given this was an Amish inn, she would have to overlook that.

While watching him decide his next move, Trina realized how much she desired this man's friendship. She wondered, with hope, if more might be in store for her with handsome Gavin.

He's been the only good surprise of this bungled trip. She reached for one of her checkers, wanting to win this game, yet knowing it really wasn't essential for her contentment.

Chapter

24

The afternoon light had been subdued by a covering of clouds as Trina shopped at the Log Cabin Quilt Shop on Route 340 later that Saturday. She had been wanting something special for her sister, something more than a souvenir of this trip. Janna had seemed over the moon about the prospect of having an Amish-made quilt.

She would love all this Amishness, Trina thought while picking through embroidered tablecloths and matching napkins. She recalled last night's dinner date at the Taj Mahal in Lancaster, where Gavin urged her to pretend she was somewhere exotic. During the course of the evening, they had shared their life stories over shrimp biryani and eventually closed down the place.

After returning to the inn last night, Trina had sat down by the coal stove to text Janna. *Gavin wants to keep in touch with me.*

And? Janna replied quicker than usual.

I'm deciding.

What's wrong with him? Janna asked, including a smiley emoji.

Nothing. That's why it's so hard. Then Trina added: *He's wonderful*, but quickly deleted it before sending. Instead, she wrote, *Well, gotta catch some z's. More later!*

Presently, Trina spotted a pretty quilted table runner done in creams and greens. She picked it up and perused it closely with her sister in mind.

Since I can't spring for an expensive bed quilt, she thought, heading for the cashier.

.... ❀ ....

Mandy panicked late that afternoon, beside herself with her workload and knowing she could not use the Lord's Day to catch up. Working on Sunday would ruin what little standing she had with Jerome and the rest of the family, if they somehow got word of it.

Desperate to clear her mind for a few minutes, she donned the oversized black coat she'd claimed as her own, as well as the scarf, black bonnet, and knitted mittens she'd found in her mother's belongings prior to setting aside some sentimental items for Jerome to take to Arie.

The fierce wind had died down as she stepped outside. And while the sun was beginning to set over the not-so-distant snow-covered hills, it was evident that winter had taken up residence. She walked out toward the springhouse, past the large gazebo her father and brothers had built years ago, wanting to pray but not knowing where to start. So many thoughts ran through her head, and sheer exhaustion colored everything.

She sighed and took another deep breath. *Even though the timing of this seemed like a godsend with my job loss, I should've reconsidered*, she thought now, recalling the stipulations Jerome had laid out. Yet she'd gotten herself into this yearlong agreement; she had no one else to blame.

While Mandy walked, she dared to look across the way toward Arie's house, and seeing the market wagon parked nearby, she wondered if her sister might have gone to sell some of her beautiful handiwork—crocheted doilies and needlepoint, perhaps. Arie had been a fast yet careful worker throughout their growing-up years, and Mandy had often heard Mamma speak of it to others within Arie's earshot as an encouragement. *Mamma's way . . .*

This moment, Mandy needed to empty out her thoughts and somehow navigate the oodles of work that awaited her. She knew she shouldn't have abandoned all of it to brave the cold and walk it off, as Dat had sometimes done. *"I always think more clearly out in nature,"* he would say.

"If it's not one thing, it's another, Lord," she began. "I am broken before You, torn up inside and out. Honestly, I wonder at times if I'm sleepwalking and this whole dreadful situation is a bad dream."

She sighed and pulled her scarf tighter against her neck and face as a shield from the cold.

"And I'm heartsick over Arie Mae. . . . I was too hasty in firing her." She walked along silently for a time, realizing she hadn't admitted to herself before now that she was sad about worsening the rift between her and Arie. *But it's too late to turn back,* she thought. *Too late to fix.*

Mandy began to pray again. "And, Lord, there's Trina. Maybe she's blind to it, but that woman's words can be like a serpent's venom—stinging and deadly. Dealing with her, along with everything else . . . it's too much. I honestly wish she'd leave."

Walking on, Mandy continued to pour out her anguish to God. "I'm so tired and discouraged. . . . I need help. I can't hold on here alone any longer. Will You send someone to help me before I collapse? Please, Lord."

She stopped walking and leaned against the horse fence and wept, cold and despairing.

Returning from the quilt shop with a driver the travel company had lined up, Trina walked around toward the back of the B and B, curious to see Ol' Tulip and Gertie up close and personal. She'd had a surprisingly good time on the sleigh ride with Gavin and the other inn guests last weekend, but she hadn't had the chance to get a good look at the horses that Gavin had described as *"uncommonly gentle."*

She swung the sack with her sister's gift inside, feeling surprisingly carefree and marveling that Gavin's overly optimistic attitude seemed to be rubbing off on her. She glanced over at the old farmhouse. *Is that possible?*

Turning toward the stable, she heard someone talking in the opposite direction and glanced to her right, past the large white gazebo. There was Mandy, all in black, her mittened hands folded as if praying. Trina paused to listen as the young innkeeper seemed to be conversing with someone, but no one was in sight.

At the edge of the yard, Trina saw that Mandy was quite alone. *She's praying,* Trina realized. *And not just any prayer . . . she's losing it.*

Sheepish suddenly, Trina determined not to eavesdrop on such a personal moment, but then a snippet she heard stopped her in her tracks. *She's talking about* me!

Startled to hear herself referred to as a snake, Trina stepped closer, listening intently to the not-so-prayerful rant.

She swallowed, now more tempted than ever to simply turn and run. *Is that what she thinks of me?*

Secretly, she was relieved no one else was around, and finally she found the wherewithal to leave. Dumbfounded and mortified, she headed toward the house, trudging into the kitchen and back to the room where she was staying.

How dare she! Trina thought, stricken. *I'm the wounded one.*

Then, flinging her purchase for Janna onto the bed, Trina

rehearsed everything that had happened since she'd arrived, every interaction with Mandy that she could recall. Up until now, she would largely have described Mandy as kind and attentive, generous and patient.

She went over her own words to Mandy, searching for something that might have pained her. *I've just been myself,* she thought suddenly. But a deeper, more troubling realization crept in. *Maybe that's the problem.*

Trina wiped away a tear. *What am I supposed to do?*

Convicted, she began to utter her own heartfelt prayer. And afterward, she considered how Mandy had literally pleaded with God for help. *To think she was so hurt by me that she prayed about it. . . .* And that gut-wrenching sobbing! The young innkeeper was obviously in a bad place.

Another thought occurred to her, one born from Mandy's obvious desperation.

She needs help. Trina went to the window and saw Mandy still out there, sobbing into her hands. *And giving help is something I'm good at.*

"She needs *me,*" Trina whispered. "And I owe it to her."

Chapter

25

M andy stayed up into the wee hours that Sunday morning, folding sheets and ironing pillowcases, then mixed some batter for a sweet bread for a simple breakfast, all the while thinking ahead to her meeting with Jerome on Monday. As a result, she resented the alarm clock when it sounded at five o'clock. She stretched out the length of her bed, knowing that if she was going to have time to shower and dress for church, get coffee going, and bake the bread, she would have to get up right away.

Suppressing a moan, she dragged herself out from under the warm quilt, briefly recalling the seemingly easy life she'd had in Scott City. How appealing it seemed now. It had been a while since she'd thought about using the money from the sale of her mother's home to start up a florist shop someplace. Along with that dream, Mandy had lost sight of her goal of making it to the finish line.

When Mandy was ready to start preparing the guests' breakfast, she headed groggily through the dim hallway and noticed the light from the gas lamp in the kitchen, already glowing.

Quickening her pace, she could see Trina Sutton standing next to the gas range, setting the teakettle on the back burner. The coffee was brewing, too. What was going on?

"'Morning, Mandy," Trina said, turning around when Mandy walked into the ring of light.

"You're up early, ain't so?"

Trina shrugged. "I wanted to talk to you before the other guests came down for breakfast."

Ach, *what now*? Mandy braced herself as she went to preheat the oven for the loaves of sweet bread.

"I've noticed how shorthanded you are."

Casually, Mandy adjusted her long apron and wondered where Trina was going with this. "*Jah*, but that'll be fixed soon."

"Well . . . maybe I can help you fix it."

Mandy frowned as she pulled the bread batter out of the refrigerator and poured it into three greased loaf pans.

Trina smiled. "I need something to do. And I know my way around a kitchen."

Mandy cringed. *I'm not hiring her, Lord!*

"You need me," Trina said.

"That's all right, but thanks." Mandy tried her best to keep her refusal firm yet polite. "Besides, have ya forgotten how much you dislike bein' here?"

"Well, it's growing on me."

Mandy gave her a skeptical look.

"Try me out for a few days, and if you don't see my value, we can part ways," Trina said, her tone earnest.

Mandy could scarcely believe what she was hearing. Was the woman serious? "You have a home back in Minnesota, though."

"I'm between patients, so I have nowhere to be presently," Trina said. "Let me offer my help for a while. If you accept, I'll work out the details."

"But I need someone who's Amish," Mandy persisted.

"I can be as Amish as you are," Trina replied, raising her eyebrows.

Mandy wondered how to respond. *Am I actually desperate enough to consider this?*

She was, of course. And when the oven beeped, signaling it was ready, Mandy placed the pans inside and closed the door. "I wouldn't expect you to dress Plain if you worked here," she said, thinking aloud. "That would be deceitful."

Trina shrugged. "You mean, *more* deceitful." An almost imp-ish smile appeared on her face, one Mandy decided to ignore as she counted out the necessary utensils, then carried them into the breakfast room.

"You'd have to wear long skirts and modest tops," Mandy said when she returned for the plates and cereal bowls. "And if you're going to be cookin', you'd have to put your hair up."

"Hadn't thought of that," Trina said. "So basically you want me to look semi-Plain?"

Mandy grimaced. "I guess so . . . if you were to work here."

"I'm just being direct, Mandy," Trina said. "Most people don't understand that."

Jah, Mandy thought, suddenly feeling trapped.

"You're running yourself ragged," Trina said when Mandy went to the cupboard for the juice glasses. "And I honestly want to help. Just say yes, and I'll stick around."

Mandy sighed and pondered Trina's unsolicited offer, knowing what a huge help another set of hands would be. *Can we really work together?*

········ ❀ ········

Mandy sat in her usual spot at the community church, next to a family of four. The school-age boy and girl sat silently, smiling at her prior to the service starting with congregational singing. Recalling her earlier resistance to Trina Sutton, she felt like a choosy beggar.

I did ask God to send someone to me, she thought later, bowing her head for the prayer before the sermon. *Is Trina meant to be the answer, Lord?*

Mandy followed along in her Bible as the minister read from the wooden pulpit, but in the back of her mind, she could still hear Trina practically imploring her for the job.

After church, Mandy took the long way home, by way of Belmont Road, with its lovely old covered bridge over Pequea Creek. Slowing way down as she approached, she remembered how, when Josiah had first started courting her, he had once dared to point out it was a *"kissing bridge"*—and in Arie's hearing, of all things. Arie had let it slip later to Mamma, who had declared such talk, so early in a courtship, irresponsible nonsense, earning *Mandy* a scolding.

Turning on the radio, Mandy took in the beauty of the wintry landscape as she meandered back to the inn. *If I don't hire Trina, I'll soon have no choice but to quit*, she thought. *These could be my last few days here.*

Pondering her predicament, Mandy crept along, taking note of the picturesque white barns and the waterwheels, the newfangled "wedding house" erected on one of the smaller farms, and the Amish families on foot or riding in buggies to visit relatives on their off-Sunday from Preaching.

On Old Leacock Road, she slowed again when she came to the bridge over the railroad crossing, recalling how bumpy it had been to go over the tracks in a pony cart years before.

I would not regret leavin', she tried to convince herself. *I gave the inn my all. Did my best.*

But that's not exactly true, she thought now. *Keeping Arie would have solved everything.* Mandy fought back tears at the thought of her sister, though she still felt letting her go was warranted. *Nearly the moment we were reunited . . .*

When she parked her car, Mandy stared at the house where Arie lived with Josiah, wondering what Arie's life was like these days.

She sighed and contemplated where she should live next. Kansas was out, wasn't it? Despite her friends in Scott City, it was too dry and brown there a good part of the year, and there simply weren't enough opportunities.

Then, suddenly remembering her financial situation, Mandy fought against the notion of quitting. *Not yet.*

.... ✿ ....

"If you're sure you want to help here, we could give it a try," Mandy told Trina when they were preparing a light lunch together. Trina hadn't said if she'd gone to church again with Gavin or not, and it was of no concern to Mandy.

Trina nodded, seemingly pleased, although she didn't crack a smile. "First and foremost, I want to do all the cooking," she said as they sat at the kitchen table over coffee and a ham and cheese sandwich.

She's already taking over, Mandy thought, chagrined.

But instead of fussing about it, she agreed—Trina was certainly the better cook. "And tomorrow, once the guests check out, we'll each take a bedroom to redd up."

"Won't it go faster if we work together in the same room?" Trina asked, clearly full of her own ideas.

Again, Mandy didn't argue. "Don't forget, no jeans or pants . . . only modest skirts and dresses."

Trina raised one eyebrow as if about to speak, then seemed to reconsider. Instead, she said rather casually, "Guess I'll have to do a little shopping today, then. And Gavin will have to get used to seeing a new me."

It occurred to Mandy that Trina might be eager to remain while Gavin was still there at the B and B. Could that be why she was offering to help?

Doesn't matter, Mandy realized, feeling strangely relieved as they hammered out the details of Trina's employment.

········ ❀ ········

Jerome had a big talk on when he came for breakfast the next morning. "No new snow in sight," he said as Mandy poured his coffee and gave him some apple juice, too.

She presented him with a tasty breakfast casserole made by Trina, who'd broken the rules yesterday and gone out on a Sunday to shop for the ingredients to the various recipes she'd selected from the inn's treasured recipe notebook. Even though she'd loaned Trina her car to do so, Mandy decided to remain mum about that.

Jerome's eyes lit up as he took a bite of the casserole. "*Ach,* this is *wunnerbaar-gut!*" he said, still chewing, his expression one of rapture.

That's when Mandy introduced Trina to her brother, saying, "I almost gave up on finding a *gut* cook."

"Givin' up ain't something we Dienners ever do," he said, nodding at Trina, who offered a polite greeting before going to make some last-minute whipped cream to top her dishes of autumn-spiced fruit compote.

With Trina nearby, now was no time for Mandy to recite the struggles of the past five weeks to her brother. It went without saying that if she was going to hire an *Englischer,* she must be desperate—or downright crazy.

Chapter 26

One guest after another raved about the delectable break-fast, and one woman even assumed that Mandy had made it. "You've been holding out on us, young lady!" she exclaimed while Mandy was refilling coffee in the cheery breakfast room.

Humored by what was in effect a backhanded compliment, Mandy was pleased with the turn of events.

"May I have the recipe?" the same woman asked. "It's Amish, right?"

"*Jah*, and one my mother made quite a lot, as did my grand-mother," Mandy answered truthfully before going back to the kitchen, where she announced to Trina that her breakfast was an amazing success.

"What did I tell you?" Trina said happily. "Cooking is my thing!"

Stifling a smile, Mandy busied herself with running hot water into the sink to wash the dishes.

"When do you start decorating for Christmas around here?" Trina asked as she carried the empty casserole pan over to the counter near Mandy. "It's already kind of late in the season." And before Mandy could answer, Trina started in on some holiday decorating ideas she had "to liven up the dreary place."

"Oh . . . but Amish people don't put up trees or garland and whatnot," Mandy informed her as she squirted dish soap into the water.

"Well, that's a bummer." Trina frowned.

"It's our tradition, so the guests here don't expect it." Mandy said, worried that Trina was going to make this an issue for debate. "The most I'd consider doin' is maybe buying a few poinsettias."

At that, Trina merely scoffed. "Hmmph."

"This is an authentic Amish inn, remember?"

Trina shook her head and looked at her dubiously.

Finally, Mandy put her foot down. "There will be no Christmas tree or plastic Santas here."

Shrugging, Trina looked away and went to pour some coffee for herself. "Just sayin'."

Maybe say less, Mandy thought, yet was still happy with the results of Trina's cooking. The woman's talent for it was even greater than Mandy had hoped.

"If you stick around long enough, you'll see this place is anything but dreary once the butterfly meadow is filled with newly blooming wild flowers," Mandy said, wondering if Trina would still be here. "It's quite the sight."

"I can't wait," Trina said.

"The day you see both a butterfly and a hummingbird draw nectar from the same red zinnia is a red-letter day, believe me."

"I'll take your word for it," Trina said, preoccupied now with digging through a stack of drawers. "Where's your citrus zester?"

Mandy showed her, and Trina followed up with another half dozen questions as she searched here and there for the various kitchen implements she wanted in order to make lemon bars for an afternoon snack, seemingly more impatient by the minute.

Oh dear, Mandy thought. Considering Trina's mood, she was relieved when a few of the guests began to check out later that morning. It had been challenging to keep her contained in the kitchen. All Mandy needed now was for people to find out that the amazing Amish breakfasts were being prepared by anyone but an Amish cook!

········ ❀ ········

"It's too bad you slept in today," Gavin told Trina later that afternoon. He was standing near the sideboard, wearing jeans and a long-sleeved gray-and-white-striped polo shirt, refilling his coffee cup. "You missed out on a terrific breakfast."

Trina simply smiled, mindful of Mandy's desire for secrecy. She asked what his favorite part of the meal had been, guessing what he might say.

"The breakfast casserole was something out of a cooking show," Gavin told her, taking a sip of coffee. "The perfect blend of potatoes, sausage, spinach, and cheese."

Inwardly pleased, Trina said, "You sound like a connoisseur."

"Well, due to my frequent travel, I eat out quite a lot. Eventually, you figure out what you like and what you don't, I guess."

"With so much traveling, when do you find time to write? Besides here, that is."

He waved his hand. "I squeeze in articles when I can, but the poetry is just a hobby, more to unwind than anything. Keeps me human, I suppose."

She hesitated. "Well then, when are you going to grace me with one of your creations?"

He laughed. "As soon as I'm convinced you won't make fun."

This brought laughter to them both.

"I'll look forward to it," Trina said, wanting to wait till he left before she removed the tablecloth to be washed in the third load of laundry so far today. She didn't mind hanging the sheets and things out to dry on the line outdoors, thankful for the sunny day, no matter how cold.

Gavin asked, "Say, since you're checking out the day after tomorrow, I'd like to take you out for dinner tonight . . . one last time."

She drew a deep breath, hoping she didn't appear too pleased. "Actually, it looks as though I'm going to be staying on a bit longer."

"Oh, now that's a surprise," Gavin replied, probably remembering her litany of complaints.

"I'm just . . . uh . . . going to help out for a while," Trina added.

His eyes narrowed, and the truth seemed to dawn on him while she grinned and batted her eyes, affecting innocence.

Finally, he gave a triumphant smile. "I thought something was up. So . . . let me guess, *you* made breakfast today?"

Trina slid two fingers across her lips. "It's a secret."

Seemingly amused, he folded his arms as she explained that Mandy needed some major help. "So you can't tell a soul."

"Well, after *that* breakfast, you have my word." His smile expanded to a grin. "How long do you plan to stay?"

"I'm playing it by ear."

"No hurry to get home?" he asked, clearly bemused.

"Nothing pressing," she said, not revealing that she'd already spoken with her boss today about a leave of absence, uncertain when she might return to Rochester. Gail Anderson had actually applauded her decision, saying she thought the extended change of pace would be good for Trina, and thankfully, a neighbor had agreed to keep an eye on her place.

"Is that a yes for tonight?" Gavin asked.

"How about the weekend? Once I've caught up a bit."

"Okay, especially since it now seems as if you can't avoid me, even if you want to." His twinkle was endearing.

"Smooth talker, aren't you?" She liked his style. "Well, back to work."

"For both of us," Gavin said, heading for the stairs with his coffee. "I've got a midafternoon phone conference. One of my clients is having HR issues with a restaurant merger."

Trina hurried back to the kitchen to begin her lemon bars, trying to wipe what must surely be a silly grin off her face.

.... ✿ ....

Two very hectic days passed, and amid all the changing of bedding and washing and hauling wood and coal, as well as feeding chickens and gathering their eggs . . . and the general cleaning of the B and B, Mandy appreciated Trina's help. But there were times when Mandy was so exasperated with Trina's ideas about the so-called proper way to do things that it was an added chore just to work alongside her. Even worse was that Trina was so often right. Considering she was new to all this, that was maddening!

Mandy did her best to ignore the little things and focus on the basics, attempting to work together as a team. *Like two mules pulling a load of hay.* She smiled at that ridiculous image.

"What's that smirk about?" Trina asked as they made up the bed in the Yellow Room.

"Oh, just thinkin'."

"Something funny?"

Mandy presumed she would keep pressing, so she told her.

Trina laughed. "That seems fitting. I actually like that, because I feel like a mule. Strong, persistent . . . yep, that's me!"

Mandy stifled another smile as they leaned over to make square corners on the clean sheet.

"And that's really what you were smiling about?" asked Trina, straightening.

"Perty much." Mandy breathed in the fresh, clean scent of the bedding. "Ever smell something so *wunnerbaar*?" she asked, changing the subject and referring to the sheets.

Trina put her nose to the bedding, sniffed, then grimaced. "I don't know—a chocolate cake beats sun-dried sheets to pieces."

This struck Mandy as funny, and she couldn't help but laugh out loud.

Eventually, Trina began to laugh with her.

"So what's your favorite fragrance?" Trina asked, putting the pillowcases on the feather pillows. "Is it really sun-dried sheets?"

"Fresh-cut hay is high on my list of favorites."

Trina grimaced. "Hmm, I wouldn't have guessed that."

"My twin sister and I liked to run out to the field and watch our father and brothers run the baler."

Trina frowned.

"My siblings and I always ran barefoot from early springtime till the first frost," Mandy said when they had finished putting on the pretty yellow, white, and orange bed quilt. She sighed as she let the memory wash over her.

"Where are all these siblings now?"

Mandy waved. "You might not believe it if I told ya."

"Try me."

"They all live within a few miles of here."

Trina stopped for a moment and put her hands on her hips, as if thinking. "Okay, but . . . I've only met Jerome. He seems nice."

"Oh, he is." *Nice enough*, Mandy thought.

They moved next door to make up the Green Room, where earlier Mandy had left the folded clean sheets on the stripped bed.

"You mentioned something about . . . a twin sister," Trina said, gesturing for help in raising the mattress so she could slip on the bottom corner of the fitted sheet.

"*Jah*, Arie Mae," Mandy admitted, leaning down to help.

"Where is she?"

Mandy pointed toward the big farmhouse. "Right over there."

Trina made a horrified face. "Wait . . . your sister lives next door?"

Mandy merely nodded, wishing their conversation had taken a different turn.

"And you're over here killing yourself?" Trina exclaimed and stopped to stare at Mandy. "What's *wrong* with this picture?"

"It's a long story," Mandy said, hoping Trina would drop it. *Unlikely*, she thought.

"Doesn't Arie know how much you're struggling?"

"Oh, I'm quite sure she knows."

Again, Trina frowned. "But doesn't your twin care what happens to you? Or the inn?"

Mandy blew out an exasperated breath. "If you must know, I let her go."

"You *fired* her?" Trina's expression looked as though that was the last thing she'd expected to hear.

"I had my reasons." Mandy flinched, then let a welcome silence play out. She pointed to the lightweight blanket. "Trina, would you adjust the length on your side?"

"Mandy? Don't leave me hanging, okay?"

Mandy sighed. "My sister and I were very close for many years."

Trina nodded. "Now we're getting somewhere."

"But I'd rather not talk 'bout it."

"Can't you tell me anything?" Trina's eyes showed concern.

Mandy took time to smooth out the quilt before finally revealing, "We had a big falling-out."

Trina was nodding. "That's the news flash?"

Mandy sighed.

"And?" Trina looked on expectantly.

"I've said too much already." *No need to tell her more*, Mandy thought.

Trina pursed her lips, as if readying her next question, but before she could say more, the telephone rang, giving Mandy the perfect excuse to leave the room.

Chapter

27

Mandy had been amazed at the variety of Mamma's breakfast recipes Trina had made over the past week. True to Trina's word, Mandy found her to be incredibly helpful in the kitchen.

Also, Trina had not inquired further about Mandy's issues with Arie Mae. As awkward as things had been between her and Trina at times, so far running the inn with Trina was going along well enough. When it came to accomplishing tasks, things seemed to go better if Trina called the shots, but Mandy didn't mind. *Not as long as I'm getting more sleep,* Mandy thought, smiling.

It was late in the afternoon Friday, an ideal day for drying clothing, considering the brilliant sky and a gentle wind. Mandy had run two loads of washing early that morning while Trina made breakfast and was heading outdoors to see if the clothes were dry on the line.

Just then, one of the horses began to neigh loudly, and Mandy looked toward the stable and saw Yonnie coming toward her as fast as his short legs would carry him.

"Dat's with Gertie," he said, his little face worried. "She's real sick."

Together, they went across the yard to the stable door. "What's wrong with her?" she asked Karl. The mare was lying down in the stall, mouth gaping.

"It's the colic," Karl told her, squatting near Gertie's head.

No. Mandy closed her eyes in frustration.

"As you prob'ly remember, it's not uncommon in the winter, when horses aren't out grazing," Karl said.

Indeed, Mandy well recalled that colic was the most common cause of death in horses. "My brother Sammy lost one of his horses to it," she told Karl.

"I'm awful sorry," he said. "I've been sprinkling some hay in with the horses' feed since the start of the coldest weather, hoping to ward off somethin' like this." He stroked Gertie's mane. "I talked to the vet a day ago, and he stopped by after dark to look in on her."

"Never heard him—it must've been late."

"Considerin' the hour, Merv pro'bly didn't want to bother ya." Karl pulled up his sleeve to look at his watch. "I 'spect he'll be by any minute now for a follow-up."

"What can be done besides keepin' her from eating much?"

"It's wait and see right now. She has no appetite, and she's been given a laxative and some pain medication, too." Karl leaned closer to the mare. "I took Ol' Tulip out the past couple days for the sleigh rides for the guests so Gertie here could rest . . . recover *zimmlich glei.*"

Very soon, Mandy thought, hoping so. "I'd hate to lose her . . . she's been like part of the family."

"Oh, I understand. Ain't easy to see a beloved horse suffer so." Karl's expression was thoughtful. "Merv and I are doin' everything we can to get her back to normal."

"*Denki,* Karl. This means so much." Mandy bent low to stroke

Gertie's nose and whispered to her. "*Gut* girl . . . you're such a *gut* girl."

Karl gave Gertie a pat, as well, and then took her pulse. "She's at forty-five beats per minute—still higher than she should be, but an improvement from yesterday. I think she's going to pull out of it."

"I pray so."

Karl looked at Mandy, his eyes soft. "Not to bring up a tetchy subject, but you seem a bit more settled these days. Glad to see it."

She paused, startled he'd say something so personal. "Well, I've been getting more sleep at night."

"I was concerned—my heart went out to ya, honestly." He continued stroking Gertie, whose eyes were now closed. "I was wondering if maybe I might help more round here."

She was touched by the suggestion. *He wants to do more?* Without responding directly to his offer, she explained that Trina had been helping out lately.

"So that's the young woman who sometimes hangs out the washing—the *Englischer*?"

"*Jah*, she's just assisting for the time being," Mandy said, guessing Karl would have a hard time understanding why she'd want to employ such a woman. "Trina came as a guest, and as much as it surprises me to say, she seems to be an answer to prayer."

"Well, you can thank the Good Lord."

Mandy nodded, surprised that Karl seemed to care when it really wasn't his worry.

The vet, Mervin Zimmerman, arrived shortly thereafter, sporting a five-o'clock shadow and a dark blue denim shirt visible beneath his open jacket.

Mandy and Karl stepped aside when Merv entered the stall to do the required examination. Afterward, he insisted that Gertie be given additional water. "Force the liquids and get her up and moving around. That's critical now."

"I'll walk her out to the barnyard right away," Karl said, going immediately into the stall, where he talked to Gertie in soothing tones.

"She should be feelin' better soon," Merv told them. "But give me a jingle if she's not. Night or day."

Mandy and Karl both thanked him, and with some effort, Karl managed to encourage the ailing mare to her feet.

Suddenly, Mandy remembered the washing she'd come out to take off the clothesline. It was getting chillier now, the sun drifting slowly toward the horizon. *Maybe Trina already brought it in*, she thought.

"You've been very helpful, Karl, to Gertie . . . and to me," Mandy said, somewhat at a loss for words.

Unexpectedly, Karl followed her out the stable door, then hesitated, holding his hat in his hands, glancing down at it, then back at Mandy. "I mean it 'bout helping more. Just give me a holler."

"I appreciate that," she said simply, glad for the vet's caring manner and the good prognosis. But despite Karl's offer, she really didn't know what to think of him. Perhaps he was just a sympathetic and friendly fellow. Or was there more to it?

Mandy couldn't be sure, but whatever it was, she needed to nip it in the bud if anything romantic was going on in his head. *He is really nice, though*, she thought. *I'll give him that.*

And handsome, she pondered further. *And his little boy is adorable.*

Mandy sighed. *But he's Amish, and I'll be leaving next November, once I sell the inn.*

········ ❀ ········

That Saturday noon, while Mandy helped to make salads and turkey and Swiss cheese wraps, Trina announced that she had plans for supper that evening.

"With Gavin?" Mandy asked.

"For some reason, he has this fascination with me."

"Silly him," Mandy jested.

"Don't read too much into it," Trina was quick to say as she carried their plates over to the table.

"He's obviously attracted to you." Mandy took a seat across from her. "Must like your spunkiness."

Trina turned and gave Mandy the funniest scowl. "You crack me up."

"*Nee* . . . he's sweet on ya." Mandy smiled. "Seriously."

Trina frowned as if Mandy had just given her something profound and mysterious to ponder. She folded her arms, still seemingly perplexed. "I'm not real comfortable with—"

"Well, Gavin's a lovely man, from what I gather," Mandy interrupted. "And Mamma thought the world of him, if that's any endorsement."

Their eyes met, and Trina looked away, her suddenly dark mood deepening.

"What's a-matter?" Mandy asked.

"Nothing," Trina said, her eyes still dim.

A few minutes passed as they bowed their heads for the table blessing, then began to eat in silence until Trina wiped her lips and murmured, "The shoe is on the other foot, I suppose." She inhaled slowly. "My fiancé died in a car wreck more than a year ago."

"Oh . . . I'm awful sorry," Mandy quickly replied. *No wonder she's hesitant about Gavin!*

"Sounds like both you and I have suffered big losses," Trina said softly, telling Mandy more about the accident that had altered her happy plans. "But I'm determined to move forward. That was part of the reason I took a chance on a mystery trip."

Trina refilled their water glasses and then changed the topic to her elderly friend, Gail Anderson, with whom she'd spoken that morning.

"What a sweet lady she must be," Mandy said.

"Is she ever. And someday, if she's strong enough, she's exactly the type of person who would enjoy an inn like this—she and Gavin would hit it off," Trina said, laughing.

"It's good to have a friend who understands you so well," Mandy mused.

Trina gave her a concerned look. "What about you? I take it you don't have time anymore to attend all the work frolics and other activities I hear the Amishwomen around here enjoy."

"No worries. I don't need to sit around stitching up quilts," Mandy said, attempting to brush off the question. "If I'd wanted that, I never would've left this life behind."

Trina seemed to consider that. "So . . . where did you go when you left?"

"Western Kansas. A little flat, perhaps, but with lots of very nice folk."

Trina whistled. "A long way from here."

Mandy recalled the hours and hours of driving. "You can say that again."

"This is really home for you, then, isn't it?"

Not anymore, Mandy thought, instead answering, "More so now that I'm not runnin' round like a chicken with its head chopped off."

"Thanks to me," Trina said without missing a beat.

"I *am* feeling far less frantic."

"Yes, well, and thank *you* for not requiring me to wear Amish clothing." Trina glanced down at her long skirt. "As it is, I feel like someone out of a prairie romance novel."

Mandy gave her a smile. "Well, I think you would've made a fine Amish cook!"

Trina laughed and picked up her napkin. "I may not be Plain, but I wouldn't have let you get rid of me without a fight," she said unexpectedly.

"*Ach*, Trina—"

"Okay, okay, enough—I'm just telling you that I didn't have it in me to leave you hanging by a thread here, Mandy." She folded her hands. "And I'm not even related."

Mandy sighed, thinking back to her first day home. "Arie Mae's not a terrible person."

"Could've fooled me." Trina frowned. "You said you fired her for a good reason."

Mandy shrugged, suddenly melancholy. *Did I?*

.... ✿ ....

That evening, while cleaning up after a too-quiet solo supper hour, Mandy realized again how far she and Trina had come in such a short time, and by sheer trial and error. Not necessarily a trial by fire, though, as she'd found Trina far easier to manage than initially expected.

For sure and for certain, working with Trina day in and day out meant that disagreements lurked around every corner, but Mandy was glad for the woman's conscientiousness, and the guests were beyond delighted with the breakfast offerings.

An acceptable trade-off.

Chapter

28

It was a particularly cold morning the Wednesday before Christmas when Gavin carried his bags downstairs. Checking the breakfast table while her famous egg bake was in the oven, Trina caught a glimpse of him and felt a wave of nerves. She hurried to the front door and opened it, stepping outside, onto the stoop, and watched Gavin load his things into the car.

Is he leaving without saying good-bye? she wondered. Based on his kind, caring response Saturday evening when she had told him about her engagement and Shawn's sudden death, she couldn't imagine that.

Just now, he spotted her and gave her a smile and a wave.

"You're still staying for breakfast, right?" Trina asked, shivering in the bright blue morning as he came back up the walkway. She hugged herself, her breath wisps of warm air in the cold. "It looks like maybe you're in a rush."

Gavin chuckled and put an arm around her shoulders. "You can't get rid of me that easily. Now, let's get you inside."

Whew. She felt rather ridiculous chasing him outside as she had, but his reassuring manner put a quick end to that as they headed back indoors, where she excused herself and made her way to the kitchen. Mandy eyed her curiously but said nothing.

An hour or so later, Trina was delighted when Gavin came looking for her in the kitchen, ready to make his departure. Mandy was clearing off the table in the breakfast room.

Gavin reached for her hand and held it gently. "I'll be in touch, okay?" he said with a wink.

"Okay," she said, wishing she dared to say more. After she heard the front door latch, she crept into the entryway to watch him walk down to his car and drive away, sad to see him go.

········ ❀ ········

Gavin texted Trina the next two days and called her in the evenings when he was home from work.

Then, on Christmas Eve, she received a package containing a framed poem entitled "The Strong-Willed Woman." At first reading, Trina didn't think of it as the most romantic gift she'd ever received. But then, rereading it, she realized it was a unique expression of Gavin's affection and appreciation for her, and she was so taken with its creativity, she asked Mandy if she could hang it up in her room.

Mandy gave her that knowing look, and Trina could hardly disguise her own smile. "Maybe you're right . . . maybe he does like me," she admitted, to which Mandy nodded emphatically.

A card had arrived from Janna, asking when Trina was ready to give up her country gig, a smiley face after the question mark.

Not for a while, Trina thought, considering that even with her and Mandy both working fast, they were still just barely keeping up. But it was nice to be missed.

I miss you, too, sis, she thought.

Each day, Trina worked steadily alongside Mandy without stopping, except for lunch, eight hours straight. Trina wasn't necessarily thrilled with the minimum wage she was earning, but helping Mandy had never been about making money. Trina had a purpose again, and she felt appreciated and valued as a person. And Mandy was good at promptly showering her with compliments, no strings attached, even when obviously frustrated with her.

And each night, when Trina leaned her head on the plump feather pillow on the bed that had once belonged to Mandy's twin sister, Trina could sigh happily, knowing she was accomplishing something good for another human being, just as she had with Gail. Trina thanked God for the opportunity to make a difference in this very rural bend in the road.

.... ✿ ....

Weeks passed, and January and February turned into March. Now that spring was on its way and the ground seemed to be thawing, there was plentiful mud everywhere, the reason for the name of the popular annual auctions held in Strasburg, Gordonville, Refton, and Bart. The mud sales were used to raise money for the area fire departments, and things got so busy that Mandy had to turn down a number of people calling to book a room. Gone were the days when she'd worried over her mother's regular clientele drying up and disappearing.

To Mandy's relief, Trina continued to stay on, making no mention of when she might return to Minnesota. Little by little, Mandy and Trina began to find a more focused rhythm to their days. Along the way, they also got to know each other better, here and there sharing stories from their childhood, although Mandy had only shared about the good times. Amazingly, there were occasions when Trina didn't respond quite so abrasively. In fact, Mandy had been seeing her softer side more recently, enough so that she sometimes dared to allow Trina—*Englischer* though she was—to interact with guests.

········ ✤ ········

In mid-March, winter made a sudden reappearance. It was a snowy Thursday when Trina drove Mandy's car to Bird-in-Hand with Mandy in the passenger's seat, as was usual these days.

A herd of the neighbor's cattle huddled together near the fence lines where hay had been scattered, looking miserable. When the women arrived at market, the snow made it hard to see across the parking lot as Trina and Mandy got out and hurried inside.

They shook the snowflakes from their coats and scarves, glad to be out of the storm. Trina removed her gloves and stuffed them into her coat pockets. She was caught by surprise when Mandy abruptly changed course, touching her arm and redirecting her.

"What is it?" Trina asked.

"Just trying to avoid an unpleasant situation," Mandy replied.

"What?" Trina replied, still resisting Mandy's efforts.

Giving in, Mandy sighed, leaned closer, and whispered, "It's Arie Mae. Over by the baked goods."

Attempting not to appear obvious, Trina glanced over and spotted Mandy's twin sister. Now that Mandy had pointed her out, Trina realized she'd seen this young woman before, right here at the store, in fact. She was surprised to notice that Arie was quite pregnant.

While Mandy went to get a shopping cart, Trina followed Arie Mae with her eyes. Mandy's twin seemed tentative as she moved slowly toward the first aisle, as if taking everything in. Various people waved and smiled at her, and while Arie appeared friendly toward them, she was not as demonstrative as Mandy. *She's less outgoing,* Trina decided. *Shy, maybe.*

Mandy returned with the empty cart. "Prob'ly shouldn't stare, *jah?*"

"I really want to meet her," Trina replied.

"Ain't a *gut* idea," Mandy urged, shaking her head.

"Oh, c'mon—how bad can it be?"

"*Nee,*" Mandy said abruptly, her face suddenly pale.

Trina was shocked at her response. "Okay."

Mandy looked relieved. "*Denki.*"

Trina reached for the cart, following Mandy, who quickly led her in the opposite direction.

List in hand, Trina eyed the produce section, wanting some green onions for the skillet breakfast she'd seen in Mandy's mother's recipe book. "We're almost out of garlic, too," she told Mandy as she reached for several papery bulbs.

Trina next headed to the spice aisle for the paprika, then on toward the baking supplies as Mandy went back to the produce section for some green peppers, leaving Trina alone and wondering whether Arie Mae was still in the store. And just then, she spotted her a few yards away, coming Trina's direction. Their eyes met briefly, and Arie actually smiled before turning away again.

As if driven to do so, Trina began to push the cart toward Arie at the same time Mandy wandered up behind her.

"Trina, what are you—"

By then, Trina was within earshot of Mandy's sister. And Trina suddenly realized she had no idea what to say to this stranger who was their closest neighbor, especially not with Mandy still following her. A forced encounter could very well be traumatic for both sisters, she thought. *Am I walking into a hornet's nest?*

"Trina!" Mandy whispered loudly at the exact moment Trina came to her senses and was about to reverse course.

But it was too late. Arie had turned around again, this time with a curious expression . . . and Trina had no choice but to go ahead. "Excuse me, aren't you Arie Mae?" she said, approaching her.

Arie's gaze shifted from Trina to Mandy, and immediately her pretty face broke into a smile. "Hullo, *Schweschder. Wie geht's?*"

Her friendly response startled Trina, and poor Mandy seemed to be struggling to produce a smile.

"Hullo, Arie Mae," Mandy said. "This is Trina Sutton—she's been workin' for me awhile now."

"Jerome has spoken kindly of you, Trina," Arie said softly, still smiling at them both. She glanced at Mandy. "He's mighty impressed with your tasty breakfasts."

Trina was taken by her gentle charm. "I love to cook, so it's a good fit," Trina replied, noticing the blush on Mandy's cheeks. Arie, however, was as pleasant as any sister might be when running into another.

"How've ya been, Mandy?" Arie asked, her hands gripping the shopping cart, half filled with groceries.

"Oh, busy."

"Which is so *gut* to hear, considering . . ."

"*Jah*, lots of guests, many repeats like before, but many more new ones," Mandy said, her voice sounding unnatural and forced.

The sisters just stood there, apparently at a loss for words before Arie and then Mandy said something in *Deitsch*. Fascinated by their similar mannerisms, Trina observed the twins closely, not sure she should interrupt.

"Well, it's nice to finally meet you," Trina said when it seemed clear both were done talking. "When's your baby due?"

"Mid-June."

"Not very long now," Trina said.

"Real close to Mamma's favorite season," Arie said, looking sweetly at Mandy just then and turning to address Trina. "You'll get to see the butterflies return by the hundreds only a few weeks before then—every imaginable color and kind."

"Mandy's mentioned what a sight that is; I'm looking forward to witnessing it for myself." Trina glanced at Mandy, who she could see was eager to get going. "Well, we have a long grocery list, so . . ."

"*Ach*, of course," Arie said, nodding her head. "I'm glad we met, Trina. And it's so nice to see you again, Mandy Sue."

"Have yourself a *gut* day," Mandy said, seeming to have trouble getting the words out.

Arie turned to head up the aisle, her long green dress and matching apron swishing against her legs as Trina hung back a bit.

"That wasn't so bad, was it?" Trina murmured to Mandy.

Mandy was dead silent.

"I'm sorry," Trina said now. "I shouldn't have looked for your sister, hoping to bump into her like that."

"*Jah*," Mandy said, gesturing toward the left.

They walked through the store to the checkout as Trina pondered what had just happened. She knew one thing: Unless Arie was a pro at faking it, she was nothing like Trina had expected.

"*Not a terrible person*," Mandy had recently said.

No doubt about that, Trina thought. Yet it was clear that something terrible had happened to the two otherwise kind and caring sisters. The way they'd interacted so woodenly, as if nervous, it was hard to believe they had once been very close.

.... ❀ ....

On the tense ride home, Mandy felt all in and hoped to divert Trina's attention from the chance meeting. But Trina would have none of it, and Mandy felt the onslaught of questions coming. Trina was going to push her nose into things.

"So that was really weird, huh?" Trina said. "Arie seemed so happy to see you."

Mandy shook her head. *I can't do this,* she thought. "You agreed to leave things be."

"You're right," Trina said. "I'm just too nosy for my own good."

They were silent for the remainder of the trip home. Trina pulled into the lane leading to the inn, drove around to the back, parked, and turned off the car, yet neither of them made any move to head inside.

The only sound in the car was a ticking as the engine cooled. The landscape surrounding them was a fresh sea of heavy snow. Was spring really only a few days away?

At last, Trina spoke. "I know I'm overbearing sometimes," she said softly. "I've heard it my entire life, but I'm trying."

Mandy shrugged. "It's okay. I mean . . . we've gotten along well, and I've appreciated your help. But this thing 'tween Arie Mae and me . . . you have to let it go."

A silent pause fell over them again, the wind rustling through the stark black tree branches, bringing more snowflakes with it.

Trina tapped her fingers on the steering wheel. "Look, it's really not my place, okay? I'm sure your sister did something dreadful, but have you considered that maybe she wants to make up?" Trina turned now, her eyes piercing Mandy. "Maybe she's hoping you'll forgive her. That's all I'm saying." She removed the key from the ignition.

Mandy shook her head. "It's too late for that."

"Too late?" Trina looked shocked. "You're a goodhearted person, Mandy—one of the nicest I've ever met. People like you don't hold grudges."

"It's not a grudge."

"Then what?"

Their eyes met again, and neither of them spoke for a prolonged moment.

Finally, Mandy reached to open the door, knowing Trina was right. *It's just not very easy,* she thought.

"Let's get the groceries inside," Mandy said, bracing herself for the wintry blast.

········ ❀ ········

That night, when Mandy slipped into bed, she had some difficulty praying but still managed to thank God for helping her make it through yet another day in Gordonville. She recalled running into Arie earlier, looking quite pregnant now, and remembered the way Trina had stumbled through the awkward situation. Arie had responded so kindly, even glancing over at Mandy from time to time, as if pleased by the unintended meeting.

"Arie seemed so happy to see you," Trina had insisted to Mandy.

Sighing, Mandy reached for the large flashlight and shone the light on her wall calendar, where she had been marking off the days, one by one, and thinking ahead to next November.

One day closer to my goal . . .

Chapter

29

The next morning, after the departing guests had checked out, Trina offered another meager apology while she and Mandy stripped beds together. "Whatever's going on between you and your sister isn't my business. But I gave you my opinion, and you can decide what to do with it."

Mandy had to smile. Even when apologizing, Trina could be rather pushy. "There's more to the story," she said.

"There usually is," Trina replied, but she dropped it right there. And they worked together for the rest of the day in relative calm while Mandy wondered when, or if, she would ever become accustomed to Trina's frank approach.

.... ✿ ....

Weeks passed, and by the time April arrived, the many blossoming trees and bushes gave a sweet aroma to the air.

One mild Sunday afternoon, after they had returned home from the community church, where Trina had also settled in since Gavin's departure, Mandy showed her how to hitch Ol' Tulip up to the family carriage. Gertie, who'd long since recovered from the colic, was content to graze in the nearby meadow while Mandy hauled the guests around on the short jaunt with Trina assisting in Karl Lantz's stead. From what Karl had said a few days ago, he and Yonnie planned to spend the afternoon in Ronks, so Mandy was thankful that Trina was willing to help out, despite the fact a farm animal was involved.

"Next, I'll teach ya how to hold the driving lines and direct the horse," Mandy suggested as she and Trina unhitched Ol' Tulip after the guests had enjoyed their buggy ride.

Trina pulled a face. "Hold your horses!" She laughed as she helped to unhook the holdback straps.

"You need to learn how to do this, *jah*? In case I need help."

Trina grinned.

"I know that grin," Mandy replied with a smile.

"Were you thinking you might need help in case Karl's not around?"

Mandy frowned. "Well, sure . . ."

Still smiling broadly, Trina gave a quick nod. "Uh-huh . . . thought so."

"Now what're you talking about?" Mandy held the shafts steady as the unhitched horse walked out.

"Well, from observing the two of you together in the stable—"

"*Ach*, Trina . . ."

"Hey, he's obviously interested—"

"I doubt that."

"I don't."

"He's *devoutly* Amish."

"And you're not?" Trina asked.

"Well, *you* said I wasn't." Mandy gave her a goading smile.

"I'm not so sure anymore," Trina replied.

"Why?"

"Let's call it a hunch."

Mandy led the mare toward the stable. "Here we go again," she said over her shoulder.

Trina followed her inside and helped to freshen the straw in the stall. "You can't tell me you aren't fond of Karl."

Mandy ignored her. "What 'bout you and Gavin? Are you two fallin' in love?"

"Don't change the subject. Amishwomen are supposed to be meek and mild, remember?"

Mandy laughed. "I'm learnin' from you how to dish it out. So let's talk more about Gavin."

Trina took a breath and slowly let it out. "Okay, so we're being real."

"Honest, *jah*." Mandy nodded, noting Trina's sudden shift.

"I'm not sure what's going on."

"With you or with Gavin?"

"With me, I guess," Trina replied. "Because he wants to see me again soon." Reaching for the grooming brush, Trina sighed loudly. "If God has anyone new for me, it's likely Gavin. I mean, he's the most patient person I've ever met. And he's kind, smart, and sensitive."

"Good-lookin', too," Mandy added. "Don't forget that."

"Oh, I agree that he's handsome. But most important, he's unflinching in his faith. I've really enjoyed some of our long conversations, even though lately they've all been by phone."

"Then, what's the problem?"

Trina paused. "I don't know. Maybe it's just that he's so different from Shawn." She was quiet for a moment, then looked up at Mandy. "Sometimes, I wonder what he sees in me."

Perhaps he's attracted to a strong woman. Mandy thought of the poem, smiling. "I hope you realize how much you have to offer Gavin."

Trina began to groom the horse, starting by loosening the

dirt and hair with the curry comb, not answering for a time. At last, she said, "I don't know. Something's holding me back." She frowned. "It might just be too soon for me."

"Is that really the reason?"

Trina looked shocked. "What do you think it is?"

"*Ach*, I'll give this a try," Mandy said softly, taking her time . . . wanting to get the words right. "I think you're afraid of losing him, Trina. Like you lost Shawn."

Catching her eye, Trina scowled fleetingly but didn't reply. Pressing her lips together, she continued brushing, but she looked like she might explode. Suddenly, she stopped her grooming and gave Mandy a thoughtful look. "What if things don't work out?"

Mandy felt for her. "I still think you should give him a chance."

Frowning now, Trina looked right at Mandy. "Is this what *I* sound like when I'm pestering *you*?"

Mandy tried not to chuckle as she picked up the soft brush and helped Trina groom away the loosened dirt from Ol' Tulip, talking softly to the mare as she did so.

"Part of me does want to give Gavin a chance."

A silence pervaded the stable. Then Trina added, "I wish you could give your family a chance, too, Mandy."

"Trina . . ."

"For starters, why not think about going to worship with your sister and the rest of your family?"

"To Preaching service?" Mandy couldn't begin to consider it.

"Far as I can tell, that's the missing part of the equation between you and the People," Trina insisted. "Besides, you'd get to see all your relatives gathered in one place."

"Trust me, they're not so keen on seein' me."

"I think you might be wrong."

"How would you know?" Mandy asked, frustrated. "You must understand by now that I haven't actually *joined* the Amish church." She went on to mention that her Dawdi and Mammi Dienner had told her that they and the rest of the family had looked on her as disrespectful for abandoning her widowed Mamma. "They were real leery of me." She sighed and recalled how she'd felt when her grandfather gently reprimanded her. "The People think I'm a rebellious soul, in need of saving."

"Well, why not prove them wrong?" Trina said, studying her. "After all this time, wouldn't it be wonderful to get back into their good graces?"

Mandy was taken aback. "That's not an option."

"Why not?"

"It just ain't," Mandy insisted.

"So . . . who's afraid of losing now?"

Mandy considered all the times she'd looked across to the nearby farmhouse, where Arie Mae must be preparing her nursery for the coming baby. To think Mandy would never really know her new little nephew or niece. Heavyhearted, she replied, "What Arie Mae and I had is long gone. And there's no point in discussing this further."

Trina stepped closer. "I'm not asking you to fix things with your sister. Just go back to your former church and see where it might lead."

Mandy shook her head.

"Just one time?" Trina persisted.

Their eyes met, and Mandy couldn't believe she was actually considering the surprising suggestion. Despite the welcome quiet, she wished she could brush off the unsettling conversation. Yet it lingered in her mind for the rest of the day.

Jah, *maybe I'll go once,* she thought, *but just for old time's sake.*

Chapter

30

On certain afternoons, Mandy enjoyed some momentary quiet to read or write letters, having become more accustomed to taking a little time for herself since hiring Trina. Winnie Maier was one of Mandy's favorite people to correspond with, and occasionally she also emailed a note to Eilene Bradley or Karyn Fry, just to keep in touch.

One thing hadn't changed, though. Mandy still found herself glancing out the window, across the cornfield, wondering about her twin, and remembering the years when things were so much better between them. And then she would catch herself and shake off the cobwebs. *Just take it day by day . . . then you can leave and not be surrounded by so many reminders.*

"You're daydreaming again," Trina said the third Monday in April while walking across the yard to help Mandy finish hanging up the towels and washcloths.

Mandy smiled. "I s'pose you're right."

"I'm right a lot," Trina replied, reaching for the clothespin bag and situating it closer to her. The response made Mandy smile.

Weeks earlier, she would have groaned inwardly, but she'd gotten a better handle on who Trina was—the bravado was more about covering up her pain than anything else.

"Even so, ya prob'ly shouldn't boast 'bout it," Mandy joked, waiting for a typical Trina comeback, but there was none.

"Well, just so you know, Gavin and I had a good long talk by phone last night," Trina said. "Can you guess what that means?"

Mandy had wondered when she might find a way to revisit this. "So, did ya agree to see him?"

Trina smiled. "I actually did."

The two of them worked without talking for a time, then Trina eyed her, asking, "Have you thought more about attending your old church?"

"Well, I'd have to find out who's hosting it first," Mandy said, thinking that if Josiah and Arie were having it over there, she definitely would not go. It was hard enough to even consider going.

"What's that have anything to do with it?"

"Each *Gmay* or church district rotates services throughout all the homes in its community," Mandy explained. "So in the space of a year, every family hosts Preaching in its house or barn once."

Trina glanced at the inn. "Did you have Preaching services in this house, or out in the barn?"

"Before Dat passed away, we held church in the house, because the kitchen, breakfast room, and adjoining sitting room were one large room. When Mamma got the idea to open the B and B to bring in some needed income, my brothers added the walls to divide up the space on either side of the existing fireplace."

Trina reached down to get another towel to pin to the line. "And you really haven't seen your other brothers very much since you came back last fall?"

Shaking her head, Mandy said, "Oh, we visit now and then,

but it's ever so uncomfortable, is all. Without you to talk to . . . or the guests, I'd be real lonely."

Trina turned to look over toward the stable. "What about Karl and Yonnie? You interact with them nearly every day."

"As friends," Mandy said, making it clear.

"I guess that's another reason to start going where your people worship."

"Why?"

"That way, Karl can see you're not just playing Amish."

Mandy sighed. She wasn't going to reveal her secret. Because if Trina knew of Mandy's plan to sell her childhood home and leave Gordonville, she might wonder why she was working so hard to help out. No, she would never understand.

.... ❀ ....

Together, Mandy and Trina hitched up Gertie to the carriage the following Sunday, and Mandy headed off to attend the nearby Amish service with a real measure of anxiety while Trina took Mandy's car to the community church down the road.

This is so odd, Mandy thought, wondering why on earth she'd agreed and feeling increasingly nervous the closer she came to Preacher Stoltzfus's farm.

Even though Trina might have thought Mandy's world could be righted by this single act, Mandy caught herself praying all the way and tried to pace the horse so she wouldn't have to hurry later on, so different from driving a car. *If I'm ever going to get more help,* Mandy reasoned, *I do need to be attending.*

But it was a poor excuse to go, and she knew it.

At the preacher's house, she turned into the long driveway marked on the north side by a bank of poplar trees, then handed off the horse and carriage to the hostlers, the six teenage boys responsible for looking after all the horses. One of the deacon's grandsons, dressed in black trousers, vest and coat, and a long-sleeved white shirt, led Gertie to a large watering trough.

Now that she was there, Mandy continued to pray under her breath, preparing for the possibility of encountering her sister again. Gingerly, she made her way over the freshly mown grass, lumpy with age-old tree roots. Silvery brown slivers of honey locust pods, some a foot long, were lying all over the ground. The morning was still fresh and dewy this early. Mandy hadn't arrived for church so near to eight o'clock for the longest time, but she hoped doing so might help her get into an attitude of worship.

Rounding the ivy-strewn white farmhouse, Mandy could see that the women's line was already beginning to form. Observing the older women toward the front, Mandy noticed they kept their heads bowed slightly, not looking around. Some had devoutly folded their hands, and most were dressed in royal blue or black dresses with full black aprons and capes, the younger unmarried women and little girls in white organdy aprons.

Except for the white organdy *Kapp* that she'd sewn for herself just a day ago, Mandy had donned all black, out of respect for the traditional mourning period.

The first Dienner relative she spotted was Jerome's very blond wife, Hannah, whom Mandy had seen a handful of times since her return. Their daughters, Gracie and Marian, however, had sprouted up remarkably since Mandy had last seen them. Mandy found herself blinking twice to make sure the school-age girls were actually Hannah's.

Determined not to draw attention to herself, Mandy slipped into the very back of the line, knowing she would be expected to walk in with the other unbaptized young women.

So far, all's well, she thought, feeling much more tense than she ought to on this lovely Lord's Day. If her mother were still alive, she would want Mandy to show the proper reverence prior to filing in to the temporary house of worship, something Mandy had been taught from her earliest days. So as Mandy inched forward to make space for the latecomers, she lowered her head and kept her eyes trained on the back of the black shoes of the young woman in front of her.

Once both the lines of men and women had filed inside through separate doors, they all sat on hard wooden benches facing each other—the men's side of the *Gmay* facing the women and little children.

Several of the young women with whom Mandy had once attended Singings initially gave her surprised stares from where they sat near her on the back benches. But in just the space of a moment, their expressions changed quickly to acceptance when they understood that Mandy was present to join in worship.

By the time Mandy had sung the familiar second hymn, *Das Loblied*, she realized she was standing behind her nineteen-year-old cousin, towheaded Ella Dienner. She considered how five years had made a marked difference in the appearance of certain of her kin, and hardly any in others, such as Danny's and Joseph's respective wives, tall and slender Rosanna and pretty Ruthie.

The first sermon dealt with daily bearing one's cross with patience and humility, as instructed by the Lord himself. The word *humility* particularly stood out to her, and while she was tempted to ponder others' faults, she knew how much more important it was to attend to her own.

While kneeling at the bench for the silent prayer, Mandy felt convicted in a greater way than when she'd gathered with the People for worship as a teenager. *I haven't really felt close to the Lord in years*, she realized as the old feelings of helplessness fell over her.

When the People rose in unison for the benediction, Mandy pressed her lips firmly together and willed herself not to shed a tear.

Following the Preaching service, Dawdi Reuben, Mammi at his side, encouraged Mandy to stay around for the shared meal. "It'd be chust *wunnerbaar* if you would," Dawdi said, a solemn look on his deeply wrinkled face.

"Are ya sure?" She glanced around and saw that some of the women were already setting the tables that had been church benches but a few minutes ago.

"Everyone's glad to see ya, Amanda dear," Mammi Dienner said as she reached over to clasp Mandy's hand.

"Well, if it won't cause a stir . . ." Mandy agreed.

"*Nee*, the People are willing to forgive," Dawdi Reuben whispered as he leaned near.

Over helping the other men to set up the tables was Karl Lantz, his young son standing in the far corner of the room with another little boy his age. Karl caught Mandy's eye and gave a quick smile and bob of his head, then returned his attention to the remainder of the benches.

"A fine fella, I daresay," Dawdi Reuben remarked, his voice quiet.

He must have caught me looking at Karl, she thought, her face blushing.

"A right *gut* catch, your Mammi here thinks."

Mammi gave a knowing smile, matching what must have been on her mind.

"Dawdi, please . . ." Mandy stepped back from her grandfather, trying to discourage any more such comments.

"Better watch out. Dawdi's one fine matchmaker," Mammi said, looking bright and well rested in her Sunday best. "And Yonnie's such a well-mannered child."

Mandy told her that she'd enjoyed talking with Yonnie on many occasions. "He's fond of my hot cocoa," she said without thinking, which gave Mammi the titters to the point she had to fan her face with a white hankie she pulled from her dress sleeve.

Good thing Trina's not here, Mandy thought as she followed her grandmother across the room to where the older women were waiting for the cold cuts and pie to be served.

About that time, three of Mandy's sisters-in-law, Hannah, Rosanna, and Ruthie, wandered over to greet her. Each of them gave her a brief hug, and Mandy felt sure it was sincere on their part. Still, it was hard to believe when they'd had so little interaction during Mandy's months at the B and B. Would all of that really change simply because she had come to Preaching? Mandy supposed it might, if she continued to attend for the months ahead.

Trina's opened a can of worms, Mandy thought in that moment, but she knew the real test was yet to come.

Mandy avoided making eye contact with her sister when Arie Mae took a seat next to Aunt Martha down the table a ways, and Mandy hoped she could keep it that way.

"Are ya doin' all right at the inn?" Jerome's daughter Gracie asked as she and Mandy were finishing up their snitz pie.

Mandy had always been closest to Jerome's family, and she was relieved to have talkative Hannah and her eight-year-old daughter Gracie sitting on either side of her. "I'm thankful to have some very *gut* help," she said before taking another bite of pie and putting her plastic fork on the table.

"Are ya talking 'bout that lippy *Englischer* woman?" Gracie said.

Mandy sighed, recalling the many opportunities her oldest brother'd had to observe Trina. Obviously, Jerome had shared some of his early thoughts about Trina with his family. Lately, though, he and Trina seemed to get along quite well—especially since she'd discovered his favorite breakfasts, all in a regular rotation for his Monday meetings with Mandy. "Well," Mandy replied, "Trina can cook circles around me."

"And she's following Mammi Saloma's recipes?" Gracie asked, reaching for her water glass.

"So far we haven't served anything outlandishly English." Mandy had to chuckle, thinking of Trina. "And the guests are, well, eating it up."

This must have struck Hannah as funny, because she covered her mouth with her hand, then coughed a little, which seemed to catch Arie's attention, since she suddenly looked their way. But Mandy glanced down at her plate, not up to making a connection with her, not when completely surrounded by the People . . . nearly all of them related to her in one way or another.

Later, when two of Preacher Stoltzfus's nephews helped her hitch up Gertie and get on her way, Mandy thought, *That wasn't so terrible, was it?*

She directed the horse toward the road and then glanced back to see her brothers Joseph and Sammy still in discussion with several other men in the side yard of the preacher's house.

Mandy was surprised at how accepted she'd been made to feel today—as though she belonged with the People.

Chapter

31

Mandy headed home, appreciating the sunshine and the warmer weather as she held the driving lines. She spotted a handful of horses in a nearby meadow, basking in the afternoon sun, and recalled having overheard some of the womenfolk at the table talking about planting green beans and snap peas, as well as cucumbers, all of them itching to get their hands in the soil once again.

It was easy to reminisce about what such a Sunday afternoon buggy ride had been like for her and Arie Mae as little girls sitting in the back of the carriage, their father in the driver's seat. They would occupy themselves by pointing out which farmhouse on the familiar route had the tidiest yard and flower gardens. And, during this time of year, so close to the splendid month of May, they would see which farmers already had the most wood chopped and stacked for the next winter, well before they dug their kitchen vegetable gardens. Mamma, jovial as she had been back when Dat was still alive, would softly chuckle at their observations, especially since both girls usually concluded that their yard and gardens—and their woodpile—were among the nicest around.

Gone are those happy days, Mandy thought as she came up on Karl and Yonnie Lantz walking along the roadside. Slowing the horse, she deliberated whether or not to offer them a ride. *Will it seem forward?*

Even so, she decided, Karl's house was on the way to the B and B from here. *Wouldn't it be impolite not to stop?*

Yonnie turned just then and looked at her. And seeing his little hand go up to wave and his dimpled cheeks lift into a big smile, she directed Ol' Tulip onto the shoulder and halted the horse.

"Would ya like a ride?" she asked.

Before Karl could answer, Yonnie ran to the buggy and hopped into the front seat next to her. "Looks like you found yourself a buddy there," Karl said, going around to the passenger side and getting in, then putting Yonnie promptly on his lap. "A mighty fine day for a walk home from church," he said, making small talk.

"I'll say," Mandy replied. "I wish I could've walked to church myself, but I didn't want to be late."

"It was a *gut* surprise, seein' you there," Karl said as he patted Yonnie's shoulder.

"It's been a while," Mandy said, but when the words came out, they sounded almost unfriendly.

Karl seemed undeterred and asked whether she liked driving the buggy around again.

"I kind of missed it—it's so peaceful, and I don't feel cut off from everything like I do in a car." Even to herself, Mandy had to admit it *was* nice to be able to hear the birdsong, or to smell the scent of spring blossoms carried on the breezes.

Karl seemed pleased, then asked if she needed any help with the kitchen garden.

"Would ya have time this week to till it up for me? If not, I'll ask Jerome."

"I'm sure I'll have time," Karl said. "Anything else I can do for ya, Mandy?"

She had to smile at his ready offer of assistance. It was kind of him to ask, and his thoughtfulness drew her to him all the more. "If something comes up, I'll be sure to let ya know. *Denki*."

They continued talking, and when Karl inquired whether Mandy had been attending church in another Amish district, she managed to divert his question when Yonnie asked something at the same time. But then Karl asked if she would be attending the next Preaching at her family's church, and she confessed she hadn't thought that far ahead. As for next week, she'd simply supposed that she and Trina would likely go to the community church together, since it would be a no-Preaching Sunday.

"Over there's the bishop's *Haus*," Yonnie said, pointing toward the newly painted white farmhouse.

Karl nodded. "I was over there helpin' prep the house a few mornings last week. Took Yonnie along to play with Bishop's youngest grandchildren, visiting from New Holland."

"Bishop's been so kind—the one who let us have electric put in the side of our house where the guests sleep. That was a real help to Mamma, believe me."

"I'm sure she appreciated that."

"Oh, did she ever."

Karl removed Yonnie's straw hat and set it on the boy's knee. "Couldn't see through ya, son," he said, and Yonnie's laugh was so merry, like a song, that Mandy quickly joined in.

"Our house is just up there," Karl said as Yonnie leaned forward.

Mandy felt a little forlorn when she pulled over to let them out at their driveway.

"*Denki*," Karl said with a wave. "Have a restful afternoon."

Yonnie tugged on Karl's sleeve and whispered something in his ear.

"Yonnie *hot dich sehne welle*," Karl said, grinning at her.

"And I want to see *him* again, too," Mandy replied, waving. *And his father*, she mused.

They headed toward their house, where Mandy couldn't help noticing the rows of dazzling yellow tulips in full bloom. With a smile, she signaled to the horse to pull out onto the road, then settled in for the rest of the ride.

Clip-clop-clip. She delighted in the sound of Ol' Tulip's trotting more than at any other time since she'd returned home. Did it have anything to do with the fact that Karl Lantz was so very pleasing to be around? And his son . . . *ach*, what an adorable child! Goodness, how embarrassing it would have been to drive past them in her car today, had she decided to take it to Preaching.

Truly, Mandy was very glad she had decided on the buggy this beautiful day.

.... ❀ ....

That afternoon, Trina received a text from Gavin.

Would you mind checking on the availability at the B and B for next Saturday? he asked.

Sure, I'll let you know.

If there's no room, I'll find a place elsewhere. A smiley emoji followed that.

I'll be in touch, she texted back.

Thanks, Trina.

She went out to the sitting area, away from her room, which still seemed annoyingly stark and dreary at times. While Mandy napped, Trina recalled how friendly the people around her at the community church had been today. One woman had even invited her out to lunch, which Trina found amazing. *A great way to connect with visitors.* She wondered if this was something the young minister had perhaps instigated.

Trina slipped out to the kitchen, took a cookie from the jar, and stood at the back door, staring out at the landscape springing to life before her eyes. Each day, she noticed additional buds bursting forth and more grass greening up.

A breeze rippled through the butterfly meadow. *Am I really ready to see Gavin again?* she wondered.

Chapter
32

As it turned out, there *was* an opening at the B and B for the very day Gavin had requested. So Trina quickly penciled his name into the reservations book and immediately texted him.

She moved through the week quickly, the days varying only in the breakfast menus she prepared for the guests. Tired of the same recipes she had been following from Mandy's mother's notebook, Trina thumbed through another Amish cookbook, looking for something more challenging yet equally delicious. *And something perfect for the season.* The day before Gavin's scheduled arrival, she made a large quiche with fresh asparagus and Amish farm cheese, garnering rave reviews all around.

.... ⚜ ....

Trina made sure she was caught up with all of her work by the time Gavin arrived that Saturday afternoon, wanting time to shower and freshen up before they went out for dinner together that evening.

When Trina left the inn, Mandy encouraged her by whispering, "Give love a chance."

Trina rolled her eyes, but as she walked with Gavin to his car, Mandy's words were ringing in her ears.

Gavin drove north of Lancaster to a lovely restaurant where he had made a reservation only after checking the menu with Trina beforehand, which impressed her. As they were shown to their candlelit table for two, she began to feel more relaxed, thankful for how comfortable she had become with him.

"This is perfect," Gavin said, looking drop-dead amazing in his navy dress pants and tan jacket, his shirt open at the throat.

"Our table . . . the restaurant . . . or something else?" she asked coyly.

"Everything," he said, smiling at her. "You, our surroundings. Just being with you again is fantastic."

"Well, it's nice to see you, too," she replied, accepting the menu from the waiter, who then shared the chef's specials.

"As often as I eat out, I appreciate fine dining and an attentive wait staff," Gavin told her when they were alone again.

"In other words, you appreciate being spoiled." She smiled.

Gavin laughed. "Perhaps you're right."

They talked until the waiter returned for their beverage order, and then the waiter turned to Gavin, who also ordered an appetizer to share.

Might be a long and interesting evening, she thought while perusing the extensive menu and thinking ahead to a salad, entrée, and likely dessert. *And that's fine with me,* she realized. *I've missed this man!*

Over their appetizer of stuffed mushrooms, Gavin asked if she was still enjoying her work at Butterfly Meadows. "I am . . . but I'm going broke," she said, thinking of the mortgage payments on the condo. "But Gail no longer needs me and the work here keeps me busy." *And Mandy would fall apart without me*, she thought. Then, curious, she asked how business was going at his consulting firm.

He mentioned a couple of his recent trips. "It's been more hectic than I would like lately . . . one of the reasons I'm glad to be here tonight with you." He stopped short of saying how pretty she looked, though he seemed to be saying so with his adoring eyes.

Then, surprising her, Gavin said, "What would you say about taking our relationship to the next level?"

Although taken a bit off guard, Trina had to smile at Gavin's businesslike way of introducing such a romantic topic. She narrowed her eyes playfully. "What would that look like?" she asked.

Instead of answering her directly, he asked how long she planned to work for Mandy. She hadn't anticipated that and said she didn't know, although she *had* thought about it recently. "I can't stay there forever."

"Well, I have the impression you aren't in a big rush to return to Rochester," he said. "Might you be willing to move somewhere new . . . like Maryland?" He pinned her with his eyes.

This was a real surprise. Trina looked at him, stunned.

"I'd like to date you properly," he added, taking another mushroom and putting it on his appetizer plate.

Properly? "Long-distance isn't working for you?" she teased.

"That's why I'm here." Gavin's eyes were so sincere, she was sorry she'd joked. In so many words, he was asking her to meet him halfway.

"I'll have to think about it," she said. "Pray too."

Gavin mentioned that he had been spending time talking to the Lord about her ever since he'd left the inn back in December. "If you're open to it, my sister has a guest room you could rent. I hope that's not too presumptuous," he said with a smile. "You'd be very welcome."

She nodded and reached for her glass of ginger ale, wondering how he always seemed so poised.

"Texting and phone calls are fine," he said, "but I'd much rather see you in person."

He looked at her across the table, where the candle flickered and the soft background music made the setting seem like something out of a wonderful love story. Except it was happening to her.

Isn't this what I've longed for? Trina thought, averting her gaze, worried that she could lose Gavin if unwilling to take the risk and accept his offer.

"What are you thinking right now?" he asked as he reached across for her hand.

"To be honest, I'm terrified." She let it tumble out.

All the care he seemed to feel for her radiated from his dear face. "I think you've taken the first step." His head tilted as if to emphasize his remark. "Otherwise you wouldn't be here tonight . . . right?"

Trina felt conflicted, wishing she could immediately get on the same page with him, yet knowing she really did need some time to pray about this. She recalled how much fun they'd had the last time he'd driven down to visit her, last month. And she pondered a recent sermon at the church. "*Sometimes, love means letting go . . . letting God be in control,*" the minister had said. The words had struck a chord in her.

"I do like how I am when I'm with you," she managed to say.

This brought a momentary smile and a twinkle to his eyes.

She continued, "Not so long ago, we fought like cats and dogs."

"Wait a minute—*who* was the fighter?" Gavin chuckled and gently squeezed her hand.

She shrugged and smiled. "Touché."

The waiter appeared and removed the appetizer plates and

brought the dinner salad of fennel and watercress, as well as a basket of dinner rolls.

When they were alone again, they quickly resumed their conversation.

"Seriously, though. Why would you choose someone like me?" Trina asked. "You're so independent and . . . busy. You have the world by the tail."

"Well, it might seem that way."

She considered that, hesitant about spoiling things. "How would it work?"

Gavin shook his head as if puzzled. "Where are you going with this?"

She sighed and finally came out with it. "I mean, it's not like you need me."

He frowned. "But I *want* you, Trina. We're equals."

"But I—"

"I care deeply for you." His expression underscored his appealing words. "Sure, I have a successful firm, but my life isn't complete—I want to share it with someone whose friendship I value . . . someone I admire."

She felt almost silly for questioning him.

"Would it be so bad to be in a relationship based on love and companionship rather than need?" he asked so sympathetically that Trina had to hold back tears.

After a prolonged silence, during which their entrées were served—glazed roast ham for him, and steak Milanese for her—they agreed to talk again tomorrow, following church and lunch. After that, Gavin would head back to Maryland for work on Monday.

.... ❀ ....

That night, when Trina contemplated everything that seemed to be happening between her and Gavin, she felt strangely at peace. *I'm definitely crazy about him,* she thought, surprised to realize she could feel so attached to another man so soon after Shawn.

If it was God's will, she knew she wanted to cast her fear aside for him. *We can have a future. . . .*

The next morning, as they drove to church, she was conscious of a similar tranquil feeling.

After lunch, as Gavin said good-bye to her in the entryway of the inn, Trina suddenly felt overwhelmed by how much she was going to miss him. She opened her mouth to tell him just as Mandy came in the hallway and started to ask her a question, then backed away, sputtering her apology.

"What were you about to say?" Gavin asked, slipping his arm around Trina's waist.

"Just that I'll . . ."

He leaned near and kissed her cheek. "Don't be afraid, Trina. Okay?"

She nodded. "I'll be missing you," she said at last, tears spilling down her cheeks. Then, feeling foolish, she brushed them away.

He pulled her gently near and kissed her. "That's good-bye . . . for now."

And hello, too, she thought, wishing he could stay longer. There was still so much to work through before she could commit to his idea.

She stood in the doorway and watched him walk to his car, and when he turned back unexpectedly to wave, she smiled through her tears. And realized her days in Gordonville were definitely numbered.

I want to move to Maryland, she thought.

But how would she break this to Mandy?

Going to the coat closet, Trina removed her lightweight jacket and put it on, then poked her head into the kitchen to let Mandy know she was going for a walk. "I won't be gone long," she promised.

"All right," Mandy said, not looking up as she sat at the kitchen table writing a letter.

Wanting to avoid questions, Trina chose to leave by the front door. She spotted the familiar farmhouse across the way—its windows gleaming in the sunlight—and she was thankful for the breeze and the sun, and the sound of birds returning from southern climes.

Trina took the shortcut to Arie Mae's house, heading straight through the cornfield. It seemed like the perfect moment to do what she'd been considering for some time. *Perhaps it could actually work,* she thought. And after meeting Mandy's sister, Trina had a hunch that Arie would be all for it.

Chapter

33

E arlier on this particular Sunday afternoon, Mandy had
 taken Jerome up on his recent invitation and walked up
 the road to visit her eldest brother and his family. Her
nieces Gracie and Marian ran out to meet her, chattering in
Deitsch about what they were learning in school. Gracie even
took Mandy's hand.

They're welcoming me back, she thought.

Hannah, too, had been very considerate, also inviting her to
come to church again next Lord's Day. Between that and Karl's
interest in her returning for worship, Mandy didn't know how
to answer. Because, while she was enjoying reconnecting with
her family and her friendship with Karl, she didn't want to let
herself become too intertwined with the People. Not considering
her long-term plans.

She had actually lost track of time when the back door burst
open and Trina reappeared from her walk. Mandy jumped,
startled.

"*Ach,* you're back. Would ya like something to drink?" she
asked, pushing her chair away from the table.

"No thanks, but I do want to talk to you," Trina said. She looked like she'd been crying.

"Are ya all right?" Mandy asked, concerned now. She went to the fridge and poured a glass of lemonade for herself.

"I'm fine," Trina assured her. She sat down in the spot she'd claimed since that first suppertime meal. "Mandy, I've come to realize something."

"*Jah?*"

"I've been standing in your way."

"Of what?"

Pausing, Trina ran her palms along the table, as if searching for the right words. "Of making things right with your sister."

Mandy was stunned. "My sister? What are you talking about?"

"What I'm trying to say is . . . I'm leaving, Mandy. I'm moving to Maryland."

Mandy's thoughts were spinning. "I don't understand. Did I say something?"

"Not at all," Trina protested. "Everything's fine. Everything's *great*, actually. Gavin says he wants to date me 'properly.'"

Though Mandy was happy for Trina, she felt terribly sad. Unbelievable as it seemed, in the space of only a few short months, this difficult young woman had become her friend. And now, just like that, she was leaving? "When are ya goin'?"

"As soon as I can book a flight home," Trina said, her face earnest.

"But this seems so sudden. . . . You've become my right arm!" she protested. "How am I—"

"You'll be fine," Trina interrupted. "I wouldn't think of leaving you without help."

"But that's exactly—"

"Arie Mae wants to talk with you." Trina blurted out the words. "She's coming over in a few minutes, in fact."

"*What?*" Mandy's mouth dropped. "You talked to Arie 'bout this?"

"It's okay," Trina said, motioning with her hands as if to calm a child.

"Aw, Trina, what did ya go and do?" Mandy felt ever so frustrated as she reached under her sleeve for a hankie—one of her mother's, with a perfectly embroidered S. *Arie's coming over?* she fretted. *Now?*

Glancing out the window, Trina said, "It's best if the two of you talk alone."

Mandy followed Trina's gaze, still unable to comprehend the pending changes. "I'd rather hear whatever's up from you," she insisted.

"You don't have to worry, Mandy. I'll let Arie explain . . . then you two can decide. C'mon. It's time for some new beginnings." Trina paused to smile at her. "And if you search your heart, I think you'll agree."

A gentle knock came at the back door. And although Mandy had been expecting Arie Mae, it was still disconcerting. This had been their home for years, and now her sister was *knocking*.

Because of me, thought Mandy guiltily as she opened the door. Arie waited there in a loose-fitting green dress and matching apron, her strawberry blond hair neatly parted down the middle and twisted back on the sides, a black bandanna tied over her hair bun.

The moment seemed surreal, and for the longest time Mandy simply stared at her as Arie's eyes met hers.

Arie's face broke into a contagious smile. "Is this a bad time?"

"*Nee*," Mandy somehow managed to say, surprising herself. "*Kumme* in."

She offered Arie Mae some lemonade, but Arie simply shook her head. "*Denki* but *nee*," she said almost too softly to hear.

Another awkward moment passed as Mandy fumbled about, searching for the right words.

"I s'pose ya know I had an unexpected visitor this afternoon," Arie began, arching her back as she lowered herself slowly into the chair, great with child as she was.

Mandy nodded and took a seat at the head of the table. Just then, all she could think of was confronting Arie Mae five years ago about Josiah—and how Mandy had left within a day for Kansas. "Trina mentioned you were droppin' by, but she didn't go into much detail. None at all, really."

Arie's eyebrows rose. "Oh dear, so this is—"

"Rather unexpected, *jah.*"

Arie hesitated, then said, "Really, I'm all for it," before she even began to share what Trina had proposed. "But only if it meets with your approval."

Here, Mandy frowned, hardly knowing how to respond.

Arie went on, saying, "Trina asked if I'd talk to you 'bout taking her place in the kitchen, at least till the baby comes."

Of course, thought Mandy, *that would be Trina's primary concern, considering my less-than-stellar cooking.*

"I'm not askin' for my old job back," Arie added, "just offering to help out part-time till maybe Betsy Kauffman or another young woman in the community would want to step in." She paused, folding her arms. "Does that sound workable?"

Her sister was being very accommodating, and Mandy couldn't help being curious about it. Did Arie honestly want to do this? And if so, why? Mandy swallowed hard, remembering the difficult days before Trina started working there.

"Mandy, I believe you're still angry at me," Arie said now.

"*Nee* . . . listen," Mandy interrupted, coming to a quick decision. "Based on what's happened between us, I think this arrangement could only work if we agreed not to discuss the past."

Arie seemed to consider this, then gave a slow nod. "All right, then. I'm willing to wait till you're ready to talk 'bout it." She reached up and let her finger slide over her bandanna. "And just so ya know, I won't accept any pay."

This surprised Mandy. "Why wouldn't you want to be compensated?"

Arie leaned her elbows on the table. "Well, honestly, I don't."

"If you insist," Mandy said, still finding this rather peculiar. "So I'll let you know once Trina goes," she said, rising to conclude the conversation. As she watched her sister struggle to get out of the chair, she added, "I appreciate your willingness to help out in a tight spot."

"It'll have to be a day-by-day thing. The baby's due in only six weeks, but surely you'll have someone else lined up real soon," Arie said, smiling sweetly.

Mandy nodded and watched her move slowly toward the back door.

Arie turned just then. "It was *wunnerbaar* seein' you in church again, sister."

Mandy nodded, feeling guilty again. *All the pretending I've been doing.* "Have yourself a nice day" was all she could say now, still baffled as to how things had come to this . . . or why she was allowing it.

Just for a short time, she decided, anticipating a trial ahead.

She happened to glance out the back window after Arie Mae left the house and saw Josiah there waiting to help her into the carriage.

Mandy had to look away. *This is surely a mistake*, she thought, wishing with all of her heart that Trina would stay.

Chapter

34

The very next Wednesday, Trina was scheduled to fly home from Harrisburg. She had stepped outside to ask Mandy a question for one of the guests and found her out hanging up the daily washing.

Suddenly, Trina came to a dead stop, frozen on the stoop, her eyes wide as she took in the colorful sight of dozens of luminous wings in the butterfly meadow. "They're here," she whispered. "Mandy!" she called.

Mandy hurried to her side. "Didn't I tell you they'd come?" she said as she gazed with her at the wide meadow beyond. "And just in time, too."

"I was beginning to think it was just a myth!" Trina exclaimed, shielding her eyes from the sun as she took in the amazing display.

Mandy laughed. "It's been years since I've see them."

Trina could see that the sunny butterfly meadow was abundant with many varieties of wild flowers, most of which had only recently started blooming. A large butterfly-shaped garden bordered the meadow on one side. Along the north side, a row of mature trees provided shelter for fragile wings on windy or rainy days.

"As a child, I loved walking through the meadow. Every springtime was like the first we'd ever seen. Mamma always advised Arie Mae and me to tiptoe around the flowers so as not to disturb the butterflies." Mandy went on to mention a few of her mother's favorites among the plants—the pink- and red-flowered dianthus, the purple-flowered sweet alyssum, but especially the milkweed. "That attracts the monarch butterflies."

"I love that they came the day I'm leaving," Trina said, sitting down on the step to take a few pictures with her phone.

"It's a special farewell," Mandy said, touching Trina's shoulder. "Just think. These butterflies are the descendants of the very first ones my Dawdi William Dienner saw so long ago." She mentioned again the blessing her great-grandfather had so strongly believed in.

"That's a beautiful thought." Trina sat there with Mandy, the two of them looking in the same direction. And in that moment, Trina realized that the botched mystery trip had been anything but a mistake. *God planned for me to end up here,* she thought, a warm sensation coming over her. *He certainly has a unique way of getting my attention!*

"Are you all right?" Mandy asked, looking at her. "Your face is flushed."

"Something just dawned on me."

"Somethin' *gut,* I hope."

Trina smiled and glanced at Mandy. "Something very good."

She never would have believed it, but Trina would miss cooking and cleaning in this old house. Even more, she would miss the peace she had surprisingly found here.

.... ❁ ....

During their last meal together, Mandy and Trina lingered at the table, where Trina had served a surprise dessert of rhubarb

264

cream pie, one of Mamma's favorite recipes. "She only made it on special occasions," Mandy told her.

"Then I think today qualifies," Trina said, forking up another bite and closing her eyes as she seemed to savor the taste.

"It was Arie Mae's favorite, too," Mandy said softly. "We loved when Mamma would make it. We'd take turns slicing pies for Mamma, always serving her first."

"It sounds like you and Arie were really close."

She nodded. "We were."

Trina took a bite of pie. "Mandy . . . what happened?"

Mandy shrugged. "It seems silly to talk 'bout now, after all this time."

Trina put sugar in her coffee, which Mandy had never seen her do. "Try me."

Mandy held her own cup with both hands and took a sip, then measured her words. "It was all because of Josiah, which I'm sure you've figured out. I loved him since the first day he talked to me at recess, and we quickly became best friends. We did everything together long before we were old enough to date. I wasn't much older than thirteen when I told Arie Mae that I was ever so sure I was goin' to marry him."

"Well, so how did she end up with your guy?" Trina asked.

Mandy breathed deeply as she considered that painful day. "Everything changed the Sunday I was too sick to go to Singing. I stayed home to nurse a cold. But then, as the evening wore on, I started to feel better, so I decided to show up to surprise my beau. I wanted to see Josiah's eyes light up . . . the way they always did when he first spotted me somewhere."

Trina's expression was intent.

"I went on foot, and when I entered the barn during the fellowship time of refreshments, I saw Arie and Josiah together talking. At first, I didn't think a thing of it—we were all friends, after all, but then, observing them for another moment, I realized something was off. Arie Mae was acting very different, all flirty and whatnot, poking his elbow, laughing like he was the most amusing guy there. And Josiah seemed to be enjoying it . . . a lot, even leaning forward to whisper in her ear a time or two. It sure didn't seem like they missed me."

"Didn't Arie have a boyfriend, though?"

"She had always acted like she wasn't too keen on havin' a steady beau. Until that moment, that had actually seemed strange to me."

Trina grimaced. "Because maybe she was interested in *yours?*"

Mandy sighed. "I left before they saw me that night, and waited to see if Josiah would drop her off at home later. And when he did . . . after she came inside, I confronted Arie about what I'd seen."

Trina was frowning. "And did Arie admit to it?"

"*Nee.* We had a long, long conversation, and she convinced me that nothin' was going on between them. She insisted that being true to me, as her sister, was more important than any fella could ever be." Mandy paused and then pressed onward. "And she promised to stay away from him. 'Even as a friend,' she said."

"And did she?"

Mandy took in a breath and let it out slowly, terribly embarrassed suddenly. *I can't believe I returned to the past like that,* she thought, apologizing as she got up to clear the table. "I know it has to sound like grade-school stuff—two girls fussin' over the same boy—"

"No," Trina said simply, shaking her head. "Not in the least. But what made you leave home?"

Mandy slung the tea towel over her shoulder and leaned against the sink with a great sigh. She pressed her lips tightly together, still not sure she could utter the words. Glancing out the window at the sky, she turned back to Trina and said quietly, "I found Arie Mae with Josiah another time—two weeks later, after another Singing. I can't even remember why I bothered to walk round the back of the barn . . . maybe I suspected something. And that's where I found her, my dearest sister, with the boy I'd always loved, locked in a close embrace. They were kissing, and not just little pecks." Mandy shook her head at the painful memory. "Worst of all, Josiah had never kissed me the whole year we were court-ing . . . said he wanted us to wait."

Trina tilted her head, her expression sad. "Oh, Mandy . . ."

"*Nee*, I don't want sympathy," she insisted, going on to describe how Arie Mae had opened her eyes and, seeing Mandy there, had pushed Josiah away. "She actually had the nerve to try to explain, upset about being caught, I s'pose. But I didn't give her any leeway. . . . I dashed around the side of the barn and all the way home. I could hear her runnin' after me, calling my name again and again."

Trina was silent as she came over to the sink and stood there, touching Mandy's shoulder.

"By the next afternoon, I was gone," Mandy told her. "I mean, I could hardly breathe in this house, round Arie Mae. And then Mamma, of all people, said it was none of my business who Josiah wanted to date . . . made it clear I *should* leave for a while. Weeks and months passed, and pretty soon it was two years already. When Mamma wrote to say that Josiah and my sister were engaged, I realized it was better to stay put in Kansas, where I'd made a new life for myself. And . . . before I knew it, five years had come and gone."

The kitchen seemed more expansive as the silence settled in. And then Trina asked, "You're still mad at Arie, aren't you?"

"Not really."

Trina frowned, her brow furrowed. "Are you sure? Or are you saying you've forgiven her?"

"I'm sayin' that what she and I had is broken, Trina."

"But that's not what I'm asking you."

"We can't fix what happened," Mandy insisted. "It's impossible, whether I forgive her or not. Don't ya see? We can never go back."

"True, but you can move forward, right?"

Mandy pondered this, exhausted with all she'd revealed. "And now Arie Mae will be here tomorrow mornin' to cook breakfast for the guests . . . in your stead."

Trina said nothing more as Mandy turned to run the water for the dishes.

Chapter

35

Mandy had left her windows open all night while she slept, and waking up, she yawned and stretched to the lovely scent of rain. Worrying about having confided so much in Trina, she hoped she'd done the right thing. Trina had been surprised, that was certain. And before leaving, Trina had wrapped her arms around Mandy, showing amazing care. And she had tactfully urged Mandy again to consider that maybe it was time to forgive, since Arie and Josiah were married, after all. *"Remember, this wound isn't beyond the scope of God's grace."*

Then Mandy had said a reluctant good-bye, and she and Trina parted ways.

Looking back on Trina's time there, Mandy couldn't help but have warm feelings. She was curious how the flight to Rochester had been, having never flown on an airplane, nor having any desire to do so. Mandy also wondered how it felt for Trina to be home again. *Gone so long.* Mandy remembered how strange it had been for *her* to return to Gordonville last fall.

Then, recalling that this was the morning Arie Mae was coming to cook breakfast for the guests, Mandy got moving quickly, rising to close the windows, the damp morning chill pouring into the room.

········ ❁ ········

Instead of waiting for Arie Mae to knock, Mandy made sure the door was standing open to greet her as Arie walked up the stoop and into the kitchen.

"It's another beautiful spring mornin'," Arie said, a bright smile on her face after Mandy's hullo.

Mandy agreed and remembered that her sister had always been a morning person, seemingly cheerful no matter the weather or the circumstance. *Mamma said Arie Mae was born happy,* Mandy recalled unexpectedly, and she wondered how her sister could seem so pleased to be working at the inn under Mandy's nose.

While preparing to cook, Arie opened the tall cupboard door and started to giggle. "Remember how Dat would measure our height on the back of this door when we were really little?"

Mandy hadn't forgotten. Marveling at how comfortable Arie Mae truly appeared, Mandy answered, "*Jah,* and Mamma told him never to restain over it, ain't so?"

Arie nodded. "Look—when we started first grade, we were the exact same height." She pointed to the pencil marking and the date on the back of the door. "After that, he measured us every six months."

"You'd be a hair taller, then I would be . . . back and forth." Mandy smiled.

"We should measure each other now, just for fun, even though we prob'ly haven't grown any since the last time." Arie gestured toward the cupboard. "Do you wanna be first?"

"Like when we were kids?" Mandy asked. Arie had often insisted Mandy go first, since she was older by ten minutes.

"Why not?"

So Mandy stood very still, her shoes off and feet flat on the floor as their father had always said to do, while Arie marked her height on the back of the door.

Next, Mandy marked Arie's. This close, she could smell her sister's light perfume, the same she'd worn since she was old enough in Mamma's eyes.

"Be sure to write the date," Arie said, stepping away, "like Dat always did."

Mandy complied, aware of Arie's gaze on her, and wondered if they really could simply pretend nothing had ever happened. Even though their heights hadn't changed, everything else surely had.

But as the early minutes wore on, Mandy felt more at ease, their conversation flitting easily from one safe topic to another as they waited for the guests to stir upstairs.

And, despite a few initially awkward moments, Mandy wondered if this could possibly be a new beginning for them, just as Trina had suggested.

.... ✿ ....

The guests seemed to enjoy having two Amishwomen serve them breakfast. Arie Mae even offered to play "Amazing Grace" on her harmonica, which was a big hit. Mandy, too, enjoyed hearing the lyrical melody after so many years. And when one of the women asked if Arie would play an encore for her birthday, Arie obliged.

"Josiah says I'll be playin' lullabies to our baby soon," Arie Mae said later as she helped Mandy to redd up the breakfast room and kitchen.

"'Jesus Loves the Little Children' is a sweet one," Mandy added softly. "Mamma sang it to us and to Jerome and Hannah's little ones, too. Remember?"

"*Jah*, her first grandchildren." Arie sighed. "Makes me sad sometimes to think my children will never know Mamma or Dat."

By the time Arie was to head home to cook the noon meal for her husband, Mandy was feeling more comfortable with the arrangement. She wasn't prepared, however, when Arie paused with her hand on the doorknob, a look of tenderness in her eyes. "Mandy, I realize I mentioned Josiah earlier, and I hadn't planned to—"

"It's all right," Mandy said quickly. "Really." *Josiah's your husband . . . end of story.*

Arie Mae smiled and then looked a bit uneasy. "It felt real *gut* to be back here workin' with ya, sister."

Mandy nodded and returned the smile. *It's all rather unbelievable,* she thought as she watched Arie walk home. They were almost back on sure footing, but Mandy knew God expected more from her.

········ ✿ ········

The next day went surprisingly well again, with Arie Mae working best as she could, considering how cumbersome she must feel. Mamma had quietly mentioned once that she and all of her sisters had worked right up until they had their babies, so Mandy didn't worry that Arie was overdoing it, although she limited most of her work to cooking.

Earlier that morning, when Arie had first arrived, she'd shown Mandy the piecework for a cradle quilt she was making. Mandy had oohed and aahed over it, oddly happy to be included, and when Arie asked her about the color scheme, she agreed that the soft greens and yellow worked well for a boy or a girl.

"Would ya mind if I stayed for the noon meal?" Arie surprised Mandy by asking. "Since . . . uh . . . Josiah's gone to an all-day farm auction over in Terre Hill."

"All right," Mandy agreed, recalling the countless mud sales and consignment auctions they'd attended as a family.

Arie Mae was being so dear, and they were getting along as they always had before the blowup over Josiah. *Perhaps this arrangement really will work,* Mandy thought as she went about the day.

.... ❀ ....

When the next Preaching Sunday rolled around, Mandy found herself thinking of Trina, of all people, missing her help especially when hitching up the horse and buggy by herself. She was curious how long it might be before she heard from her, yet there had been no commitment about keeping in touch. Still, Mandy was curious if Trina and Gavin would marry someday, excited that Gavin had suggested the move to Maryland.

Sometimes, Mandy still contemplated how Trina had landed here instead of where she'd hoped the travel company would send her. *I'm thankful she came,* Mandy thought, not forgetting how taxing their relationship had been at first. She remembered how Trina had told her later that the limo driver had declared Trina must be there for a reason.

Just then, Ol' Tulip reared her head, rattling the tack and traces, and Mandy snapped to it, leaving her musing behind. "You're ready to get goin', aren't ya, girl?" she said, stroking Ol' Tulip's thick mane.

.... ❀ ....

While waiting for the common meal after church, Mandy stood outdoors with Arie Mae, who looked rather uncomfortable today, bless her heart, in a flowing blue dress, black apron over her middle. "I've noticed you're still wearin' black," Arie said, stepping closer. "For Mamma?"

Mandy nodded. "It's been longer than six months, true."

"Well, how long you wear it is up to you." Arie glanced toward some of their girl cousins, standing all in a bunch, most either engaged or about to be, according to the grapevine. "Have ya thought of goin' to Sunday Singings again, maybe?" Arie asked, offering a smile.

"Honestly, not sure I have the time. I try to catch up on my Bible reading and, well, rest come Sundays." *She thinks I should be dating. . . .*

"I can imagine, what with all the cleaning and grocery shopping and all." Arie eyed Betsy Kauffman, who was talking with Cousin Kate Dienner. "You might approach Betsy and Kate 'bout working at the inn. I don't know if Betsy has another job or if Kate's interested, but I can find out."

Mandy smiled. "*Denki* for thinkin' ahead. It means a lot." She did mention that Cousin Kate hadn't been too keen on even talking to Mandy when she first returned. "Maybe seein' me here at Preaching with you might help."

Arie reached for Mandy's hand and squeezed it. "It's so *gut* to have ya back, sister."

Mandy was pleased by Arie's open affection.

Later, when Mandy was ready to head home, her teenage cousins Jonathan and Davey seemed especially friendly and eager to help her hitch up Ol' Tulip. Mandy thanked them as she got into the carriage.

A half mile or so down the road, Karl Lantz passed her in his gray family buggy, and Yonnie waved at her. She smiled and waved back in return, and farther up, where the road widened, Karl pulled over and gestured out his window for her to stop.

"Mind if we drop by later with homemade ice cream?" Karl asked once their buggies were side by side.

"It's chocolate chip," Yonnie said, eyes sparkling.

She might easily have said she had other plans or politely

refused, but Yonnie's eyes were so hopeful that she didn't have the heart to disappoint him.

So she agreed they could come by in an hour or so, which meant Mandy would have little time to herself that afternoon. Yet, truth be told, Mandy couldn't have been more delighted.

Chapter 36

Mandy was rather surprised how, after the first couple of weeks, she and Arie had fallen into their former roles, Mandy continuing with her regular domestic chores, and Arie as head cook in charge of the kitchen—at least until Cousin Kate was to start when the baby was born. Betsy had also agreed to return, rather happily, too, and was already assisting Mandy in redding up after guests, as well as keeping up with all the mowing and her beloved hens. Betsy had even exclaimed how much she'd missed caring for the chickens, which had made Arie laugh a little. "*I mean it*," Betsy had replied, and Mandy couldn't help noticing that Arie was trying not to burst out laughing all the harder.

It was Arie who suggested offering suppertime meals to the B and B guests. "For an extra charge, of course. It used to be a real draw, much like the carriage rides are now," Arie mentioned to Mandy as they were at market together one Saturday afternoon in early June, tending the table where Arie's embroidered items and colorful needlepoint wall hangings were displayed. "It's up to you, Mandy."

Since Betsy had started working again, Mandy had a less hectic schedule, and had come along to keep Arie company, not wanting her to be alone as the mid-June due date neared. "Do ya honestly want to cook for these suppers?" Mandy asked, wondering why Arie would want to take this on.

"We used to do three a week—I think I can handle that as long as you help with the cold food items. How does that sound?" Arie asked, going around to straighten the pillowcases, making sure they were in sets.

"What, like Mamma's canned chow chow?"

This brought a laugh from both sisters. "Since you put it that way, it might be *safer*," Arie teased. "You could slice the pickles, too . . . things like that." She came around and took a seat next to Mandy behind the table.

"You really don't think I can cook much, do ya?" Mandy said, conscious of the sticky buns and other donuts in the next booth over, as well as an adjacent display of German sausages. The glorious aromas were making her hungry.

"Did I say that?" Again, Arie had to cover her mouth to suppress her laughter.

They teased each other back and forth until Arie remarked how Karl Lantz seemed to be coming around more frequently than before. "And why might that be?" Arie asked, giving Mandy a knowing grin.

Mandy played coy. "Well, his little boy is fond of me."

Arie nodded. "His son, *jah*."

Mandy glanced at Arie, uneasy about any conversation involving Karl or any man, for that matter. It still felt too raw, too close to what had damaged their relationship in the past. They had managed to move forward, though, and how they were getting along felt good most days. But there were other times when Mandy wondered if they had merely covered over a festering wound, hoping it would just go away.

Arie continued, "Jerome said that he and Karl were chewin' the fat at one of the farm sales here recently. Come to find out, Karl is related to my husband."

Mandy mentioned she'd heard from Betsy, back last November, that Karl had relatives here. "She wasn't sure which branch of Lantzes he was related to, though."

"He's Josiah's second cousin."

"Well, how 'bout that," Mandy said, still wondering why Arie had her mind on Karl.

"Jerome says Karl's an honest man . . . and as conscientious as Dat was." Arie waved at one of her regular customers, who waved in return while strolling past the market table with her children.

"I believe he is, too" was all Mandy said. The direction of their conversation amused her. *And to think that Karl and Josiah are related, and not too distantly either!*

.... ✿ ....

As market closing time neared, Hannah and her girls, Gracie and Marian, came over to Arie's table to visit. "What're *you* sellin' today, *Aendi* Mandy?" asked Gracie, her hands tucked behind the back of her rosy pink dress.

"Oh, I'm just keepin' Arie Mae company."

But Gracie was apparently intent on an answer. "I wondered what sort of handiwork you like to do best."

Arie spoke up. "Mandy likes to darn socks. Ain't so, sister?" She turned to look at her, giving a wink.

"Well," Mandy said, "there was a time when I helped your Mammi Dienner darn your father's socks—well before you were born."

"And before I even met your Dat," Hannah told Gracie, who looked surprised that Mandy was that old.

"Honestly?" Gracie said, mouth open.

"Ain't exactly what you'd call handiwork, though," Mandy said, poking Arie for fun.

"*Nee*," Hannah said, "but it's a necessity, and from what Dat says, your Aendi Mandy was the best sock darner around."

"You ain't pullin' my leg, Mamma?" Gracie asked, the corners of her mouth turning up.

"Oh, she wouldn't think of it," Mandy said seriously. "And if you'd like to learn how, just come over after your chores are done. I'll show ya."

Hannah was nodding her head. "I think she'd like that, wouldn't ya, sweetie?"

"Am I old enough?" Gracie asked, eyes sparkling. "*Gut* enough with a needle?"

Arie spoke up again. "Mandy was your age when our mother taught her to mend."

"Did you mend with her?" asked Gracie as she stepped forward to look at the wall hangings.

"Rarely," Mandy said, laughing. "Arie was busy cookin', another necessity."

They stood there talking awhile longer, and then young Marian picked up a set of pillowcases and asked her mother if she could learn to embroider like that.

Hannah smiled and touched Marian's little head. "When Gracie's over at Aendi Mandy's darning socks, you can go to Aendi Arie's to learn to embroider."

"And cook!" Mandy added, which brought a big smile to her younger niece's shining face.

"They're such cuties," Mandy said as they waved good-bye to head down the aisle toward the fudge display.

"*Jah*," Arie said, watching them go. "Reminds me of us at that age."

Mandy remembered going to market with Mamma numerous times and having strangers stop them to ask if they were twins.

"Do you remember getting lost at Root's Country Market?" Arie asked.

"You thought I planned it so we could go around and get samples of food and goodies," Mandy said, remembering it plain as day.

"Well, didn't ya?" Arie was laughing again, having herself a good time in the midst of showing her wares.

"I might have, but I felt awful nervous in that big crowd, not knowin' how to get back to Mamma."

"I was more frightened than you, I think," Arie claimed, taking a sip from the water bottle she had tucked under the market table. "You were always the adventuresome one, remember? The tree climber . . . the *daring* one."

Mandy shook her head and pulled up a chair next to her. "There was never any danger at Root's, though."

"Say what you will: We were plumb lost, and it took hours for us to find Mamma, or for her to find us."

"Hours?" Mandy was shocked that her sister believed this. "It was a few minutes, if that."

"Well, I remember it differently," Arie said gently.

Mandy let it go. There was no need to have the last word over something that took place so long ago.

.... ❀ ....

As they traveled home later in Arie's buggy, Mandy could sense her sister was weary, the driving lines slack in her slender hands. Still, Arie seemed fairly talkative as she reminisced about her last visit to market with Mamma.

"How was Mamma's health before she died?" Mandy asked now. "Jerome said she kept going, not wanting to slow down much, even though she wasn't well. Wouldn't see a medical doctor."

"Oh, Mamma kept busy enough, but we all noticed she tired easily. Even so, caring for the guests was her lifeblood."

Mandy contemplated that. "So do you ever think about Dat's brother's visit after Dat passed away?"

Arie hesitated. "Sometimes. I still remember how surprised I was, and him bringin' his little sons, too. Seemed ever so odd, so soon after the funeral."

Mandy nodded, tempted to ask, *Do you still think we made a mistake?*

"*Onkel* Albert," Arie said softly.

Only a few months after Dat's death, Onkel Albert Dienner had arrived with his youngest sons to help Mamma get the inn up and going, taking it upon himself to visit for an extended time. And without any warning that he was coming, no less.

Even though she was only thirteen years old, Mandy had felt uneasy about it from the moment he and his boys arrived, given that his wife had died in childbirth not more than eight months prior. And while her brothers didn't seem to have a problem with him and their boy cousins staying in the upstairs bedrooms, it was Mandy who had panicked one afternoon when she happened upon Uncle Albert helping Mamma hitch up Ol' Tulip. From everything Mandy observed, the man was out of line, getting too close to Mamma, who was still very much grieving Dat.

So Mandy had dug in her heels and insisted that Uncle Albert must have ulterior motives for wanting to help establish the inn, and she'd told Arie Mae so in the privacy of their room. "*Just ain't right,*" she'd said. "*Somebody's gotta stick up for Mamma.*"

"*Who are we to say we know what's best for her?*" Arie had protested.

"*We're her daughters,*" Mandy had replied indignantly. "*If anyone knows what's best for Mamma, it's us.*"

That had calmed Arie down some, and after Arie, too, had

witnessed something similar in the kitchen one morning, when no one was around but their uncle and Mamma, she and Mandy had told Jerome of their concerns. Thankfully, their big brother believed them and had intervened, for which both Mandy and Arie were grateful—and relieved.

The very next day, Uncle Albert and his boys had packed up their things and were on their way. Much later, Mamma had shared with Mandy and Arie that Albert had gone so far as to declare his affection for her in those few weeks, which made things awfully awkward for Mamma, who hadn't suspected anything of the kind.

Yet with the passage of time and the girls' maturity, Mandy and Arie Mae had sometimes second-guessed their actions, especially when Mamma seemed lonely.

She might have found some added happiness with our uncle, Mandy thought presently as she and Arie rode home together.

"I think we were prob'ly a bit selfish," Arie Mae commented now as she made the turn up the long lane to their childhood home. "We wanted Mamma to ourselves, and we were bein' loyal to Dat."

Mandy nodded, surprised that Arie would admit it. *We didn't see how anyone could replace him.*

Those memories flooded her mind as they came to a halt behind the familiar farmhouse. *Yet as sisters, we always stuck together . . . at least back then.*

Before getting out of the carriage, Mandy invited Arie in for some meadow tea, but Arie was ready to return home. As Arie drove away, Mandy wondered if she'd ever feel comfortable asking Arie the question that nagged at her the most, at least regarding Mamma. One that had nothing to do with Onkel Albert.

Why did Mamma leave the inn to me? Mandy thought for the hundredth time. After all, her twin sister had stood by Mamma's side, working every day with her . . . the loyal daughter. *How come Arie doesn't seem hurt . . . or miffed?*

········ ✿ ········

Trina was surprised at how well settled she already felt with Gavin's sister, Melanie, after moving from Rochester, where she had packed up her things and put her condo on the market. Melanie's brick row house in the Otterbein neighborhood of Baltimore was small compared with the Butterfly Meadows Amish Bed-and-Breakfast, and located on a rather busy street, which made Trina appreciate the tranquility of Amish farmland all the more. *How swiftly one's perspective can change!* she mused.

She had immediately applied for recertification as a home health aide in Maryland, and in the meantime, she enjoyed evenings out with Gavin, who'd cut back some on his travels to spend time with her. The nights she stayed in, she relaxed in the beautifully restored living room while Melanie played the piano—everything from ragtime to Mozart to classically arranged hymns.

One such evening, Trina was reading a few of Gavin's most recent writings—and finding she was developing a taste for his style of free verse—when her phone rang. It was Gavin, asking her out on a special date the following weekend, since he had some travel pressing this week and would miss seeing her. "Very uptown," he said, a lilt in his voice.

"Okay, I'll wear a dress and heels," she said, wondering what was up. While they hadn't been dating long, she and Gavin had already gone for a premarital counseling session, although she didn't expect this "special date" to be the night Gavin would propose. Not yet. But the thought struck Trina that she might *eventually* be proposed to—and for the second time in her life.

Chapter

37

The following Tuesday evening, the breakfast room was resplendent with candlelight—several block candles marched across the mantel, and tapers graced the middle of the nicely laid table. All of the guests had enthusiastically signed up for the Amish meal, and Mandy and Arie were pleased to serve a three-bean salad to start, then the main course of creamed chipped beef over mashed potatoes, green beans with ham, and homemade potato rolls with melted butter. For dessert, Arie offered both steamed banana pudding and a delicious lemon cheesecake.

"You obviously have your mother's flair for cooking," one of the male guests said. "If you offered these dinners every night, you could retire early," he added as he indulged in Mandy's offer of seconds on dessert.

Arie Mae smiled and accepted the compliments with her usual grace.

Another guest asked for them to say the Lord's Prayer in German, which they both did. Mamma had never denied such a request, saying it was a precious way to honor their heritage of faith.

When the meal was over, Mandy and Arie worked in tandem to redd up. Then, tuckered out, they sat together in the kitchen to each have a small piece of cheesecake. "Was it worth all the extra work?" Mandy asked, concerned for her sister, who was rubbing the small of her back.

Arie nodded. "It's a *gut* way to spread word 'bout the inn, *jah?*"

"True. And *gut* money, too," Mandy said absently, thinking that the next owner would appreciate all that had gone into building positive word of mouth. She wondered when she should inform Arie of her plans to sell and leave the area, dreading the conversation.

"The extra money will come in handy for repairs and whatnot," Arie replied and mentioned that Josiah had recently said the stable roof needed to be replaced, as it had weathered one too many hailstorms. "None of them were bad enough to warrant replacing the whole roof, so he just kept patchin' it."

"I'll do what has to be done," Mandy agreed. "But I still say you oughta be paid for your work here," she added.

"I told Jerome what I'm doin', and he didn't seem to mind. And I've been thinkin' that I'll need to take some time off after the baby is born," Arie said, sipping some water. "When I'm ready, I'll bring him or her with me in a Pack 'n Play, or maybe get the old cradle down from the attic here."

Mandy was surprised, since they'd agreed that Arie would work only up to the delivery.

"Well, let's see how ya feel—take it a day at a time, maybe?" Mandy also knew that Cousin Kate could step in to cook breakfast, and possibly two to three dinners a week, if they decided to continue that. "I'm concerned that you're workin' too hard."

"*Puh!* I feel great," Arie said, laughing. "I really do, but it's awful nice of you to fret over me."

"Mamma would've, that's for sure."

"Jah, our dear mother hen," Arie said, smiling sweetly as she glanced at the wall hanging with the Scripture verse. "I miss her every day."

Mandy nodded, thinking the very same.

When they'd finished eating their dessert, Mandy insisted Arie take the leftovers home to Josiah, then offered to drive Arie home, since it was dusk.

"Oh, would ya mind?" Arie said, and there was that beautiful smile again.

"I'll bring the car round the back."

Arie waved her hand. "You're pampering me unnecessarily."

"I'll be the judge of that," Mandy said. "Mamma's not here to look after you, remember. So, here, let me take the leftovers so your hands are free." *Arie and I act like when we were youngsters, getting along wonderfully,* she mused. She breathed in the fragrant twilight as she headed out to the parking area, glad to have this chance to perhaps drive the back roads, once Arie was safely home. She had some thinking to do, and it wasn't always easy when there was so much going on at the inn, booked solid now every single night.

Arie was waiting for Mandy in the backyard, her arms folded across her ever-expanding middle. "This is so kind of you, sister," she said, getting into the front seat.

"You'd do it for me, *jah?*" Mandy said, then added with a smile, "Just not with a car."

Laughing softly at first, Arie was quiet once she was buckled in. She leaned forward and touched the dashboard. "Makes me wonder, sometimes, how long you'll keep it."

"This car?"

Arie nodded.

"It's not becoming of me, I know." Mandy had wondered when

this might come up with Arie, considering Jerome had already expressed his disapproval a number of times.

"Preacher Stoltzfus was askin' about it . . . guess he wonders if you're thinking of taking baptismal classes this summer, now that you're home again."

Mandy didn't want to admit that she had no plans to, because that might lead to an undesirable discussion. "Like you, once your baby comes . . . I'm takin' things one day at a time," she said, glad to have thought of something that might keep the peace.

She pulled up close to the back walkway at Arie's house and let her out there. "Don't forget the leftovers," Mandy reminded her, even saying she could carry the containers for her, though Arie wouldn't hear of it.

"*Denki* again."

"*Denki* to *you*," Mandy replied, then waited till Arie was in the house before backing out of the lane and turning north onto Old Leacock Road. Her mind wandered as she thought ahead to November. *My return to modern life,* she thought, her feelings more mixed than she would have anticipated.

During some leisure moments on recent Sundays, Mandy had found time to research towns around Maryland and Pennsylvania as options for places to live and possibly open a florist shop. She'd taken particular interest in smaller communities like Hagerstown, Maryland, though she recalled that the Frys hadn't felt they could do well with the big-city competition encroaching upon them. Mandy had kept that in mind. Truth was, she thought she might actually prefer to run a B and B somewhere. After all, a large portion from the sale of Butterfly Meadows would have to go toward the purchase of a place to live, as well as start-up costs. Perhaps she should just look for another small inn. . . .

Then why not just stay? She sighed. *Am I that ferhoodled?*

Pushing it out of her mind, she meandered along until she decided to pull over and give Trina Sutton a quick call. She parked in front of Leacock Shoe Store and dialed.

When she heard Trina's voice, Mandy said, "Hullo, it's Mandy Dienner."

"Mandy *Dienner*! As opposed to all the other Mandys I know?"

Mandy laughed. *Sounds just like her.*

"It's about time you called me! I was beginning to feel like chopped liver."

Again, Mandy had to chuckle. "I've been thinking 'bout you. Are you glad ya moved to Maryland?"

"Well, Gavin and I were engaged last weekend, and we're talking about an autumn wedding."

"Engaged! *Ach,* I'm so happy for ya."

"Who'da thunk it?" Trina asked. "But the real question is . . . how are you?"

She filled her in on Arie's return and how they were getting along again. "And Betsy Kauffman, who worked here before, is helping out, too."

"So, how are you and your sister really getting on?" Trina asked.

Wonderfully, Mandy thought, feeling a strange stab in her stomach. "We're fine," she said.

"Fine?"

"*Jah,*" Mandy said simply, feeling a little deceitful.

Trina went silent for a moment, and Mandy braced herself for one of her friend's direct comments.

"I worried how you'd manage with just you and Arie, since she's pregnant."

"Well, let me tell you . . ." Mandy mentioned what a fast and hard worker her sister was, adding that they were even offering special evening meals now.

"You'll soon be rolling in it." Trina was laughing.

Mandy had to laugh, too, at her friend's candor.

They exchanged a few more remarks about the inn, then Mandy asked, "Are you workin' yet?"

Trina paused. "Waiting for my recertification presently, but I help Gavin's sister around the house when she's at work—cooking, you know. And I've been enjoying Gavin's church, making new friends there."

Mandy was thrilled to hear it. "Well, I hope you'll come an' visit soon."

"That would be so much fun. But first, I need to make some money!" Trina laughed once more; then they said good-bye.

Mandy sat there, marveling at the difference in the young woman who'd first shown up at her door that wintry evening last November.

Trina's question lingered in her mind: *"How are you and your sister really getting on?"*

Mandy sighed and thought of Arie Mae. It was as if they'd painted over the wall without patching up the holes first.

.... ❀ ....

On the drive back to Butterfly Meadows, Mandy noticed several buggies parked at Arie's, and all the windows were aglow with gaslight, too. A car drove up, and a woman hurried into the house. *The local midwife?* she wondered, not sure who else it could be at this hour. *Is the baby coming early?*

Not wanting to be in the way, Mandy didn't stop. Yet she was curious and found herself praying for a safe delivery for Arie's new son or daughter.

Before getting ready for bed and then again before putting out her lamp, Mandy checked to see if the house lights were still on over at Josiah and Arie's, feeling increasingly tense, wondering if something was amiss. *Surely not,* she thought. *Arie's strong*

*and healthy and has a good midwife. She wanted to work right up
till her delivery.*

Nevertheless, Mandy decided to stay dressed and rest on top
of the bed with a lightweight quilt over her, praying that all
would be well.

········ ❀ ········

Suddenly, in the stillness of the darkened room, Mandy awakened. She felt a sense of urgency and wondered if the Lord had
nudged her awake. Reaching for the flashlight, she shone it on
the windup alarm clock. *Two-thirty.*

Raising a window shade, she saw that Arie's house was still
alight, and she hurried down the hall to the coat closet for a
sweater and a bandanna, whispering prayers as she moved about.
"Give Arie a safe delivery . . . and a healthy baby," she prayed,
heading out the back way.

The moon was only half full, so she carried her flashlight
and took the slightly longer way since the cornfield was muddy
from recent rain. Down the sloping driveway and out to the
road, Mandy made her way, accompanied by the never-ending
chirping of crickets.

The air was filled with the scent of freshly cut hay, and a
breeze rustled in the canopies of the trees, but not a single car or
carriage passed by as she rushed toward the farmhouse, praying
with all of her heart for Arie Mae.

And then she saw Josiah running toward her. "Come quick!
Arie Mae's been askin' for ya!"

Chapter
38

I s she all right?" Mandy asked, hurrying to keep up with Josiah's long strides.

"I pray so," he said. And together, they dashed up the lane, neither saying another word.

The back door was ajar as they stepped up onto the porch. Josiah let Mandy pass through first, his hair disheveled, his pale blue shirt rumpled.

Josiah's father and Hank and Willie—two of Josiah's older brothers—were sitting in the kitchen talking in low tones at the table. Pausing there, where they were obviously awaiting word of the birth, Mandy felt out of place. Josiah's father looked worried, his perpetual frown deep and hard. Mandy's stomach churned. Most likely Josiah's mother and sisters-in-law were already with Arie Mae.

Mandy followed Josiah up the stairs, pleading silently, *Please keep my sister and the baby safe, O Lord.*

In the hallway, Josiah's two sisters-in-law were sitting in folding chairs, apparently praying, their heads bowed. And in the bedroom, Lois Ackerman, the Mennonite midwife, was in a chair on the far side of the bed. Clad in a dark blue jumper and white blouse, she rose just then to blot Arie's forehead with a cold washcloth. Josiah's mother sat near, her hands folded and her expression concerned.

Josiah moved a chair closer to the bed. "Go ahead and take a seat near Arie Mae," he whispered, and Mandy did so as Josiah went to stand beside the window, his back to the room.

The room felt stuffy and closed up, and she wished Josiah or Lois might open a window, but it was not her request to make.

Arie Mae's head turned slightly toward the midwife. "Where's Mandy Sue?" she murmured. "Is she comin'?"

"I'm here," Mandy said, quickly reaching for her sister's hand. "Right beside you."

Arie gazed at Mandy without making a sound, almost as though in a daze—until the next hard contraction came.

Hearing the intense moans, Mandy's heart went out to her sister.

"It's too soon to push," Lois said, standing over Arie now, leaning near. "Work with me the way we discussed, dear."

When the contraction ceased and a calm came over the room once again, Mandy wrapped both her hands around Arie's and felt how cold and clammy they were. "You've been in my prayers tonight," Mandy said softly.

"Just routine, the midwife says. . . . *Puh*, could've fooled me!" Arie said.

"You'll be fine," Mandy said. "I just know it."

Arie nodded weakly.

Lois removed the washcloth from Arie's brow and went to the dresser, where she poured more water from the blue-and-white-speckled pitcher into a large matching bowl. Returning, she once more placed the cool cloth on Arie's forehead.

Sighing loudly, Arie whispered, "Mandy Sue, if somethin' should happen and I don't make it . . ."

"Please, ya mustn't talk like that." Mandy kissed the back of her hand. "Remember what Mamma always taught us when we were little? God is with us always. Never will He leave us; never will He forsake us. The Lord is our help and strength in times of trouble."

"But it happens." Arie gasped. "Remember Uncle Albert's wife? She died in childbirth."

"But she was much older, sister."

Arie gripped Mandy's hand as she groaned again, a long, low sound that caused Josiah to turn abruptly from the window and step to the foot of the bed. "I'm gonna call for an ambulance," he announced.

Lois frowned, clearly not in agreement. Even so, this was Josiah's first child, and Arie Mae seemed in a terrible way. And because Mandy had never been in the room during the delivery of a child, she didn't know who was right—Josiah or the midwife.

Josiah did not wait for his declaration to be validated; he left the room, and Mandy glanced again at the midwife, wanting to know what she thought. But Arie grabbed Mandy's hand again, lips moving without a sound, and Mandy leaned close.

"Do ya remember when you had bronchitis?" Arie asked now. "When I sat by your bed?"

Mandy had never forgotten. The roles had been reversed then, with Mandy confined to her bed and Arie Mae sitting with her by the hour, reading aloud from her favorite books, changing the cloth to cool her fevered brow. *But she's my twin,* Arie had protested when Mamma had voiced concern that they'd both come down with it.

"I really need to talk 'bout some things, Mandy." Now Arie was crying.

Mandy reached over and wiped the tears from her cheeks. "Shh . . . just try an' rest, all right?"

Shaking her head, Arie became even more restless. "I'm sorry, Mandy . . . for all the pain I caused ya. For what I did."

"Please don't think of that now," she told Arie Mae, trying to soothe her.

Arie strained to raise her head off the pillow. "But do ya forgive me?"

Of course I do, Mandy almost protested, but something stopped her. *Do I?* she wondered, looking into her own heart and remembering the day Arie had returned to work at Butterfly Meadows. Mandy had insisted on not discussing the past, but in so doing, she had denied Arie the chance to unburden herself.

Tears sprang to her eyes suddenly. "I forgive you, my precious sister. I do," she insisted, meaning it.

Arie tugged on the sheet, practically knotting it in her duress. "There's something more," she whimpered. "Mamma was wrong. . . ."

"Arie, you mustn't—"

"*Nee,* listen to me. It was in the heat of the moment—she didn't mean to tell you to leave. She always regretted it." Arie gasped now, her face beet red as she tried not to scream in pain while the next contraction overtook her.

"We can talk 'bout this later," Mandy said, eyeing Lois, not sure how to calm Arie Mae.

Josiah's mother came to Arie and talked softly through the contraction, assuring her that the pain was normal and wouldn't last much longer.

But Arie shook her head, eyes wide with fear as she looked only at Mandy.

Seeing her sister in such awful straits, Mandy clenched her jaw. "You'll be holdin' your baby in your arms ever so soon," she said as she moved to sit on the edge of the bed once the contraction had let up. "Your wee babe is comin', sister."

"Do ya believe . . . what I told ya?" Arie Mae pleaded.

"I certainly do." Mandy gently told her that their mother had written an earnest apology years ago. "Maybe ya didn't know."

Arie shook her head. "*Des gut* . . . Mamma didn't tell me. Ah *gut* . . ."

The sweet smile that was Arie's alone spread across her lips, and when she closed her eyes, her slender hand felt warm and relaxed in Mandy's.

········ ❀ ········

Lois Ackerman asked that the room be vacated, except for Mandy, and within the hour, the sound of the baby's first cries echoed from the rafters all the way downstairs without an ambulance ever being summoned. Mandy wondered if Josiah's Dat had eased the young new father's fears, and she was glad that any interference from the outside world had been unnecessary.

Mandy had the unique pleasure of calling for Josiah to come and meet his healthy baby daughter. Arie Mae snuggled with the wee one, pressing her face next to the infant's, tears falling onto her head like an anointing as she thanked her dear Lord and heavenly Father for this most precious gift.

Mandy believed with all her heart that she was supposed to have witnessed this miracle of life—her tiny niece, so pink and plump and strong.

Had the Lord awakened Mandy to be there for her sister? Mandy believed so, and she watched fondly as Josiah took his daughter in his arms for the first time. When Arie Mae asked him to give the baby to Mandy, the cherished moment was forever embedded in her memory.

Later, as the sun's first rays began to rise from the eastern horizon, Mandy reluctantly left her sister's little one to walk back toward the inn, embracing the new day.

········ ❀ ········

Though tired from the absence of a full night's sleep, Mandy felt sustained by the truly remarkable experience. And for the first time in years, she felt free.

I was foolish to wait so long to forgive, she realized. *Forgive me, dear Lord.*

Moving to the window, Mandy looked out across the field toward Arie Mae's and smiled. *Thank You for keeping my sister safe.*

With renewed joy, she went about the morning sharing the baby news with her guests. One of the women asked if a name had been chosen yet, and Mandy said it was probably too soon for that.

"Don't the Amish pick out names beforehand?" another woman asked, apparently eager to know more.

"Some do, *jah.*" Mandy explained that, historically, the People had used only a few traditional first names—mostly biblical ones—but in more recent decades, Amish parents had begun to select names that were more common to *Englischers.*

This seemed to come as a surprise to some, and as Mandy talked with them further, she realized she was enjoying herself immensely.

"Will your sister permit any pictures of the baby?" asked one first-time guest.

"Well, some young parents do privately take photos of their little children." Goodness, Mandy felt almost like a teacher today.

And all the day long, Mandy felt as light as the rose petals on Mamma's white trellis, knowing she and Arie Mae had reconciled in that frightening yet wonderful hour . . . one of new birth all around.

········ ❀ ·········

The morning of the following Lord's Day—a no-Preaching Sunday—Mandy went over to spend time with Arie Mae and the baby while Josiah and his brother Hank did the barn chores. Josiah's mother took charge of the kitchen and meals as Mandy and Arie took turns holding the lightly bundled infant, soothing her cries. "Having a sister sure has its perks," Mandy said as she smiled down at her tiny niece.

"I'm so glad you were with me during the birth," Arie said softly as she stroked her daughter's soft, dimpled hand. "I was a real mess, *jah?*"

Mandy shook her head. "What matters now is that you're a mother. Such a wondrous blessing." She truly meant it; her sister fairly glowed with contentment, tired though she must be.

Arie gave her a small, shy smile. "I've decided to name the baby Amanda Mae," she said. "Josiah thinks it's real perty, too."

Mandy's breath caught in her throat. *Such a surprise!* "Ach, sister . . . I'm so honored."

"I just wish Mamma was here to meet her newest grandchild." A tear spilled down Arie's cheek as she cradled her new babe, and she reached out with her free hand to Mandy, who clasped it.

"Knowin' Mamma, she would have her arms round the three of us right this minute, ain't so?" Mandy smiled at Arie and cooed at tiny Amanda Mae, grateful beyond words to be there with them in this moment. *To think I might have missed this!*

Chapter

39

M andy was out hanging sheets and towels when Josiah dropped by Monday morning to tell her that Arie would be taking more time to rest. "Another ten days or so. She wants to get used to bein' a Mamma before returning to work," he said, dark circles under his eyes.

"*Gut* idea," Mandy said, letting him know it was perfectly all right. "Arie was so confident that she could just resume workin', but I don't want her to rush back."

Josiah nodded. "Real kind of you. *Denki.*"

"Let me know if she needs anything, all right?" Mandy said as she pinned a towel to the clothesline.

"Well, you have your hands full here, and my Mamm is with Arie, so there's no worry."

"You have a sweet little daughter," she told him.

He smiled. "Thank the Good Lord she's real healthy," he said, then turned to head toward home.

For a moment, she watched him hurry on his way. Talking with Josiah stirred something within her, but it wasn't longing or regret—or even anger. It was a profound sense of peace.

301

More than ever before, Mandy was convinced that God had turned what had been painful and destructive into something good . . . something in accordance with His will. *I just wasn't willing to see it.*

⋯⋯ ✤ ⋯⋯

Cousin Kate seemed pleased to temporarily take Arie Mae's place in the kitchen, and was all a-chatter about the newborn babe just across the way, hinting that she and Betsy wanted to go over and visit.

"I'm sure Arie will bring Amanda Mae by soon enough," Mandy said. "The guests will want to see her, too."

"You can say that again," Kate said, cracking eggshells against the mixing bowl. "Too bad your Mamma didn't live long enough to lay eyes on Arie's baby."

"I'm just tickled that Arie chose to give baby Amanda my first name," Mandy said, serving applesauce into small bowls.

"Not too many sisters would do that," Kate observed as she stirred the egg-and-milk mixture for omelets.

Well, some close sisters would, Mandy thought.

⋯⋯ ✤ ⋯⋯

Trina and Gavin strolled through the Palm House at the Rawlings Conservatory in Baltimore that Saturday morning, reveling in the lush green beauty all around.

"What would you think of having our wedding in a place like this?" Trina asked as she walked hand in hand with her fiancé.

Gavin was quiet for a second, then stopped walking and turned to look at her. "This place would actually be my *second* choice," he said, smiling.

"What's your first?"

They started walking again slowly, taking in the Victorian architecture of one of the oldest glass houses in the country.

"I'm not sure how it would set with you."

"Try me."

"Well, I know of a quaint little Amish inn. . . ."

Trina laughed. "That butterfly meadow would be a fantastic backdrop for an outdoor wedding," she said, trying to remember when Mandy had said the last of the butterflies migrated south in the fall.

"So you're not opposed?" asked Gavin. He looked rather astonished.

"Were you expecting a battle?" Trina laughed again.

"Our clashes have been diminishing," he joked.

"Must be the meshing of hearts." She smiled. "Hmm . . . that could be the title of a poem." She gave him a teasing look, thrilled to spend the day with this amazing man. "Just to be on the safe side, we could get married in early September, before the first hard frost."

Gavin seemed satisfied. "One of us should check on availability at Butterfly Meadows, though, don't you think?"

"Definitely. I wonder if they offer a Plain wedding package?" Trina gave him a playful wink.

"Let's find out."

"You call, since it was always your place to go to write," Trina suggested as they walked out to the colorful perennial gardens, which reminded Trina of the butterfly-shaped garden at the B and B.

"But Mandy is your friend and former boss," Gavin pointed out. "I don't need to get in the middle of that."

"No reason to argue over *this*." Trina grinned and reached for her phone. "I'll give her a call."

········ ❁ ········

Late that Saturday afternoon, when Kate and Betsy had finished up for the day, and after Mandy had washed almost all the windows, inside and out, she went to her room to freshen up before making supper for herself. Picking up her phone, she noticed she'd missed a call.

She was happy to hear Trina's voice on the message, inquiring about Gavin's usual suite for two nights starting Thursday, September seventh. "If possible, we'd like to have our wedding out on the lawn there, with the butterfly meadow behind us. Call me when you have a chance—I know you're busy. But isn't this exciting!"

Mandy had to listen to the voice mail twice, she was so shocked. To think that Trina, who'd once despised the inn and its surroundings, wanted to have her wedding here!

Going out to the entryway, Mandy checked the reservation book, but regrettably, the Blue Room was already booked for four nights at that time. And so was everything else.

"I could give up *my* room," Mandy murmured as she went back down the hall. On a whim, she looked in her mother's former bedroom, where only the dresser, a chair, and a bookcase remained. Jerome had taken the double bed for young Gracie and Marian so the girls could share a room, making space for their younger boys . . . and a new baby, come the new year.

In the meantime, Mamma's empty room had become a dust catcher, though Mandy had kept it thoroughly cleaned each week.

Walking through the spacious room, Mandy stopped suddenly with an idea. Then, going to the windows, she opened all of them. Surely the farmland view could rival that of any honeymoon suite in all of the county.

This could be a windfall, of sorts, she thought, knowing guests were constantly inquiring about a bridal suite. And the lack of electricity on this side of the house could even be sold as adding romantic ambience. Yes, perhaps it was possible to turn this room and Arie's into something special for Trina and Gavin. *And for future brides and grooms, too,* she thought, catching herself thinking of a future beyond November.

But, she argued with herself, *the B and B might sell faster if the rooms are combined and fixed up a bit.* Perhaps Arie's former room could become a nice-sized private bath with a claw-foot tub. Of course, Mandy wasn't in any financial position to start updating all the rooms, but combining Mamma's and Arie's former rooms into a large suite was an excellent idea—one she would talk to Jerome about first thing Monday morning.

Then I'll call Trina!

.... ⚜ ....

Sunday midafternoon, following Preaching, Mandy was reading five chapters in the King James Version of the Bible and comparing them with the same five in her mother's old German *Biewel* when she heard a tapping at the back door. Going to see who was there, she was greeted by Karl Lantz, who removed his straw hat and asked if she might walk with him over to the pasture.

"Are the horses all right?" she asked, following him down the steps.

"Just fine, *jah*." He smiled over his shoulder. "Nothin's wrong."

As they walked, he asked if she'd ever gone horseback riding.

"*Nee* . . . not since I was a little girl."

"We did occasionally in Wisconsin, but I wasn't sure 'bout here," he said, his hat still in his hands.

"Well, sometimes younger teens ride the road horses just for fun," she said, a bit puzzled.

"I was hoping you and I might go riding or walking together through the countryside," he said, not faltering but not sounding very confident, either. "Get better acquainted."

Her heart sped up, and Mandy realized how much she'd secretly hoped he might ask her. Yet she also knew it was a risk for him to be seen alone with an unbaptized woman—perhaps the reason why he wasn't suggesting a buggy ride down well-traveled roads. "Is that a *gut* idea, Karl?"

His blue eyes momentarily searched hers. "No harm in a little walk, *jah?*" As if suddenly remembering something, he reached into his pants pocket and handed her a cube of sugar. "Would ya like to give this to your favorite horse?"

"*Denki*, why not," she said, still not sure how to answer as they made their way past the barnyard and into the paddock.

He brought out another cube. "Here's one for Gertie, too."

"All right," she said, smiling as she walked beside him.

By the time they came upon Ol' Tulip, the horses had drifted out of the hot sun and under a grove of trees. Mandy greeted her, petted her forehead, then held her hand flat to offer the sugar cube. The mare tilted her long nose sideways and promptly took it. Not looking at Karl, who stood near, Mandy waited for what more he might say.

"I like ya, Mandy . . . you've prob'ly guessed it." He paused a moment. "And I'd be interested in courting, though we couldn't move forward till . . . well, you know."

Till I join church, she thought, turning to look at him, impressed by his gentle yet forthright demeanor and his heartfelt remarks. "I'm fond of you, too, Karl," she said, knowing it was true. "Will you give me some time to think about it?"

"I'd be glad to wait for your answer, *jah*," he said.

From where she stood, Mandy could see Mamma's arbor flourishing with roses, brilliant dots of red and yellow in the heat of the day. The inn stood beyond that, its red brick warm in the light, its windows thrown wide to the breezes. Summer appeared to be in full bloom, and somehow, this place seemed that much more beautiful, too . . . at this moment.

Chapter

40

"Before we go over the books, there's something I'd like to ask you," Mandy said to Jerome as she brought over his perfectly fried eggs and not-too-crisp bacon and toast.

"Well, look at this," he said, taking a seat at the table with a big smile on his ruddy face. "We've come full circle, ain't?"

"Just for you, *Bruder*," she said, putting the plate in front of him. "I've been practicing these past months." She could hear Kate coming up the basement steps with more washing to hang outside, and Betsy outdoors mowing.

Jerome bowed his head for the silent blessing, and when he said amen and picked up his fork, Mandy wasted no time sharing her idea to create one large suite from the existing two empty bedrooms. "I think there'd be a lot of interest."

Jerome considered this. "Well, turning two rooms into one isn't normally a wise idea, but in this case . . ." He appeared to ponder it a bit more as he took a bite and looked about the kitchen. "Ain't a bad idea, really."

"I'd use it for a bridal suite for Trina Sutton—remember her? She's getting married in September."

Jerome's head flew back when he guffawed. "How does one forget such a woman?"

Smiling at that, Mandy asked if he could recommend a contractor.

"Well, Karl Lantz is the best man for the job," Jerome said.

She liked the sound of it and thanked him. "Will you ask him 'bout it, then?"

Jerome said he would, then gave her a scrutinizing look. "Are ya still thinkin' of selling the place in November?" He took a few more bites of egg, then ate some bacon, too. "The family hopes you'll stay and settle down here."

Mandy appreciated his saying so. "I do have plenty of *gut* reasons to lean in that direction, true." She thought of her and Arie's renewed relationship and baby Amanda Mae . . . and Karl's interest.

"Glad to hear it." He reached for his coffee and took a drink before continuing. "But since there's been no word from you 'bout taking baptismal instruction, I'm a bit befuddled, really."

Mandy let his words sit there as she served herself two fried eggs and bacon, wishing she'd done so earlier, since the food was no longer hot. *I never imagined making a permanent home here again. Surely Jerome has always suspected that.* Truth was, she'd had her plans for so long now.

When her brother was finished drinking his coffee, Mandy went to get the receipts and financial statements for him.

The minute Jerome left the house, Mandy headed to her room to give Trina a call, letting her know there was availability at the inn on the days she'd requested.

"That's terrific," Trina said. "We were really hoping so."

Mandy kept the creation of a bridal suite a secret from her former employee, also not revealing that Trina's wedding could be the last big event to be held there before the B and B was sold.

Trina was bursting with excitement over her wedding, which would be "small but special," with only one attendant each. "Wait till my sister hears that she finally has a reason to visit Amish country!"

Mandy smiled at that, then said that she and her helpers would do everything they could to tailor the wedding day to Gavin and Trina's wishes. "Let me know what food you'd like for the brunch. I promise not to make corn bread!"

At Trina's giggle, Mandy joined in, the two of them laughing till they nearly cried.

When they hung up, Mandy went back out to the kitchen, where she found Cousin Kate finishing up the guests' breakfast. "I'll go an' help Betsy outside," Mandy told her, excited about the prospect of doing something wonderful with Mamma's and Arie's vacant rooms, still little museums to the past.

········ ❀ ········

At the tail end of the inn's breakfast hour, Josiah brought Arie Mae over in their family carriage. The day was already warm and sticky, so little Amanda Mae was wrapped only in a light blanket and wearing a small white bonnet. Mandy quickly opened the screen door and welcomed them inside. "Cousin Kate and Betsy are eager to see ya."

"Mostly the baby, right?" Arie's cheeks looked rosy.

Mandy gave her a hug. "The guests will be thrilled, as well," Mandy said as she led the way into the breakfast room and announced that someone very special had just stopped by to say hullo.

········ ❀ ········

As June became July, Mandy and her helpers spent precious hours each day tending the vegetable and perennial gardens.

In time, Arie Mae joined them while Amanda Mae slept just inside the kitchen door in the cradle Mandy had found in the attic—made by Dat more than thirty years ago for Jerome.

The coming of the garden and orchard crops also meant Mandy needed to set aside time to put up sweet corn, tomatoes, apricots, and peaches. Some afternoons, at the end of a hectic day working with Cousin Kate and Betsy, Mandy would slip over to Arie's to see her darling little namesake.

It was while taking care of baby Amanda Mae the last Saturday in July that Mandy called to talk briefly with Eilene Bradley. Right away, Eilene asked if she was considering the possibility of ever returning to Scott City. "I just thought I'd ask, because Don's thinking of selling the house and moving north to look after his parents in Rapid City, South Dakota."

"Well, if *you're* not there, why would I want to return?"

Eilene laughed merrily. "As long as we keep in touch, dear . . . isn't that what matters?"

"I agree," Mandy replied, and after they talked awhile longer, they said good-bye. Then, as sweet little Amanda Mae slept soundly in her Pack 'n Play, Mandy got busy baking snickerdoodles for the arrival of the guests that afternoon.

All the while, she pondered what Eilene had said about Don's and her plans to move away to assist his parents. *I don't want to be too far from family, either.* In fact, once the inn was sold, Mandy wished she might live close enough to make regular visits to her family in Gordonville. *I'll have financial options. . . . I'll just wait to see what God has planned for me,* she thought, opening her heart fully.

While the cookies baked, she watched her sleeping niece's tummy rise and fall, and Mandy realized that Jerome had never really doubted that she would stick it out at the B and B for the full year. Like Mamma before him, Jerome had counted on her becoming knit together with the People again to the point that she would want to return to the fold.

Mamma must have assumed that natural consequences would fall into place, thought Mandy. *If I behaved Amish, I'd eventually become Amish.*

This realization was still somewhat of a roadblock, though. *Why didn't Mamma simply split the sale of the inn between all of my siblings and me? That would've been more fair. Or why didn't she leave me out altogether?*

Even so, Mandy knew that if the Lord was, in fact, leading her to a future away from the People, He would make it ever so plain. And this time, she could leave with a clear conscience.

.... 🌼 ....

The days of Mandy's final months in Gordonville seemed to pass with snowballing speed. She'd come to think of it as a proving, of sorts. *When I'm believed worthy of the inheritance,* Mandy thought. There was an irony there, and despite her hesitation to tell Karl of her plans, she found herself spending more time with him nearly every day, especially now that he was around longer hours to put the finishing touches on the bridal suite. Karl and Jerome, and sometimes Mandy's brother Joseph, had joined together to work in the afternoons on the remodeling, respectful of Mandy's time, as well as the peace of the inn's guests.

Having forgotten how quickly and meticulously Amish carpenters worked, she was surprised at the remarkable results as the sleeping area, with a cozy sitting area off to one side, and the spacious new bathroom neared completion.

As his father worked, Yonnie, who was growing as fast as a weed, sought Mandy out all the more. Being with the expressive little boy brought her joy, but it came with a sense of impending loss. In the space of a year, she'd come to love him dearly.

One mid-August Saturday, she went with Arie Mae to look for a bed and a new mattress, as well as bedding, bath towels, and some plain off-white curtains to go over the new green shades. *I must keep some Amish trappings in there*, she thought of the shades, wanting something that would complement the multicolored Double Wedding Ring quilt she had already purchased for the space.

With Arie's input, Mandy found just the right bed, cherrywood with a substantial headboard and footboard. After looking in on Amanda Mae, left in the care of Josiah's mother, the sisters returned to the inn and stood in the middle of the large bridal suite, the sunshine making a long gleaming rectangular shape on the hardwood floor.

Stepping off the area, Mandy asked her sister, "Where should the bed go?"

Arie stood with her back to the windows, her arms folded. "You want it someplace different than where Mamma's was?"

"Maybe." Mandy noted the shift in tone from Arie's usually bright and cheerful manner. "I want your opinion. Does the bed have to be in the same spot?"

Arie stared at the space where Mamma's bed had been for as long as they could remember. "S'pose not."

"Sometimes change is *gut*, don't you agree?" Mandy forced more enthusiasm into her voice and leaned against the wall.

Arie gazed at her sorrowfully. "Mandy . . . if you're so set on leavin', why does it matter where the bed goes?"

Stunned into silence, Mandy could only shake her head. *How does Arie know?*

"I wormed it out of Jerome," Arie admitted, as if reading Mandy's expression.

"Jerome had no right," Mandy murmured.

Arie moved closer, her eyes glistening now. "I'm really hopin' you'll stay, Mandy Sue. I honestly am." She paused. "Haven't things changed for the better between us?"

Mandy wholeheartedly agreed. "Absolutely."

"So then, why not stay?" Arie pleaded. "I'd love to have you nearby as Amanda Mae grows up."

Mandy delighted in holding her adorable namesake . . . and in how close she felt again to Arie Mae, too. "It *would* be *wunnerbaar*. . . . Believe me, I'm praying 'bout this. I don't want to make a mistake."

The room was thick with emotion. "How could stayin' be a mistake?" Arie asked, her brow furrowed.

"For one thing, I'm not the same person," Mandy said hesitantly. "Years away changed me, I think."

"You've still got plenty of Plain in you, though." Her sister sighed. "I changed, too, after ya left. Mamma did, too. I remember how hard we worked, as if we were paying some kind of penance. Mamma threw her heart into this place, into the guests. She started prayin' beforehand for the people who would walk through her front door . . . she wanted this inn to mean something more than just an income. She wanted it to be a blessing." Arie stopped to wipe her tears. "But there was always a hole in our hearts. And we never stopped hopin' you'd come home."

Mandy tried not to tear up. "Mamma should've given the house to you, though. Not me—I didn't deserve it. Aren't you upset about that?"

Mandy met Arie's eyes, and for a moment, they just stood there. At last, Arie spoke. "There's more to it."

Mandy opened her mouth to inquire, but Arie was already moving away, heading for the doorway, and Mandy felt confused as she walked out of the room to the bedroom next door. There, she sat on the hard cane-back chair.

I should just let Arie and our brothers divide up the proceeds from the sale of the inn, she thought, miserable now.

She remembered Jerome's refusal to tell her exactly what would happen if she declined the inheritance. *Why is that?* Mandy wondered again.

She stepped out for a walk under the shade of the trees in the pasture, yearning for peace, the kind that Gavin O'Connor had said he'd always experienced there. She made herself breathe more slowly, missing Dat, who would know how to calm her with his favorite psalms.

Across the way, Mandy could see Ol' Tulip and Gertie lying in a patch of shade on the far side. Yonnie was there, too, walking near them, and somewhere or other he'd gotten himself a fine-looking walking stick. Spotting her, he came scampering through the grassy paddock, running so fast his little straw hat flew off and was airborne for a moment. Laughing, he stopped and caught it and pressed it down on his head, giving it a pat on the crown and wearing that adorable grin.

He commenced running again to her. "'Tis a *gut Daag* for ice cream, *jah?*" he said, and his smile stretched over his little sunburnt face.

"Any day's a *gut* one for ice cream," she agreed as he fell into step with her beneath the canopy of trees.

Yonnie swatted at his ear.

"A mosquito?" she asked.

He nodded. "I got bit on my ankle." He pushed his walking stick into the ground with each step he took. "They must like me, *jah?*"

"Rub salt and water on the bites when ya get home," she suggested absently, her thoughts still on the earlier conversation.

"Your Mamma always said to spit on the bites." He grinned at her, as though hoping for a reaction.

Something about the thought of Yonnie talking with Mamma touched Mandy. "My brothers did that, too, growin' up."

He tilted his head as he looked up at her. "You have four big brothers, ain't?"

She nodded. "And one sister."

"She says you're twins."

"That's right."

Yonnie was quiet for a moment. Then he said, "It's hot today. Dat says we could prob'ly cook an egg on cement." He wrinkled up his little nose at the thought.

"Here in the shade it's not so bad," she said, not herself at all. Usually, when Yonnie was around, she felt like smiling . . . all chatty and cheerful. "Won't be many more weeks of such muggy weather like this. Soon, it'll be fall and the days will get shorter again."

Yonnie nodded his head, dragging his stick now. "Dat asked me a funny question at breakfast. He asked if I could live anywhere, where would it be."

She smiled down at him, paying closer attention. "Is that so?"

"Want to know what I said?"

"I sure do."

Yonnie grinned up at her. "Butterfly Meadows, I told him."

She thought this was sweet. "Where I live?"

"*Jah.* What do ya think 'bout that?"

"Well, wouldn't your Dat be awful lonely?"

Yonnie shook his head. "Maybe he could sleep out in the stable with Ol' Tulip and Gertie."

She laughed, finding the boy simply adorable. "You'd put your Dat out there with the horses?"

Yonnie seemed to think on this, frowning and scratching his blond bangs beneath his straw hat. "I wouldn't *want* to, really."

Mandy wondered about the mind of a young child and changed

the subject. "If there could only be one season all year long, which would ya choose?"

"Winter," Yonnie was quick to say.

"Ah . . . so you could have my rich hot cocoa every day?"

He bobbed his head quickly. "How'd ya know?"

She glanced up at a nearby tree branch and pointed. "See the little birdie up there?"

Yonnie nodded, eyes fixed on the branch. "That birdie told ya?"

She smiled and tapped the crown of his hat. "I think I just pulled your leg."

Yonnie looked at her for the longest time, like he was awestruck. "What's your favorite season, Mandy?"

"Oh, that's easy. It's springtime, when the butterflies come."

"*Jah*, I like that, too."

They walked and talked till they ran out of shade trees, then turned back again and strolled leisurely toward the stable, where Mandy noticed that some of the horse fencing needed repairing. *Always something to mend*, she mused.

Chapter 41

That evening, Josiah knocked on the back screen door while Mandy was washing her supper dishes. Surprised, she dried her hands on her apron and went to greet him. "*Jah?*"

"Arie Mae wants you to come over, if possible" was the first thing out of Josiah's mouth. "Would ya mind too awful much?"

Mandy hesitated, not sure she was the best company for anyone this evening. Not the way she felt. "Did she ask ya to fetch me?"

"*Nee,*" he said, shaking his head and glancing back toward his house. "She doesn't know I'm here."

Mandy had no reason to mention their earlier conversation. "Are ya sure Arie wants to see me?"

"She's been tellin' me how the two of yous have grown closer again, here lately." She could hear the tension in Josiah's voice. "I daresay somethin's weighing heavily on her mind."

"*Jah,*" Mandy said, opening the screen door and stepping outside. "I'll go an' see about her."

The corners of his mouth turned up slightly. "*Denki.*"

She set out walking with him, and he suggested they take

317

the narrow field lane around the cornfield, where they'd once walked as young teens, talking about nature and their favorite Bible stories—just whatever popped into their heads.

Black crows flew high over the field, and the sun cast long shadows over the dusty road as they walked in silence. A slight wind whooshed through the tall cornstalks on their left as Mandy's bare feet pushed against the flattened dirt.

"I also came over for another reason, to be frank," Josiah said, breaking the stillness. "It's long past time to clear the air."

Mandy hadn't expected this.

He kept his face forward, hands in his pockets. "All those years of our friendship—yours and mine—I cared for ya, Mandy."

Why is he saying this now? She frowned, not wanting to look at him. She hadn't forgotten how he'd been so devoted. *Almost like a sibling.*

Josiah stopped walking suddenly and was several paces behind her before she realized it.

She turned. "What is it?"

"It's high time I apologized for what happened between us," he said, looking sheepish. "You see, I was pursuing Arie Mae even before you caught us together that one night." He sighed. "It wasn't right, yet I didn't know how to tell you, Mandy. I was immature . . . and afraid of hurting you . . . and ruining our friendship."

"Well, that explains a lot," she said, wondering why he thought it would make her feel better. Yet she had to admit that it felt freeing, somehow, to talk this out with him.

"I really bungled things up—I shouldn't have led you on, Mandy." He drew a long sigh. "It's bothered me all these years."

"Water under the bridge now," Mandy was quick to reply.

She glanced toward his and Arie's farmhouse, grateful for Josiah's desire to make things right. "I was gone much too long," she said almost as an afterthought.

"Arie Mae missed you somethin' fierce," Josiah said. "She was worried sick 'bout you, 'specially after her letters came back unopened. She pined for you even after we were wed."

Mandy considered this as they made their way out of the cornfield to his property.

"With all of her heart, your sister loves ya. Once your years away started adding up, it got to the point that Arie Mae would've done anything to get you to come back home," he said. "Anything."

As they walked past Josiah's corncrib, Mandy heard the low whir of a small airplane overhead, pushing against the humid air. Climbing the back porch steps, she was reminded of the night of sweet baby Amanda Mae's birth. "I want to cheer up Arie, if I can," she told Josiah, who held the screen door for her.

"Just seein' you—bein' with ya—will be enough," Josiah replied, motioning for her to go inside and upstairs to her sister.

.... ⚘ ....

"I was afraid I'd offended ya," Arie said, sitting in the rocking chair in her and Josiah's bedroom to nurse her baby.

Mandy laughed softly, trying to reassure her. "Nothin' to fret over."

Arie smiled as Amanda Mae continued to nurse. "I'm glad ya came."

"Josiah was worried 'bout ya," Mandy said, wanting her to know.

Nodding, her eyes met Mandy's. "We've walked some rough paths, you and I, but no matter how I feel now, I don't want you to think I'm upset about your choice to sell the house." She paused and blinked back tears. "But I'll be sad."

"Arie, I understand," Mandy said. "I'm still deciding, honest I am."

Arie sighed loudly. "And I really don't mind where ya put the new bed, either." Gently, she patted Amanda Mae's little back. "It was your idea to create the bridal suite . . . and it'll be your house to sell, if ya do."

"I'll visit . . . I promise. And often." *I don't have to be Amish to be a close sister,* Mandy thought. *But I do to be courted by Karl. . . .*

That seemed to sit a little better with Arie, who raised the baby to snuggle against her shoulder. "Maybe you'll change your mind yet," she said, eyes glistening. "I can hope . . . and keep prayin'."

Mandy hugged her, and when the twilight began to fall, she said she needed to head home. Arie Mae nodded, telling her that she planned to come Monday as usual to make breakfast for the guests.

"Only if you're up to it, all right?"

Arie agreed, and Mandy hoped Josiah might sit now with his wife and tell her all that he'd talked about on the walk over. Knowing Josiah as she did now, he surely wouldn't want any secrets kept.

········ ✿ ········

Mandy sat down with Arie, Kate, and Betsy that Monday to go over a list of instructions for Trina and Gavin's wedding reception, much of it based on the careful directions Trina had sent by mail. Following a morning wedding that would include both of the couple's parents and siblings, Mandy and her staff would serve a hot brunch in the breakfast room, including wedding cake and some sparkling punch.

Mandy counted up the number of guests in her head. "We should be able to seat everyone," she said. "And, let's see"—here she surveyed Trina's short list of items Gavin had requested for the meal—"it looks like Arie Mae and Kate will be makin' a special wedding egg bake that day."

Kate and Betsy exchanged glances, and Arie Mae rolled her eyes. "A *wedding* one, *jah?*" Arie said, grinning. "What's in that?"

This brought a merry moment, as Mandy, especially, had to laugh.

Cousin Kate suddenly frowned. "*Ach*, wait . . . we're forgetting the guests who are already booked. Where will *they* eat breakfast?"

Mandy paused to consider that. "The wedding brunch could take place in the gazebo," she suggested. "What 'bout that?"

"Perfect!" Arie Mae said. "But you'd better ask Trina, just to be sure."

"Josiah and Karl could set up some tables out there," Mandy said. "The gazebo's plenty big enough for a small wedding party."

"There's really not much else to be done," Kate said, munching on a carrot stick.

"The wedding's less than two weeks away," Mandy said, thankful the new bridal suite was ready and furnished.

"Will we need a few cut flowers, maybe?" Betsy asked.

"Oh, nice idea," Mandy said. "How 'bout some from Mamma's butterfly garden—Trina so loves that." She heard Amanda Mae waking up in the sitting room. "Arie says it will be the first-ever wedding on the premises," she noted as her sister excused herself to go and get the baby.

"Maybe the gazebo is somethin' you'll want to offer in the future—an ideal spot for a romantic breakfast or dinner," Kate said, practically grinning.

The future? Mandy thought. *Everything seems to hinge on that.*

Already she had been checking around for a good real-estate agent.

Arie returned with bright-eyed little Amanda Mae in her arms, then offered her to Mandy, who took her eagerly, a lump in her throat.

Only a little more than two months left . . .

Chapter

42

The afternoon before her wedding, Trina arrived with Gavin. Quickly, she set down her purse to give Mandy a big hug.

Mandy laughed merrily. "Goodness, I wasn't expecting that, but it's *gut* to see you again, too," she greeted her, then shook Gavin's hand. "Come on in," she motioned. "I have something to show ya. Tomorrow night, you'll both be stayin' just down the hall here," Mandy said as she waved for them to follow.

Puzzled, Trina followed Gavin and Mandy into the private family side of the inn, wondering if perhaps Mandy had run out of rooms again. *Surely not,* she thought, not relishing the idea of spending her wedding night in Arie's old room. *Not even for old time's sake!*

With a beaming smile on her face, Mandy opened the door to what had been her mother's former bedroom, and stepped back to let Trina and Gavin look inside. "Surprise! A bridal suite . . . just for the two of you."

Trina shook her head and grabbed Mandy's hand to pull her into the large space, replete with ecru-colored window curtains over the green shades and a grand king-sized cherrywood bed with a gleaming headboard and footboard. "Look at that gorgeous quilt," Trina told Gavin. "It's the Double Wedding Ring pattern, right?" she asked Mandy.

"You're right. How'd ya know?"

"Oh, my sister has been educating me about all things Amish since I returned from Gordonville. Janna's so excited about finally getting to see the B and B at tonight's wedding rehearsal." Trina recalled her sister's delighted squeal when she had learned the wedding would be at Butterfly Meadows.

Mandy smiled. "I think by now you could tell *her* a thing or two about the Amish, *jah?*"

Trina nodded and glanced at Gavin, who had walked over to the suite's sitting area, which had a nice-sized white sofa dressed up with blue and green throw pillows. "I had no idea this was here," he said.

"Well, it wasn't until just a few weeks ago," Mandy said, explaining how she'd gotten the idea after Trina called about having the wedding there. "The suite you always stay in was already booked, but I didn't have the heart to say anything."

"You're amazing—that's what," Trina said, turning in a slow circle to take in the lovely room. To think Mandy had gone to all this trouble for *them!* "We're honored to be the first couple to stay here."

Mandy gave her hand a squeeze. "I wouldn't have it any other way."

Gavin left to go to the car for Trina's bags, and while he was gone, Trina told Mandy how happy she was that their landmark celebration would be held near the butterfly garden. "God has orchestrated everything so perfectly," she said, hugging Mandy again. "He certainly knew what He was up to when He brought me here."

"And ya won't mind not havin' electric?"

Trina giggled. "Gaslight will be perfect . . . like the old days."

They headed next door to Josiah and Arie's home, where Mandy had arranged for Gavin to spend his last night as a single man, since the inn was full. And as soon as he'd settled into their spare room, Gavin suggested he take Trina to the restaurant where they'd had their first date. Oh, did she ever love this man!

········ ✿ ········

On the morning of Trina's wedding, Mandy got up early and strolled around the perimeter of the yard, thankful for the warm winds that had come in the night, and for the daybreak as bright and as pleasant as any early September Friday she recalled from her childhood. She looked about her at the familiar surroundings—the still-vibrant butterfly garden; the charming gazebo where a festive brunch would soon be laid out; the neat piles of wood stacked for winter, thanks to Karl—and felt that she was being drawn into a living portrait. *Mamma would be so pleased,* she thought.

········ ✿ ········

The small wedding near the butterfly meadow was a private one, so Mandy could only guess what vows might be spoken by Gavin to his bride, who wore a gown of lacy white. The couple made a handsome pair as they strolled hand in hand to the gazebo for their first meal as man and wife.

When the brunch was served, Mandy was happy to let Arie Mae receive all the accolades for the meal, deserving as she was. Mandy helped serve, taken with the newlyweds' fondness for each other. She was so glad that Trina had found contentment at last, a sentiment Janna had shared, as well, when Mandy met her before the ceremony.

At Arie's insistence, the next morning, during the regular breakfast with the other guests, Mandy sat beside Trina and Gavin and was served chocolate chip waffles and scrambled eggs, crisp bacon, fresh fruit, and pan-fried cornmeal mush with sausage gravy.

Trina held her hand as Arie led with the silent blessing, and later, she gave Mandy a little hint about their honeymoon location. "It's someplace warm and sandy," Trina said with a grin at Gavin.

"And nary a cornfield in sight? Electricity in every room?" Mandy played along.

Gavin chuckled. "Not that we're enamored with electricity, of course."

She laughed. "Well . . . how long must I wait to find out?"

"We're going to the Bahamas." Trina and Gavin clinked each other's coffee cups in a toast of sorts.

Mandy noticed how happy they both looked and said she was honored they'd chosen the inn for their wedding. Then, smiling, she reached for her coffee and suddenly thought of Karl Lantz, looking forward to seeing him to chat later today, as they so often did.

Ach, *maybe it's being around these two lovebirds!*

········ ❀ ········

The departure of the butterflies was something Mandy had never relished, but they would return. *As they always do,* she thought. October started out being unseasonably warm, its bountiful yield of pumpkins on display at roadside stands up and down Old Leacock Road. Now there were delicious pumpkin pies and pumpkin bread to bake for afternoon treats for the guests, as well as Arie's famous pumpkin maple whoopie pies.

Mandy heard from Karl that certain English farmers around

the county who had been fretting about getting their harvest in before the temperatures dropped were cranking up the air conditioning in the cabs of their combines. Then, of all things, a mere two weeks later, Mandy found herself having to haul coal in for the stove. She couldn't have this chill in the mornings, not with little Amanda Mae along with Arie Mae now before and during the breakfast hour. The infant was a real delight, cooing and smiling at Mandy every time she held her, and so darling in the little handmade clothes Arie sewed for her while Amanda Mae slept.

········ ✿ ········

Ten more days came and went, and as red foxes slinked through the harvested cornfield, the air held the stale scent of decaying leaves. To the north, the ridgeline of the Welsh Mountains was newly visible beyond the bare birches that lined the butterfly meadow.

On the November morning that marked the end of Mandy's twelve consecutive months of managing the B and B, Jerome dropped by for breakfast.

Mandy poured coffee for him right away as he commented that the inn was doing very well, if not better than when Mamma was running it. "Practically always fully booked," he said as he stood in the middle of the kitchen and looked about.

"I've been doing just what Mamma always did." She carried his coffee to the table and set it down. *And tried to be a blessing to guests*, she thought.

"Well, it appears that it's been a success."

She watched him amble over to the tall cupboard door and open it. Staring at the place where Dat had once noted and dated all of their heights, he coughed, then closed the door slowly, almost respectfully. "Guess this here old house is yours," he said as he moseyed over to sit at the head of the table, where he trickled some cream into his coffee. "How do ya feel 'bout that?"

"Well, it hasn't been the easiest thing I've ever set out to do."

"S'pose not."

They talked about the coming winter and the fact that Mandy and her helpers had managed to tidy up Mamma's perennial garden before the weather got too nippy, and that Karl had mulched the roses in fresh manure and seen to it that the horses were supplied with plenty of fresh hay. Most of the talk was maintenance related, and Mandy knew from Jerome's expression that he was trying to avoid the burning question. But she was glad for the company, though she suspected there would be a knock at the door within the hour, when bright-eyed Yonnie came to see if she might have some hot cocoa ready for him.

Finally, Jerome drained the last of his cup. "Sometime this week, the legal documents will be ready to sign over to you," he told her as he pushed back his chair.

Mandy thanked him. But instead of feeling the relief she'd once anticipated, she felt at that moment as empty as the frosty butterfly garden.

········ ❀ ········

The next morning, Mandy was greeting the real-estate agent she'd chosen a while back after interviewing her by phone. She gave Patti Landis a tour of the entire house, as well as the outbuildings.

"I assume your horses aren't included," Patti joked with a smile as they left the stable to return to the house.

Mandy made it clear that they were not, mentioning that one of her siblings would gladly take Ol' Tulip and Gertie when the time came.

Once the two women were seated in the kitchen, Patti ran

the marketing comps through her laptop, and in a few minutes came up with several options for a listing price based on other recent sales of similar properties in the area.

"Really—*that* much?" Mandy said, astonished that the B and B would fetch such an amount.

"Oh yes, and to be honest, I really doubt this house will be on the market for long," Patti said. "Mark my words, you'll have other Amish folk knockin' your door down to get it—likely with cash in hand."

Mandy made it clear that the acreage was not part of the deal, having already been transferred to her brothers. "Only the small meadows on either side of the house and stable go with the inn."

"Are you interested in listing it today?" Patti asked, seemingly eager to do so.

"I'd like to read over the seller's contract first, if you don't mind."

"Of course." The cordial woman pulled a copy out of her briefcase and went over it with Mandy line by line.

Chapter
43

After Patti Landis left, Mandy decided to retrace the steps of the tour she'd given the woman, savoring each room, every poignant memory. Not all were especially significant, but each was built into the fabric of her life. And as she did so, she realized that Butterfly Meadows was no longer just about the distant past.

She considered the pros and cons of joining church and staying put among the People. And she pondered returning to a less Plain lifestyle, perhaps moving to Maryland near Trina and Gavin—keeping her car, enjoying modern conveniences.

Mandy thought of her large family and of her twin sister within walking distance. And adorable Amanda Mae . . .

Yet if she stayed, she'd have to become fully Amish to fit in with the People. Karl would certainly expect it, and understandably so. She tried that on in her mind, wondering how that would seem. Would she enjoy living the Amish life once again, since she'd grown up that way, never having known anything different till her years in Kansas? And would the sacrifices be worth it? she wondered, all the while realizing there were many things about Amish life that she'd missed terribly.

Sighing, she looked out the upstairs sewing room windows and saw Karl pick up Yonnie and sling him up on his shoulders, the two of them laughing heartily as they headed home.

"What should I do, Lord?" she whispered as she gazed out at the pastureland to the south of the stable, where Ol' Tulip and Gertie loved to graze. Where Yonnie so enjoyed playing while his father looked after the horses.

All the rest of the day, the thought of putting the B and B up for sale was on Mandy's mind. Like Jerome had said, she had met the challenging conditions of the inheritance. *I made it with God's help, and the help of so many others,* she thought, feeling not so much proud of herself as truly pleased that she'd followed through with her course of action . . . and succeeded.

········ ❁ ········

While Mandy prepared a fruit compote the next morning, Arie Mae cooked breakfast, with Amanda Mae rolling around in the nearby Pack 'n Play.

Arie glanced at Mandy, her expression terribly sad. "Josiah happened to notice the real-estate company's sign on the car that came by here yesterday." She took a deep breath and then straightened. "Are ya actually goin' through with selling the inn?" she asked. "I'd hoped you wouldn't leave this time . . . at least not without sayin' good-bye."

Mandy gave her a sympathetic look. "I wouldn't do that. Not again."

Arie grimaced as she blinked back tears. "*Ach,* sorry. I promised myself I wouldn't get emotional."

Mandy placed the individual fruit dishes on a serving tray. "I've been toying with an idea, but I need your advice."

Her sister nodded. "Not sure I have much to offer, but I can be a sounding board."

"I've been praying a lot 'bout what to do next," Mandy added. "As far as business opportunities go."

"Okay." Arie Mae seemed gloomier by the second.

"But I'll need a partner if I'm going to do this right."

"A partner?"

"*Jah*, can't do it alone . . . well, I'd rather not."

Arie frowned, but suddenly, a small smile flickered through, one quickly replaced by a full-fledged smile. "Well, you'd need just the *right* partner."

"That's what I was thinkin' . . . but who?"

"Hmm." Arie played coy. "Well, it would have to be just the *right* opportunity, too, ya know. Can't be too careful."

Mandy grinned. "So . . . what do you think of this inn? I hear it's located on the most heavenly property, and the butterflies visit by the hundreds every spring. And so many guests are poundin' down the door, the innkeeper can scarcely keep up."

"Sounds exhausting," Arie Mae protested, but her eyes sparkled with fun.

"I was hoping *you* might be interested."

"Well . . . I'd have to think about it."

Mandy clapped her hands. "You have exactly five seconds."

"Okay, okay!" Arie laughed, then reached for Mandy. They hugged happily until Arie let go, still holding Mandy's hands. "*Ach!* I'm thrilled ya came home, Mandy Sue."

"Let's not get all emotional, okay?" Mandy said. "We have business to discuss, *jah*?"

········ ✿ ········

After breakfast had been served and the kitchen set back in order, Mandy motioned for Arie to sit at the kitchen table. "Let's have our first partnership meeting. Do you want something to drink?"

Arie shook her head and adjusted her white head covering. "You've become quite the kidder, you know?"

"Must be the effect this place has on me," Mandy replied with a grin, and they spent the next few minutes discussing their pending enterprise.

At one point, Mandy felt it was time to uncover a suspicion, something that had been gnawing at her from her first day at the inn. "There's something I'd like to clarify."

"Sure."

"During my initial conversations with Jerome—one of which we had sittin' right here, in fact—" Mandy said, tapping her fingers on the table, "I was adamant that Mamma should never have given the inn to me, and I told him as much."

Arie Mae was quiet, her face ever so serious.

Mandy scrutinized her sister's expression. "Anyway, Jerome seemed real uncomfortable when I pressed further, telling him that I couldn't for the life of me understand how it happened, because it should've been yours."

"I didn't want it, Mandy."

A knowing look passed between them.

"So Mamma *did* leave it to you, didn't she?" Mandy asked.

Looking away, Arie sighed softly, then gave the most innocent-looking smile.

Mandy leaned back in the chair and gazed at her sister. "Well . . . it took me twelve long months to figure out."

"I hope you're not upset," Arie said.

Mandy had to laugh. "Jerome was just so cryptic."

"Did *he* let it out of the bag?"

Mandy shook her head. "No. Things started fallin' into place after something Josiah said when we were walking over to your house one evening."

Arie's eyes were brimming with tears.

"Some pieces are still missing, honestly."

So Arie began to fill in the details, beginning with "Mamma's intentions," as she put it. "She wanted to give the B and B to us both equally upon her passing—because the boys had their own farms, and you and I had worked so closely with her. But she didn't know how to go about it, since you were gone and out of reach. She was convinced you'd lived in the outside world so long that you weren't comin' back, even though she always hoped otherwise." Arie glanced toward the window, then back at Mandy. "She was also worried we wouldn't get along, so she named me the first beneficiary. But if I was deceased or declined for some reason, the B and B would go to you."

Mandy let all of this soak in, wholly assured of their mother's love. So . . . Mamma *hadn't* neglected either of them.

Arie went to get a glass of water. "I'm sure you know that Mamma didn't want you to just sell the place. She wanted you to come back . . . and maybe stay put."

"Thus, the twelve-month stipulation," Mandy said.

"And I knew she'd put that in her will," Arie said, looking sheepish again.

Tears came to Mandy's eyes as she finally realized what had happened: Arie had been willing to give up her ownership just to have Mandy come home, if only for twelve months. *Such a risk,* Mandy thought.

Arie stepped closer and whispered, "I prayed and prayed you'd want to stay on, so we could be together." She wiped away tears. "So we could be close sisters again."

Mandy got up from the table, went around to Arie's side, and sat next to her. "I'm here now . . . and always will be." She reached for her, and they embraced again, their faces wet with tears.

Arie seemed to want to reveal more. "The night Amanda

Mae was born, I almost told you what Mamma did in her will. But afterward, I decided it was better to wait it out, to see what you decided to do on your own."

"I'm glad you did," Mandy said, kissing her cheek. "I needed to work things out for myself. And with prayer."

Arie Mae nodded, smiling that familiar sweet smile.

"You're quite the conniver, ya know," Mandy said, smiling herself.

"'Twas ever so worth it!" Arie laughed out loud.

Later, after they'd dried their eyes and set to baking a fresh batch of chocolate chip cookies for the guests—nibbling on some themselves—Arie and the baby left for home with Mandy happily strolling along with them out to the edge of the stubby cornfield. There, in Mamma's beloved meadow, she felt as light as a butterfly newly emerged from its chrysalis.

Epilogue

Goodness, I continued to stay ever so busy, though Arie Mae still cooked breakfast, and Kate and Betsy helped, too. In what little spare time I had, I loved sewing Amish clothes for myself and for my little namesake, sometimes working on wall hangings with Scripture verses on them to sell at Saturday market, though I wasn't as fond of embroidery as Arie Mae. People change, though.

Whether we were at Arie's or over at the inn, it struck me as interesting how my sister and I had wholly put the past behind us and forged new memories, with sweet Amanda Mae at the center. Thank God for His many mercies.

Josiah joked now and then that Arie and I reminded him of sister-twins, then laughed and said, *"Oh, that's right—you are!"* And Arie giggled at him, shooing him out of her kitchen.

Honestly, it was remarkable how happy my sister and I were together. We made homemade Christmas cards to send to a select few as all the while Amanda Mae tried to get her dimpled knees up under her, wanting to crawl now. I would have ventured to say our close sisterhood was almost like our early years, but it was actually better.

.... ⚘ ....

Mr. and Mrs. Gavin O'Connor booked two nights, beginning on December first, to celebrate the anniversary of their first meeting, and Arie Mae and I served them a private lamb roast supper by candlelight. It made me smile when I heard Gavin mention a special gift he had planned for her later. Of course, Trina wanted to know right then what it was, but she did not press further when he said it would be worth the wait. His love has certainly mellowed her!

I was thrilled to receive a call from my friend Winnie Maier, who booked a stay for early January, saying she wanted to catch up on my life here. She also hinted that she had some big news to share, and that it had something to do with a beautiful ring on her finger. It will be so special to spend time with her again!

As for my developing friendship with Karl, his parents came the week before Christmas from Wisconsin, and I was invited to supper at Karl's to meet them. *"To get acquainted,"* as Karl put it, a light in his eyes.

That evening, after several rounds of Dutch Blitz, we all sat at the table and had generous slices of the pumpkin spice cake made by Karl's talkative and genial mother. Karl sat across from me, looking ever so handsome in his for-*gut* church clothes. And while sipping hot coffee, we listened as Karl described walking a mile to his one-room schoolhouse in knee-deep snow, wearing so many layers his Mamm had to literally stuff him into them.

Later, by the light of the moon, Karl thoughtfully helped to get me settled into his enclosed carriage, then placed a warm woolen lap robe over me. Picking up the driving lines, he directed the horse to a surprisingly slow pace, and by night's end, I told him of my intention to be baptized next year. He seemed delighted that the day would soon come when he could formally court me. Even so, the two of us considered our relationship worth the extra time it would take; it would give us the chance to build a strong foundation of friendship before tying the knot before God and the People.

The very next day, when Yonnie came along with Karl to work in the stable, I called to him from the back stoop. "*Kumme* have some hot cocoa with me, won't ya?"

Well, he disappeared into the stable, probably to tell his Dat where he was going, then zoomed out of there and practically flew over the grass crusted with frost from the night before.

"I brought ya a present," he announced.

"It's not Christmas yet," I told him as I hung up his coat and knit hat and scarf.

I waited till he was seated to pour his hot cocoa and top it with a dollop of whipped cream. "There, how's that?"

He grinned at me, his short little legs dangling from the chair. "*Denki.*" Then he pulled something out of his pants pocket, arching his back a bit to yank it out. With a smile, he pushed a Hershey's chocolate bar across the table to me, eyes blinking as he reached for his hot cocoa, the steam rising.

"Better blow on it a bit so ya don't burn the roof of your mouth."

Yonnie nodded his head, his blond hair all rumpled from the knit cap. "That's what your Mamma always said."

"Well, she was right." I struggled not to tear up.

Yonnie stared at me a moment and grinned.

Later, as he donned his outer clothing, I told him, "I hope you have a *hallicher Grischtdaag*, Yonnie," wishing him a merry Christmas.

He reached up and gave me a hug round my neck.

It was the best gift I could've imagined.

And that night, when I counted my blessings before falling asleep, I thanked the dear Lord in heaven for all the unanswered prayers I'd prayed back when. How very grateful I was to have met Karl from Wisconsin.

I could scarcely wait for Christmas Eve dinner, when I would serve a braised pot roast with sweet potatoes to him and Yonnie. I'd been practicing Mamma's recipe a good many times and honestly gotten tired of it myself. But I wanted it to be a nice surprise for Karl, who had perhaps heard of my cooking handicap—one that I had overcome quite a bit, thanks to Arie Mae . . . and dear Mamma's precious notebook of recipes, ever so handy.

I rejoiced daily at the heaven-sent surprises along this journey called life, and I knew, without a doubt, that I would never leave the People again. I liked to think that Mamma's wishes were granted, and I'd come to terms with all of that, thankful most of all for grace. Oh, where would I have been without His mercy, new every single morning?

Author's Note

T here's nothing like a charming inn! I adore spending leisure time at a peaceful bed-and-breakfast establishment in an out-of-the-way place—the more rural, the better. My husband, Dave, and I have enjoyed many visits to lovely old inns in upstate New York and all over New England, ones with dew-drenched English gardens and tasteful old-world architecture and furnishings. So it seemed quite providential when I met Darlene Bobo, the owner of Butterfly Meadows Inn and Farm (*not*, however, an Amish inn), while on a recent book tour through the South. Interestingly enough, I began to tell her about my story idea, which I typically never do prior to writing, and quickly discovered that Darlene was an innkeeper right there in Franklin, Tennessee! We talked about our mutual enjoyment of butterflies, and because I was fascinated by the name of her inn, I asked permission to use it in this story. The rest is history, and Darlene and I still agree that our meeting seemed to be divinely appointed. If you'd like more information, you can find her beautiful Southern inn online at *www.butterflymeadowsinn.com*.

As is always true, I am so very grateful to my research assistants, readers, reviewers, proofreaders, and, of course, my longtime editors, David Horton and Rochelle Gloege, for their efforts on this book. We certainly are a team!

My husband, Dave, is the very first to see my chapters and shares in my joys and challenges as I bring the ideas that are in my head—and heart—to life on the page. Ideas that spring up while I'm making family memory albums with my sister, or tending to (and talking to) my plants in the breakfast nook, or out on a mountain hike, or spending time with our grown children, granddaughter, and each of the little ones in our extended family . . . everything holds the potential for inspiration. I never know when an idea for a scene or an impression for a particular character will come, so I am always attentive.

One of those splendid bits of inspiration for this particular book came from Aunt Beverly Fry, who enjoys taking mystery trips and has shared her exciting experiences with me. Although unlike Trina Sutton, Aunt Bev has never had any unpleasant surprises!

The work of writing also involves research. When it comes to the legal issues surrounding Mandy's inheritance, I offer a very special thanks to Beth M. Sparks and W. Bryan Byler, estate attorneys-at-law.

My enduring appreciation wings its way out to all of my wonderfully supportive prayer partners, as well as to my faithful reader-friends who affirm that they often see themselves in the lives of my story people, Amish and otherwise. You are all an essential part of this amazing writing adventure, and I thank our heavenly Father daily for each of you.

Soli Deo Gloria!

Beverly Lewis, born in the heart of Pennsylvania Dutch country, is the *New York Times* bestselling author of more than ninety books. Her stories have been published in twelve languages worldwide. A keen interest in her mother's Plain heritage has inspired Beverly to write many Amish-related novels, beginning with *The Shunning*, which has sold more than one million copies and is an Original Hallmark Channel movie. In 2007 *The Brethren* was honored with a Christy Award.

Beverly has been interviewed by both national and international media, including *Time* magazine, the Associated Press, and the BBC. She lives with her husband, David, in Colorado.

Visit her website at www.beverlylewis.com or www.facebook.com/officialbeverlylewis for more information.

The Road Home

The Next Novel from Beverly Lewis

AVAILABLE SPRING 2018

BETHANYHOUSE

Stay up to date on your favorite books and authors with our free e-newsletters. Sign up today at bethanyhouse.com.

Find us on Facebook. facebook.com/bethanyhousepublishers

Free exclusive resources for your book group! bethanyhouse.com/anopenbook

an open book

Sign Up for Beverly's Newsletter!

Keep up to date with
Beverly's news on book
releases and events
by signing up for her email
list at beverlylewis.com.

More from Beverly Lewis

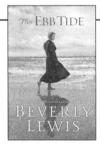

When an Amish young woman takes a summer job as a
nanny in beautiful Cape May, she forms an unexpected
bond with a handsome Mennonite. Has she been too
hasty with her promises, or will she only find what her
heart is longing for back home?

The Ebb Tide

More from Beverly Lewis

Visit beverlylewis.com for a full list of her books.

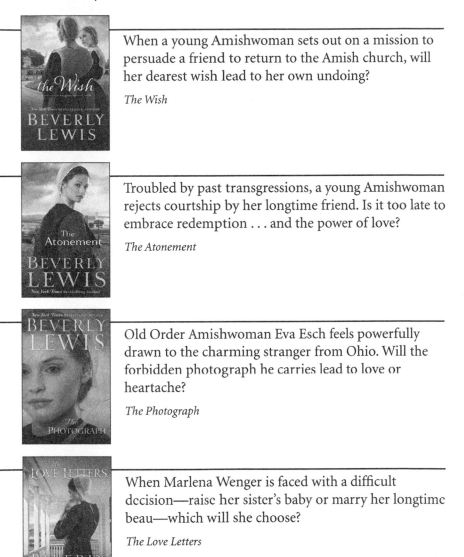

When a young Amishwoman sets out on a mission to persuade a friend to return to the Amish church, will her dearest wish lead to her own undoing?

The Wish

Troubled by past transgressions, a young Amishwoman rejects courtship by her longtime friend. Is it too late to embrace redemption . . . and the power of love?

The Atonement

Old Order Amishwoman Eva Esch feels powerfully drawn to the charming stranger from Ohio. Will the forbidden photograph he carries lead to love or heartache?

The Photograph

When Marlena Wenger is faced with a difficult decision—raise her sister's baby or marry her longtime beau—which will she choose?

The Love Letters

BETHANYHOUSE